THE MARRIAGE VENDETTA

THE
MARRIAGE
VENDETTA

CAROLINE MADDEN

PARK
ROW
BOOKS

PARK
ROW
BOOKS™

Recycling programs
for this product may
not exist in your area.

ISBN-13: 978-0-7783-8756-5

The Marriage Vendetta

Park Row Books
22 Adelaide St. West, 41st Floor
Toronto, Ontario M5H 4E3, Canada
ParkRowBooks.com

Printed in U.S.A.

To my parents, Pat and Fionnuala Madden, for giving me the confidence to go after my dream of being a writer.

To Kesia Lupo, for making that dream come true.

Note

The behavior modification techniques outlined in the following book are not based on scientific evidence or clinical research. Attempting to implement any of these techniques may result in serious adverse medical and/or psychological outcomes. (But it might be fun.)

1

If it wasn't for the photograph, I would never have gone to the marriage therapist. I didn't want to be told that my happiness was not Richard's responsibility and chastised for not making enough "me time," thanks all the same. And besides, what if the therapist psychoanalyzed away my resentment? How was I supposed to get out of bed in the morning, let alone fill all that new me time, if I didn't have my quiet seething to look forward to? And she would no doubt make me practice Better Communication Techniques and might even—dear God—force me to keep a gratitude journal. But now...well, now even I could see the time had come to seek professional help.

It had all come about at the Honey Café, which was one of those coffee shops with cutesy mismatched teacups, babyccinos for children and inspirational quotes on pegboards such as, "Don't cry because it's over; smile because it happened." To an outsider, by which I mean to a man, I'm sure it seemed like a pretty nice setup. But beneath the Spotify light jazz playlist running on a loop and the unending chatter, there was always at least one person wondering if she was about to start screaming. In fairness, it was usually me.

For me, the Honey Café's sole attraction was its location—

directly across the road from Alexis Junior School. It frustrated Richard that I insisted on schlepping theater paperwork and my laptop to the coffee shop every day when he had spent so much money upgrading the home office. He knew I felt I had to keep watch over Mara when she was in the schoolyard. That was another point on which we clashed. Regularly.

On that particular day, the Chickadee moms were reigning supreme at the long table by the cake counter. It was, I couldn't help but overhear, "Kangoo" Monday. They had come straight from the gym for post-workout spirulina smoothies, high on their audaciousness in trying something as *crazy* as Kangoo, which involved bouncing around for an hour on, no lie, elliptical antigravity boots. Mother Hen—her real name was Gina—was giving advice to a lesser Chickadee who confessed that she had dream-cheated on her husband and was wondering if she should feel guilty. Mother Hen had taken to giving a *lot* of advice since starting her Instagram account @justanothermuther39, where she posted a stream of perky stay-at-home-mom motivational aphorisms, invariably tagged #tradwife #seekingfemininity #homemaking. It was a big hit among the school moms, mainly because everyone wanted to see what her kitchen looked like.

The Chickadees paused their chatter to coo over the Junior and Senior Infants streaming out into the schoolyard for Little Break, skipping and twirling, their cries carrying in gusts. There was a yellow line down the middle that was supposed to separate the classes but they all ignored it, buzzing about to find their friends. Everywhere you looked there was constant movement. Except for one little lone figure with the hood of her purple coat pulled up against the wind that always seemed to cut right across that yard. Mara. She walked in slow circles for a while, not even lifting her head when other children bumped into her. She just moved aside and continued her circuit.

The two teachers on yard duty didn't notice at first. After a few more loops of the yard, Mara came to a stop and just stood there, the wind lifting the sides of her coat and her hair while all the other kids tagged each other and shrieked and hugged. Little shits. Not even one of them could ask her to play?

Mara was now sitting down on the gravel, all by herself. Her teacher came over and bent down beside her, asked her something. She shook her head, and he let her be. That was the worst of it: Mara never complained. When she came home, I'd ask her how school was. Fine, she'd say, smiling. And yard time? Fine. If I hadn't been watching, I'd have believed her.

Between the chatter from the Chickadee table and worrying about Mara, it was even harder to concentrate than usual, so I abandoned Richard's tax return and instead began working my way through our mail and bills.

I was interrupted by the beep of a text coming through on my phone. It was from an 083 number I didn't recognize. The message read: July 25. There was a photo attached, a grainy black-and-white shot of what looked like a hotel. I pinch-zoomed in and saw that, walking up the entrance steps of that hotel, was Richard and a woman, his face turned to smile at her, his hand sliding round her waist.

There was just one problem: the woman wasn't me.

If I'd had to predict my reaction to the possibility that Richard had caught the feels for someone else, I'd have pictured myself lounging in a silk dressing gown, long cigarette holder in one hand, martini in the other, amusing the pool boy with jaded quips about love being an illusion, that kind of thing.

But goddammit if this photo hadn't given me a shock. The same sickening feeling I used to get if I made a mistake during a concert, a jolt that would flare into a jangling of my entire nervous system, taking me out of the moment and lasting for the rest of the performance, making me horribly aware that things had gone off course.

And now it seemed that things *had* gone off course with Richard. Far more than I had thought. And, even more surprisingly, I actually cared.

Then I distinctly remembered—though I would have preferred not to—a moment from the early days. Richard and I were lying awake together in the bowed bed of our tiny attic flat in London and I thought to myself, *No one is as in love as we are.*

The text message read July twenty-fifth. Was that when the photo was taken? I rifled through my diary. July twenty-fifth was a Saturday. I had taken Mara on the train to a trad music festival in Waterford that weekend to give Richard time to write. The trip had been a disaster, as I should have known it would be. Mara had grown increasingly overstimulated and fretful and, in a crescendo of unhappiness, had vomited on the hotel bed. Richard said he'd holed himself up in his beloved home office for the whole weekend, ordered takeout and made progress with the script.

"Motherfucker."

I had said it out loud without realizing. The Chickadees turned their heads in unison like a pack of meerkats, their eyes wide in shock.

Soon, their chatter picked up again, but I knew they had filed away the incident for future reference. They had an intricate web of unwritten rules and I had just broken the most important one: never show what you're really feeling, unless what you're feeling is sunshine and rainbows. Certain minor infractions of the rules would be tolerated, but in general, behavior should be upbeat, and topics of conversation kept in check—your children's love of Gaelic football, the efficacy of Kegel weights on pelvic floor muscles, whether Center Parcs was worth the money, unverified spottings of rapists in the neigh-

borhood, how to remove shellac nails yourself if you couldn't
get to the salon and so on.

So I was pretty certain my unfortunate outburst had pushed
me into Oh-my-God-here-she-comes-don't-make-eye-contact
territory. But as the others began to exit the café, Mother Hen
paused by my table. "Mind if I have a word?"

She sat down without waiting for my response.

"Listen, it's none of my business and I don't want to overstep." Translation: I'm absolutely about to overstep. "And I
know we don't really know each other, but is everything okay?"
She tilted her head in a mock-sympathetic pose. "Earlier, you
seemed a bit…stressed out."

I could feel the advice coming.

"Trouble at home, am I right?" she prompted. "I have a sense
for these things."

Her eyes slid to my phone, then back to me. I wondered if
she had spotted the photo.

"Yes," I said. "That's it. Trouble at home. With the plumbing.
The pipes are all backed up. It's a nightmare. And the Dyno-
Rod guy just canceled—"

She touched a cool hand to mine to stop me. "Trust me, I
know what it's like," she said. "We've all been through bad
patches."

Were we still talking about the plumbing?

"If you ever want to talk…" she said in a voice laden with
false sympathy.

"That's so sweet of you, Gina. If I ever do have a problem,
you'll be the first person I'll come to." Translation: you'll be
the *last* person I'll come to. She was about as discreet as a Mat-
tress Mick ad. "But I promise you, I'm all good."

But still, Gina lingered. She wasn't going to be shaken off that
easily. In the end, I excused myself and scuttled off to the rest-
room where I could at least torment myself with this anonymous

photo in peace. When I returned to my table, Gina was gone, but poking out from under my coffee cup was a business card.

It read:

Ms. Ellen Early
Marriage Adviser
earlycounseling@gmail.com
20b Lincoln Place, Dublin 2

I reluctantly tossed it into my bag, but throughout the day I found myself taking it out, looking at it and running my fingers over the gold lettering. I searched online for Ms. Early, and then Early Counseling, but found nothing. And that night, in a moment of weakness—by which I mean after three glasses of wine—I sent an email to the address on the card. Maybe this marriage adviser could help me to decide on the best course of action. Richard, I knew from experience, was hotheaded if he felt the slightest hint of criticism directed at him. It would only put him on the defensive.

I needed to get things straight in my own mind first if I was ever going to get to the bottom of this photo.

2

So that's how I came to be standing outside a redbrick Georgian building near Trinity College, my finger hovering over a button next to the typed words *Ms. Ellen Early*. I felt a sudden urge to turn around and head home. But maybe, just maybe, I'd get lucky and the therapist would prescribe something lovely like lithium that I could sprinkle on my morning coffee. I pressed the button and heard the door click open.

I climbed four flights to the top of the building and gave the receptionist my name. She asked me to wait. There was a sofa but no magazines. I sat there trying to look like I had a rich inner life to occupy me. Ten, fifteen, minutes ticked by, and finally, she said Ms. Early would see me.

The therapist stood from her midcentury architectural chair as I entered the room. She was alone. I had assumed a previous session had gone over, but no. She didn't apologize for keeping me waiting, just shook my hand and gestured to a seat opposite her. The room was built into the rafters, airy and bare, the walls and floorboards painted white.

Her short dark hair was slicked back in a 1980s supermodel kind of way, and she was wearing an expensive-looking gray silk shirt. She had beautiful nails, shaped to a soft point like almonds. They made a small pleasing sound as she tapped them on the table next to her.

She looked like someone who might live in a brownstone in New York—married, but her husband would live on the other side of Central Park—they had decided not to live together to keep their relationship fresh. She would have high-thread-count Egyptian cotton sheets and never cook except for when she hosted dinner parties. She would share a bottle of champagne every night with friends who dropped by with takeout, and the rule would be that they weren't allowed to talk about work, only culture, travel, problems with the electoral system, whether cheek fillers could ever be a feminist choice and existentialism. She probably had no children. No, actually, she did. One grown son who called her by her first name and came to her for advice on ethical dilemmas at work. You could just tell she was a woman who would never, ever empty the junk from her car into a Lidl bag and then put that bag into the attic to be sorted out at an unspecified later date. Not that I would know about that.

"So, Eliza, how did you hear about me?" she asked, pulling me out of my reverie.

She spoke slowly, her Irish accent almost undetectable under a sophisticated transatlantic purr.

"A friend gave me your business card." My voice strained on *friend*.

Ms. Early folded her hands. "And what brings you here today?"

When I hesitated, she said, "Let's try this. Why don't you tell me what you think the biggest problem in your marriage is?"

Well, Ms. Early, the biggest problem in my marriage is my husband. And I don't know if his behavior is the result of social conditioning, millennia of hunter-gatherer genes in his DNA, his emotionally distant father, excessively high testosterone or actual clinical narcissistic personality disorder, but let's just say it's starting to grate. Oh, and to top it all off, I think he's having an affair.

I settled for, "We don't communicate well?"

She gave no indication as to whether this was the right answer or not.

I tried again. "And I suppose I'm not very good at asking for what I need. Like time to myself?"

That was always, *always* the answer to any marriage dilemma in those psychology columns in newspapers. But no. Nothing from the therapist. Not even a blink.

Then I remembered an excerpt from some article I'd read in *Cosmopolitan*. "And maybe I don't show him that I care anymore? Because I'm too wrapped up in our daughter?" In actuality, I didn't show that I cared anymore because the way he chewed was so irritating it gave me a stress headache. But you couldn't say a thing like that to a person like Ms. Early.

She drummed the table again with those elegant nails. I was annoying her, though I couldn't blame her. I was annoying myself. But what did she want?

I babbled on, hoping for some clue as to what answer would please her. "You see, Richard's under a lot of stress at work. We moved back to Dublin from the UK for this *huge* new job. He used to be the manager at Drury Lane in London, but Blind Alley Theatre hired him to produce a new play."

I waited for the typical, "You're *Richard Sheridan's* wife?" Almost everyone had heard of Richard. He was a rising star of the theater world, and now that the hometown boy was coming back to Dublin to work his magic on the beleaguered Blind Alley's fortunes, he was getting even more attention. But there was no flicker of recognition on Ms. Early's face.

I plowed on. "Richard's under a lot of pressure, and the move has been a bit of an adjustment for all of us. And I suppose maybe I'm not always there for him…emotionally?"

Puke.

"Of course, he did have a very tough childhood," I continued, rambling through the awkward silence. "His mother died when he was just a boy, and his father was—"

Ms. Early gave an irritated shake of her head and held up a palm. "Eliza, I don't give a *shit* about your husband's childhood."

Now I was the silent one.

"I, um, don't give a shit about his childhood, either," I heard myself say. And then I laughed, and so did she, and then we were laughing together. I hadn't laughed this much since they gassed me while I was having Mara.

"You've told me enough about your husband. I know his type. He doesn't interest me," Ms. Early said in the end, gazing at me. "I want to know about *you*, Eliza."

"Me?"

"Yes. Tell me, what do you do?"

"I… I mind our daughter, Mara. And I do the theater's paperwork. That takes up a lot of my time."

"And you get paid? For this *paperwork*?"

"Well, no, but—"

She shook her head and wrote something down. "What did you do before? Before you had your daughter. Before the paperwork."

"I was a concert pianist."

She raised an eyebrow and leaned back in her chair, as if to say, *now we're getting somewhere.* "Were you any good?"

Normally, I'd have slithered out of a question like this, or played down my abilities, but I appreciated her bluntness. "Yes. Yes, I was good."

She gave a nod and I sensed she was reassessing me. "You still haven't told me why you're here today."

When I didn't answer, she said, "People typically don't come to me unless their marriage is in the danger zone."

"Okay, well I wouldn't say mine's in the *danger* zone…"

"Then what would you say?" she prompted.

I'd say Richard would be wise to sleep with one eye open till sleep deprivation erased his latest transgressions from my memory.

I mean, it wasn't like I had, I don't know, set up a running-away fund and squirreled enough money to pay for a year's rent on a bijou apartment with a pastel color scheme. Not yet anyway. But a girl can dream. "We're just going through a bad patch."

"The most common crises I see are financial problems—"

"No, it's not that." We had a huge mortgage on our new house, but the theater had offered Richard a generous package to relocate to Ireland. We were sailing pretty close to the wind, but we were still afloat.

"Then what is it?" Ms. Early held my gaze while I dithered. I didn't know this woman at all. How was I supposed to share the most intimate details of my life with her?

"All right," she said briskly when I remained silent. "Let's try this. What do you think is the most important attribute in a husband?"

"Obediency?" Dammit. I hadn't meant to say that. Out loud.

The therapist gave me another dose of top-quality eye contact. "I'm trying to find out what it is that you really want. If I don't know that, I can't help you. So tell me. What do you want?"

"What do I want?"

"Yes. It is a very simple question."

I took a deep breath. "Okay. I'll tell you what I want. I want *Richard* to be the one who has to stay up till two in the morning washing all the sheets for the third time to try and get rid of the latest head lice infestation. I want *Richard* to watch over Mara all night for signs of concussion after she falls off his stupid ergonomic wheely chair. I want *Richard* to be the one stuck at home. Every. Single. Day."

Ms. Early considered this, then shook her head. "No."

"No? What do you mean, *no*?"

"I'm sure you would like all of those things, Eliza. But that's not the reason you're here."

I felt a surge of annoyance. "What's the reason I'm here, then?"

"You tell me."

I didn't reply.

"If you're not willing to be honest with me, Eliza, if you're just going to sit there and give me these tales about head lice and wheely chairs, you're wasting my time." She paused, then added, "And I do not let people waste my time."

I believed her. She let the silence between us stretch out. Sounds from the street below drifted through the open sash window. The honk of a bus, the revving of a motorbike, a shout of laughter.

Fuck it.

I took my phone out of my pocket and pulled up the photo of Richard and The Other Woman. I hesitated before handing it to Ms. Early. She slipped on a pair of gold-rimmed glasses to examine it.

"I was away with Mara the weekend that picture was taken," I explained. "He claimed he was holed up at home working on his script the whole time."

"Of course he did. Do you know who she is?"

"No."

"You haven't confronted him yet." She said that as a statement of fact.

"How do you know?"

She laughed in genuine amusement. "You're not the type."

This was more than a little offensive. But it was also entirely accurate, so I let it slide.

She was still staring at the picture. Then she handed the phone back to me. "Tell me, has he started staying out late in the evenings?"

"To be fair, he's always worked late."

"Is he very protective of his phone? Does he bring it with him when he goes to the bathroom?"

"Yes, but—"

"Has he started taking more care with his appearance?"

"No," I said, sure of myself on this one. *Got you there.*

Ms. Early remained unfazed. "Has he started going to the gym? Working out?"

"The only exercise he gets is taking the dog for walks."

"How often does he do this?"

"Most nights. He says it helps him clear his head."

"And how long are these walks?"

"Pretty long. About two hours. Sometimes longer. I mean, I'm usually asleep when he gets home so—"

"What kind of dog is it?"

"I don't know. The white and fluffy kind? Not much bigger than, say, an obese cat?"

"Two hours is too long for a dog that size. He'll get joint problems later in life."

Geez, were we auditioning for Crufts here or trying to save my marriage?

"It might be nothing," I said, trying to get things back on track. "The photo. I might be totally overreacting."

"My dear. It is never nothing."

Oh. That's reassuring.

"But the good news," Ms. Early continued, "is that I have experience with this type of situation. I know the damage it can do. I also know how to help. But first, I must know why."

"Why...what?"

"I can see you're trying to save your marriage. But why?"

"Because."

"Because what?"

"Because you don't just let your marriage fall apart! You

don't give up on something that important. You don't just walk away."

"Even if your husband is being unfaithful?"

When I was younger, I'd thought an affair would be a deal-breaker. Now that it was quite possibly happening to me, I realized it wasn't that simple. "We have a child together."

"Lots of people with children split up."

"Yeah, well, not me. I'm not doing that to Mara. She's going to have a stable childhood."

The word *stable* hung between us. Our household was many things at the moment, but stable was not one of them.

"I've read all the research and listened to all the experts and—"

"I'm sure you have."

"And breaking up our family would be too damaging. Mara deserves better."

"What about what *you* deserve?"

I was a mother, first and foremost. I didn't have the luxury of caring about what I deserved. "Mara's my priority."

"And what if I were to tell you that your daughter would be fine, even if your marriage didn't survive? Maybe more than fine?" Ms. Early countered.

"I wouldn't believe you."

"No," she said. "I don't suppose you would."

3

Mara was unsettled. She always did pick up on my moods. I had gotten back from the therapy session in time to collect her from school and take her to the playground *and* to the park to feed the ducks, but now bedtime had come and gone and she was still wide-awake. I tucked her up with her giant shark teddy, turned on the starlight projector and told story after story, but every time I thought she'd gone to sleep, she appeared back downstairs with urgent questions that couldn't wait until morning.

"How do humans mate? And how do hedgehogs mate? And if water rats can hold their breath for three minutes, can they come up the toilet?"

When she finally went back to bed, I searched in the kitchen cupboards and the fridge but there was nothing to drink except a couple of nonalcoholic beers and a bottle of Veuve Clicquot Vintage. A government minister gifted it to Richard in thanks for a private introduction to the acting cast. Richard was delighted when he'd looked up how much it cost and vowed to save it for a special occasion. I took down one of the beers and was about to pop the lid off when something stopped me. I swapped it for the champagne.

Nonalcoholic just wasn't going to cut it tonight.

I remained standing as I drank the champagne, listening to the silence that stretched from the basement kitchen—where I currently stood—up through two more floors and into the tiny servant's room in the attic. The house, a Georgian remodel, still didn't feel like home even though we'd been here three months now. Richard had found it on a preparatory trip over to Dublin and there hadn't been time for me to come and see it. "You'll love it," he'd said. "It's perfect."

Only it wasn't. It turned out that the bedrooms were so far from the kitchen that I had to get an intercom system put in just so I could call Mara down for dinner. Or, you know, make sure she was still alive. And the stairs had been designed so that, with very little effort, a small person could upend herself over the low banister and fall the entire way from the attic return to the hall. So obviously, I had to get safety nets installed, too. See also: a childproof restrictor on the attic window that led out onto the three-story-high roof; mechanical fixings for the two-hundred-kilo marble fireplace that was coming away from the living room wall; and a military-grade lock on the French doors that opened onto a Juliet balcony. But apart from all that, sure. It was *perfect*.

I took the bottle with me and wandered up to the ground floor and into Richard's study. I sat down in the ergonomic swivel chair he'd ordered on the internet after hearing that Tom Stoppard owned that exact one. I checked my phone while messing about with the chair's settings—it always drove him mad when Mara did this. No text from Richard to say he was running late. Maybe his phone had run out of battery. He wasn't a man to think of bringing a charger with him. Or keys. *Surely Eliza will be home*, he'd probably think, and he'd be right.

I was always home.

I went into my email and looked again at the message that had come through from Ms. Early's secretary an hour after our session, letting me know that a weekly slot had opened up in the therapist's diary. I was very fortunate, the secretary said, because there was normally a waiting list, and would I like to take the slot? I had not yet replied.

I drifted down the hall, followed by my little shadow, Mr. Pickles. Mr. Pickles, I should explain, was a highly strung rescue dog that Richard had arrived home with one evening and presented to Mara as a sort of quick-fix parental sticking plaster that screamed, "I realize I'm never around, but here's a small, fluffy mammal to distract you from that fact."

So there we were as usual, Mr. Pickles and I, padding about the big silent house together. Tonight I found myself wandering into the music room at the front of the house where a couple of moving boxes were piled up, waiting to be sorted. I set my glass down and started opening the boxes. Inside the first, I found bags of Mara's baby clothes that I really should have donated to charity rather than shipping over with us, but I couldn't bring myself to part with them yet. Maybe subconsciously I was hoping we might still need them.

In the next box was a pile of old programs from my European tour, with the scheduled dates and cities printed on the back. I hadn't made it to the last four cities. My tour came to an abrupt stop in Cologne. Under the programs were some press clippings, and then right at the bottom was a binder with sheet music for Chopin's *Fantaisie-Impromptu*.

I hesitated, then removed it from the box. I opened the binder and ran my hands over the pages. They were still as pristine as the day I put them into the folder eight years earlier. No dog-ears, no smudges, no notes written along the edges.

Because I never started practicing it.

I had been due to start working on this specific piece when I returned home from the European tour, in preparation for recording it in New York the following autumn. I could still remember the mixture of pride and nervousness I had felt punching holes in these pages and organizing them neatly in the folder. It was a rare honor to be asked by the Fryderyk Chopin Institute to record a Chopin piece, especially one as notoriously challenging as *Fantaisie-Impromptu*. And I had always found recording in a studio more psychologically daunting than performing at live concerts. There was no audience to buoy you up and help you sense if the music was landing as it should. And of course, there was also the pressure of doing justice to the composer. This pressure had shredded the confidence of several other pianists who had attempted to record this very piece. But even though I was nervous at the time, I also had sensed deep down that I was ready.

I put the binder back into the box and stood up, walking over to my baby grand piano still swaddled in its thick cover. It had been awarded to me as a prize for the La Palma D'Oro International Competition. I could never have afforded to buy it myself—not even close. A handmade F278 Fazioli, it was the only piano of its kind to have a *dulce* pedal—a fourth pedal that gave greater control over the sound quality.

Even though it was a warm Dublin evening, this room remained cool. I kept the heat off at all times and had a dehumidifier running to suck moisture from the air. If the environment of the room wasn't just right, it would affect the piano's tuning.

I heard Ms. Early's voice in my head: *I want to know about you.*

I peeled off a piece of masking tape sealing the protective cover. I'd been so worried about transporting it here from London after reading about a concert pianist whose grand piano was dropped by movers and smashed to pieces. In the interview, the pianist said she was grieving, that the piano was her best friend, her companion. The story had made headlines mainly because of the value of the piano, but some of the coverage implied that her reaction was eccentric. To me, it made perfect sense.

As I slowly lifted the cover, I caught the faint pine scent of the soundboard, the heart of the piano, that was carved out of two-hundred-year-old giant red spruce from the Italian Alps. I was instantly transported back to the master piano maker Paolo Fazioli's workshop, the two of us laughing as he swore he would never again make a grand with a fourth pedal because it had proved so difficult. But after I sat down and played it, he said it had all been worth it.

I shook the thought away. There was no time for reminiscing.

I fastened the cover back in place and entered Richard's study. Earlier, I had printed out a blown-up copy of the hotel photograph so I could examine it in greater detail. The woman's back was turned to the camera, but I could tell she was attractive. She wore a backless dress cut so low that it was clear she had dispensed with the need to wear anything under it. All that held the dress up was a bow tied at the back of her neck. If Richard had moved his hand from her waist and tugged on one end of the bow, the whole thing would have slithered off in an instant.

I had worn a dress like that once. Not *quite* so tailbone-exposing, but open-backed, slashed in a deep V. My father had ordered it especially for the Royal Variety Performance. The show was going to be televised, and my agent had impressed upon my father that this was our one shot at hitting the big time, and image was everything now in classical performing. Image was what made the difference between a talented almost-ran and a household name. My "look" needed to *wow* viewers, many of whom would only be able to see me from behind. And what was more *wowing* than a dress that allowed millions of people to get intimately acquainted with the upper and lower planes of my naked back? The first time I heard anything about this dress was on the day of the performance. I was fifteen years old.

I turned my attention back to the photo. Unfortunately, it was in black-and-white, so I couldn't tell what shade the woman's hair was. She appeared to be my height, maybe a head smaller than Richard. Did he have a type? Hard to say, since we were so young when we met and he'd only had a couple of girlfriends before me. Because of the angle of Richard's left hand, it was impossible to tell if he was wearing his wedding ring that day, but the woman's left hand was bare, ringless. So she was single. Great.

I searched online for apps that allowed you to identify people in photos. There were several facial recognition apps, but unfortunately nothing that worked for bums or naked backs—someone should really get on that. I refocused my attention to analyzing the hotel in the picture. No sign was visible, but at the top of the steps was an old-fashioned revolving door. Another quick internet search came up with three hotels in Ireland with this type of entrance: the Shelbourne, the Five Seasons in Dublin, and the Hodson Bay in Athlone. It seemed unlikely Richard had traveled to the midlands and back while I was gone. Although I could check the car records for M50 tolls...

No. I wasn't going to be that person. I needed to get a grip. There were a million legitimate explanations for this scenario. Richard worked with lots of women—casting directors, actresses, script writers, agents. It was entirely possible that he was attending a work-related event. Then again, why had someone felt the need to text me this photo?

Whoever it was, they clearly wanted to hint at Richard's having an affair. But was the sender trying to help me, or hurt me? There was certainly no shortage of people whose noses were out of joint with Richard. There had been several contenders for the top job at Blind Alley, each older and more experienced than Richard. They must have spent years in the trenches and felt the position was their due. And then of course there were the many actors he'd passed over for parts throughout his career. Were their grievances reignited now that he had "made it"?

Or...could it be someone who wanted to get back at me instead? I racked my brain for potential culprits. There must have been countless pianists I'd beaten at international competitions, or whose spot I "took" at prestigious residencies over the years.

But I was fully out of the game now, so why waste their time messing with me?

I mulled over some other contenders. In the early years of our marriage back in London, there'd been a few older women—wives of Richard's influential theater contacts—whom I'd had to socialize with even though they were only ever cold to me. They probably considered me an Irish nobody, but that wasn't the problem. My fault was in being a *young* Irish nobody with an on-the-rise husband who still doted on her, unlike their own husbands, who had pretty much all strayed. I sometimes even noticed these women attempting to flirt with Richard, but to no avail. He always stayed by my side, a protective arm around my waist. He always made sure I felt included.

Had one of the wives sent me this photo? A couple of them had my phone number. But why? Did they want me to know I was no better than them now?

I walked over to Richard's desk, which was in its usual state of absolute chaos. I tidied it up and cleared a space in the center. Then I set the photo down and waited.

4

It was well past eleven by the time a taxi pulled up to the house and Richard stepped out. I greeted him at the door so he wouldn't ring the doorbell and wake Mara, but he walked right past me toward the hall table. He rummaged through its drawers, muttering to himself as he gathered up coins. I handed him a tenner for the taxi driver and went back into the study.

When he came in, he clocked the open bottle of champagne and I waited for his reaction. This would be a nice little way of kicking off proceedings. "My Veuve," he'd say, emphasis on *my*—*his* wine, *his* money, *his* house—to which I'd say, "Yes, I suppose it must be annoying that someone would take something of yours without asking."

And then I'd give a nonchalant wave toward the photo.

I was ready, primed for a showdown. But instead, Richard looked at the bottle, then let out a long, weary breath and said, "Fuck it, why not?"

He didn't even bother going to the kitchen to get a glass, just poured some into an orange plastic Ikea cup Mara had left on the mantelpiece. This was very unlike him. He was big into using the right glasses for the right drink, pairing the right wine with the right food.

"I need it after the day I've had," he said, and took a mouthful while pulling off his tie and slouching onto the sofa. He hadn't noticed the photo.

I sipped my champagne. With a bit more Veuve courage, I would sort this out myself. I didn't need a therapist's help. I just needed to wait for the right moment. "What happened?"

"Bloody Majella. Who else?"

Majella. Of course. She was the theater's new Equality Director and, according to Richard, a "royal pain in the ass." He'd been forced by the board to hire her and all she'd done—according to Richard—was "shame him for being a white, straight, able-bodied cis male."

"Why?" I asked. "What did she do now?"

To date, the battles she had won included the following: the introduction of a gender-neutral casting policy, the appointment of an intimacy coordinator to keep a watchful eye on the choreographing of the love scenes in Richard's play, and—much to the horror of the theater's older clientele—unisex toilets. Each and every thing she implemented only wound Richard up more and more.

I adored her.

"Just more of the same bullshit. Believe it or not, I'm trying to run a business here, but if, God forbid, I don't go along with her *plans*, she just runs straight to the board." He drained the plastic cup and sank back onto the sofa. He looked exhausted, his skin gray and eyes sunken. It had to be said, he did *not* look like a man with the energy for an illicit sexual relationship. He looked like a man who needed to get his blood checked and be put on a good multivitamin.

"I blame those pesky feminists," I said with a shrug. "We should never have let them out of the kitchen. Speaking of which, dinner's in the fridge if you want to reheat it."

He checked himself, partly because of the feminist comment, partly because he had already ordered Thai food. I knew this because we shared an online account with the delivery company. Also, there *was* no dinner in the fridge. But I knew he wouldn't call my bluff. He wasn't into reheating. And, if we're being honest, he wasn't into my cooking, either. He'd once "joked" that he should send me to Ballymaloe Cookery School. At the time, I'd refrained from saying where I'd like to send *him*.

In any event, this pause was the moment I'd been waiting for. I took a breath and steeled myself. All I had to do was show him the photo and ask who the woman was and what they were doing together at a hotel. I counted myself down: *three, two, one,* go. The clock on the mantel ticked and a pipe rattled somewhere high in the house. I knocked back some more champagne and counted myself down again. *Three, two, one…*

"Listen, Richard, there's something I—"

"And we *still* haven't found a replacement for Anna," Richard interrupted, throwing his hands up in exasperation. Anna was initially cast as the play's lead role, selected mainly for her high profile—she'd been playing a massively popular character on a Dublin TV soap opera since her teens. She'd become pregnant after being cast and had now been put on bed rest, leaving her no choice but to step down from the role. "I just can't believe she didn't tell me she was pregnant. Some people are so inconsiderate."

Hmm, you don't say.

"She thinks she's some kind of hotshot just because she's been on Irish TV," he continued. "She wouldn't last a minute in London. She has no idea how competitive the scene is there. I mean, she's just not clued in. When I told her what Michael Gilligan said about my first play, she didn't even know who he was. I mean, Michael *fucking* Gilligan, for Christ's sake."

Not the Gilligan review again.

Michael Gilligan was an esteemed theater critic at a major UK broadsheet. His review of Richard's first staged work had been…mixed, to put it kindly. He'd said that, for the most part, the writing was self-regarding and overblown. However, he'd added that the closing monologue was close to perfect in its skewering of the British upper classes. Ever since, Richard took every chance to drop into conversation that the great Gilligan had called his debut play *close to perfect*. What Richard *never* dropped into conversation was that I'd come up with the idea for the monologue. And written most of it. He seemed to have completely forgotten this.

Richard then proceeded to discuss the many ways in which Anna—and now the entire cast—failed to appreciate how lucky they were to get the chance to work with someone as experienced as him. How people in London had warned him against moving back to Ireland and becoming a big fish in a small pond. How he was beginning to see what they had meant.

He continued in this vein for several more minutes until he noticed I wasn't responding. "Sorry. I didn't mean to unload all of this on you. I know it hasn't exactly been easy for you either since moving here. But this is the worst of it." Richard paused, then added, "I'm doing this for us. You know that, right? You, me and Mara. Once this play is done, things will be different. I promise."

Hmm, I wonder where I'd heard that before... Oh, right! Only every single time he was working on a production.

And he was *always* working on a production.

He reached for my hand, beckoning for me to join him on the sofa. I acquiesced and sat down beside him. It was only then that I caught a whiff of pints and bacon bites. So *that's* why he was home so late.

"You believe me, right?" he asked, looking at me expectantly.

"Sure," I said.

He instantly withdrew his hand, giving me a pointed look. "What's that supposed to mean?"

"All I said was *sure*."

"It's the *way* you said it. Like you don't believe me."

Of course I didn't believe him. Fool me twice, shame on me and all that.

He rolled his eyes. "Go on. Say whatever it is," he prompted, dramatically gesturing me on.

"Richard, the only reason I agreed to this move is because you promised you'd spend more time with Mara."

"And I *am*."

This was so blatantly untrue it didn't even warrant a response.

"I mean, I *will*," he corrected. "Like I said, once things calm down—"

"Your daughter hasn't seen you for five days. And instead of coming home to spend time with her this evening like you promised, you went drinking."

He drew back and settled a cold gaze on me. "I went for one drink, Eliza. *One* drink with the cast and the stage crew to keep morale up. And now I come home to this? Seriously? Do you even realize how much pressure I'm under right now? But instead of, I don't know, *supporting* me, you use it as a chance to have yet another fucking go at me."

"I can tell you've had a lot more than one drink, Richard." I knew I was right. He wasn't overtly drunk, but he was raising his voice at me and he only ever did that after a proper session. But as soon as I said it, I realized it was a mistake. I knew better than to have it out with him when he was under the influence.

"Eliza. I am the *only* man, out of everyone that went out this evening, who left early and went home to his family. I'm a fucking saint compared to the rest of them. They'll be out getting moldy till two in the morning."

Oh, well, in that case! Why didn't you just say so? "I don't care what everyone else does," I replied evenly. "This is about you and me and Mara, like you said. She deserves your attention. And I'm not going to stop bringing this up just because you get pissed off with me whenever I do."

His leg was jiggling now, something that happened whenever he got himself really worked up. Finally, he muttered, "It must be great being perfect."

I didn't reply. There was no point now that he had switched into self-pitying mode.

"Tell me, Eliza, how is it that I'm always in the wrong?"

I don't know, Richard. You tell me. "I'm not trying to have a go. But we moved here for you, and—"

"You know what? I'm getting tired of this."

"Of what, exactly?"

"The martyrdom. The constant low-level resentment."

Oh, it's not low-level, my friend.

"This isn't about Mara at all, is it?" he said. I could tell he was getting really fired up now. I wondered if our nosy neighbor Mrs. Overend could hear him. She probably had a glass pressed up against the wall.

I glanced at the photo on the desk. "No," I said. "It's not just about Mara."

"Right. This is about you."

I whipped round to face him. "What?"

"You miss the limelight."

I let out an incredulous laugh. "Richard, come on. That's not it at all."

"That *is* it, and you've got to stop taking it out on me. You could go back to work if you want."

"Good one."

"Why do you always have to do that? I'm trying to say I'll support you. We've been through this before."

"Okay, fine," I said. "Let's say my agent called me and said there was a possible booking for a three-month European tour…"

Richard waved his hand dismissively. "There's no point arguing about hypotheticals."

"Who said it was a hypothetical?"

"Ah, come on, Eliza. I mean, that's never going to happen. You don't even practice anymore."

"That's not true," I lied.

"Oh, yeah? When? I haven't heard you."

"You'd have to actually *be* here to hear me playing, wouldn't you?"

That silenced him for a moment. "I'm not getting sucked into this," he finally said, shaking his head. "No matter what I say, you're going to rubbish it. Just don't blame it on me that you're not touring anymore. This is on you, Eliza."

He locked eyes with me, and we stayed that way for about five seconds. The most eye contact we'd had in a good five months.

I sighed and changed the subject. "How's your script coming along?"

This threw him. After a pause, he said, "Eh, yeah, nearly there. I mean, there's a bit to do yet but it'll be grand."

"Maybe I should take Mara to Waterford again."

He looked at me blankly. "Why would you do that?"

"That's why I went to Waterford the last time. To give you space to write."

He glanced away, pretending to rack his brain. "Oh, you mean the weekend you went to that trad music thing? No, I wasn't working on the script. I had a big private equity investor meeting that weekend." He paused, then added, "I told you that."

"You never told me that."

He was on his feet now, pacing about the room and slugging from the orange cup. "I did, Eliza. You're always forgetting things."

"No, you said—"

"Jesus Christ, Eliza, will you drop it already? What does it fucking matter?"

His eyes were roving about the room. I knew that look. He was trying to find something to criticize, to turn the argument back on me.

Then his gaze fell on the desk. My heart quickened, and I braced myself for whatever came next.

But then he just said, "You messed with my stuff."

"I just tidied the papers. I didn't throw anything out."

"How many times do I have to tell you not to touch my desk?"

"How am I supposed to do the theater's admin if I can't touch your desk?"

"They're my private papers. And I have a system. Now I won't be able to find anything."

His *system* was to let all the letters, bills and random shit he didn't want to face pile up and up until it all slid onto the floor. Where it continued to pile up. But I knew better than to give any reaction. He wanted to get a rise out of me so he could then point out what an angry person I was.

"You're right, Richard. I'm sorry. It won't happen again," I said coolly.

"You don't *sound* very sorry."

I forced myself to take a deep breath instead of responding. No matter what I said next, he'd find a reason to pounce on it.

He continued pacing back and forth, stewing in the silence, then tried a different direction. "You better not have thrown anything out. You're always doing that. The last time you went at my desk, I wasn't able to find that contract. I had to pay the lawyer to do it up again."

I didn't point out that Majella had eventually found the original contract. In his office. At the theater.

"How would you like it if I messed up your precious music room?" Richard asked icily. He then abruptly threw the orange cup to the floor, splashing champagne on the rug, and walked toward the door. My throat tightened.

"Richard, don't."

And just like that, he had me. He knew it, too. The piano was my weak spot.

"I'll do what I like in my own house, Eliza, thank you very much. The house *I* fucking paid for."

I bit the inside of my cheek to stop myself from reacting. If it wasn't for my trust fund, we never could have bought the house in the first place. And he knew it, too.

"Go on," he said. "I can see you want to say something. Just say it."

I willed myself to keep calm.

"Who pays the mortgage, Eliza? Who pays for everything here?"

Don't let him get a rise out of you. Don't let him win.

But he kept going. "Who paid for your trip into town yesterday, where you took out two hundred euros for God knows what?" His eyes flicked over me. "You certainly didn't use it to get your hair done."

I ignored the slight, instead racking my brain for why I had indeed gone to the ATM.

Oh, right... I'd needed cash for therapy. Shit. "Wait, how did you—"

"Online banking, Eliza. Someone has to keep an eye on what we're spending," he said, rolling his eyes. "So what was it for, then? The two hundred euros?"

I hesitated. If I made something up, he'd know I was lying. And I couldn't tell him the truth. "I—"

I was quite literally saved by the bell. The doorbell, that is. His Deliveroo was here.

Then the intercom crackled to life. "Mama? Is someone at the door?"

Richard looked at me and I looked at him. He let out a harsh laugh. "Right," he said in the end, shaking his head as he walked out of the study.

★ ★ ★

I took a beat before going upstairs, wiping at the corners of my eyes. I checked my reflection in the mirror to make sure I didn't look like I'd been crying before entering Mara's bedroom, where, for the next half hour, she tried convincing me to buy a pet Burmese python to deter water rats—which, as she argued, posed a very serious threat. It was only once I'd adequately reassured her that Mr. Pickles was more than up to the job that her eyes finally closed.

But even after Mara was fast asleep, I stayed in her room. My hands were trembling, and my chest felt like something heavy was pressing down on it. I slipped my phone out and scrolled back through Richard's texts until I came to the ones I was searching for from this past summer.

July, to be exact. The days leading up to the trad music festival.

As I predicted, there hadn't been a word from him about an *investor meeting.* And then I found the incriminating text: Sorry have to bail on that festival thing. Under pressure to get last act nailed down. Will make it up to you I promise.

I was right.

I left it another ten minutes before coming back down. Richard was snoring on the sofa, cradling the takeaway carton in his arms. A single thick udon noodle dangled over the edge of the container.

He shifted in his sleep and some dark sauce spilled over the edge of the carton and began oozing its way down the noodle until it dangled from the tip, suspended over his favorite silk-and-wool-blend cream Armani sweater he'd bought because he once heard that Michael Fassbender had ten of them on rotation as his uniform. Any stains had to be immediately hand-washed out or it would be ruined. I watched as the drop swelled, then plopped onto the front of the sweater, followed by several more drops.

I went over to the desk, picked up the overlooked photo and put it back in my bag.

I *should* have gone to bed at that point, but instead, I stayed up late thinking, by which I mean stewing, and googling the symptoms of a nervous breakdown.

If I'd had some Xanax handy at the time, everything would have been fine. But I didn't, so I instead self-medicated with the rest of the bubbly. And possibly a Baileys nightcap.

Or three.

5

I woke to sunlight streaming in through the window. I sat up, rubbing at my eyes, and turned to face the other side of the bed, where I'd expected to find Richard fast asleep.

But he wasn't there—which was highly unusual. Had he already left? He rarely surfaced before me.

And that was when I realized I'd slept through my alarm.

When I went downstairs, the study had been cleaned. I could smell my favorite lavender spray and there was no sign of the takeaway boxes I'd expected to find lying about.

As I went down to the hall, I was startled by the rumble of the washing machine. Someone had set it going. In the kitchen, the dishwasher had been emptied and the coffee machine was plugged in and heated up, my favorite cup already slotted into it.

On the island sat Mara's lunch box, fully packed with a balanced, nutritious lunch. Next to it was a handwritten note:

Eliza,
Last night is bit of a blur, but i remember enough to be appalled at how i acted. i know how much you've given up for me, and because of my career, you've had to shoulder the load of bringing

up Mara. i know that most of the time, you're doing it alone. Sometimes i think that i don't deserve you. Please forgive me.
Rx

He was right to be appalled by his behavior. I was appalled, too.

But… I had to admit I was touched, despite myself. This was the first time Richard had ever really acknowledged that I'd sacrificed anything for our family, that I'd put my needs aside so he could chase his dream. But this note showed that he got it. He understood.

And if he understood, maybe things could get better.

Plus, he'd been drunk. Was it fair to judge him for things he barely remembered doing, things he would never do sober?

Either way, I realized then that the weight that had been pressing down on my chest since the night before had lifted.

You must never, ever be late, or flustered, at school drop-off at Alexis Junior School. The principal is actually pretty laid-back about punctuality, and the teachers, too, but the Chickadees? Not so much.

But suffice to say this particular morning, we were late—half an hour late, to be exact.

I parked the car and brought Mara into reception, hugging her tight before the classroom assistant led her away. The secretary asked me to sign in to a ledger and give a reason for our tardiness.

Hmm, what to write… *We were late because I stayed up half the night self-medicating with alcohol because I got it into my head that my husband is quite likely having an affair?* Or maybe, *We were late because I seem to be descending into an existential crisis after a therapist simply asked what had become of me?*

In the end, I just wrote *life.*

And that was that, except who had to walk in the door at that very second but my nemesis, Busy-Working-Mom.

Busy-Working-Mom, real name George, and I had met during Mara's first week at school, and she had been initially friendly, asking how we were settling in. I said I was glad we'd got a place at Alexis because it finished an hour earlier than most other schools, which made it an easier sell with Mara. "Well, it's a right pain in the ass for us working parents, I can tell you that," she replied, before stalking off. And she'd been cold to me ever since.

"Oh," she said, when she saw me now in reception. "Did you forget the Friday treat, too?" She brandished a tiny Kinder bar. "Tim would be raging with me. It's his favorite part of the week."

Damn it, damn it, damn it. Mara loved the Friday treat. And I had forgotten it. I could already see her crestfallen face when she opened her lunch box.

Busy-Working-Mom must have read my expression, because she said, "I have tons of spare Kinders. I always keep a stash of them in my bag for bribes. If Mara likes them, she's more than welcome?"

It was kind, and it was heartfelt, so I said, "Yes, thank you, that would be great."

Just then, my phone buzzed. "Sorry," I said to her. "I'd better check this."

It was a message from Richard: Sorry slammed at work. Won't make it home for movie. Tell Mara I'll make it up to her I promise.

So that was how it was going to be, was it?

When we'd moved back, Richard had promised to do something special with Mara once a week. She said she'd love to stay up late on Fridays with him and watch a movie. She'd get to choose the film and they'd make popcorn. With Maltesers mixed in.

But even after our fight. Even after his groveling apology, he just Could. Not. Be. Arsed.

"Mother*fucker*," I said out loud for the second time that week. The secretary looked at me over the top of her glasses. George slid the Kinder bars to her under the Perspex glass and then said to me, "Here, I'm going to grab a coffee. Why don't you come, too?"

"Oh. That's really nice of you, but I don't think—"

"Look. I know I've been a bit of a cow to you."

"What? *No*."

"We both know I have. And I've been feeling bad about it. So please. Let me buy you a coffee."

The Honey Café was already buzzing with the après-school run crowd, pairs of moms thronging the counter area waiting on takeaway coffees for their 5ks, listless mothers of toddlers killing an hour in the kids' corner and, at the long central table, a couple of inner-circle Chickadees—Nikki and Nicki-with-a-*c*—splitting a sweet potato brownie.

"Want to sit here?" George asked, gesturing to my favorite table inside the front window, and I nodded.

"That day I met you," she said, "you mentioned how it was convenient that the kids get out so early from school. And you had all this expensive yoga gear on…" She stopped, then tried again. "You see, there's a certain type around here…"

"My husband bought me that gear. I don't know why. I've never done yoga in my life. I think it must have been a hint. Can you believe he doesn't like my 'homeless granny chic'?" I said, gesturing to my outfit, which, owing to the rushed morning, consisted of saggy gray leggings teamed with a saggy gray cardigan that boasted a ratty faux-fur collar.

She laughed. "Almost as glamorous as *my* outfit," she said, shrugging her coat off to reveal loose blue scrubs. "I'm a midwife. At Holles Street. The day we met, I'd just come off a really long shift. And the minder had quit because the twins were going through a phase of being absolute little fuckers.

And when you made that comment, and when I noticed your yoga gear, I thought…"

I nodded toward Nikki and Nicki and said, "You thought I was a Chickadee."

George inclined her head. "Chickadee?"

"You know. One of the glammy mammies?"

"Ha, very good. Yes, I admit, I momentarily mistook you for one of them and for that, I am deeply sorry. Now, let me get you that coffee."

"I'll have a low-fat soy latte. With caramel syrup. And just a half a shot of coffee. I have caffeine sensitivity."

She hesitated and was about to say something, then changed her mind and nodded. She was getting up to go to the counter when the waitress arrived at our table and said to me, "Here you go, your usual. Triple espresso."

George gave a great dirty laugh. "I deserved that." She asked the waitress for the same. Then she said, "I've seen you here working on your laptop. My guess is you do something creative?"

"No, no. Nothing creative. Very boring, really."

"Oh yeah?" She wasn't letting me off the hook.

What to say, what to say. I could tell her I was actually a professional pianist, but that always sounded pretentious. And it was also kind of inaccurate now.

"I'm a failed concert pianist," I found myself saying.

"Whoa," George said. "I think I'm going to need some chocolate cake with that coffee."

"Sorry. I'm a bit hungover. I don't normally overshare."

"Ah, overshare away. A bit of honesty is refreshing around here." She tilted her head in the direction of the Chickadee table. "It's my fault anyway for prying. My husband, Mossy, is always telling me I'm a nosy wagon."

"I *was* toying with describing myself as Mom-in-Chief but—"

"But really only Michelle Obama can pull that off."

That's what I'd been about to say. "Exactly! Really, I'm just a glorified PA for my husband."

George gave a little snort, then said, "Aren't we all?"

I looked at her properly then, her scrubbed-clean skin and her eyes that were both tired and full of humor. I had been wrong about her, too, I realized.

"So…not to be all nosy again," she said, "but it seemed like you were having a bit of a shit day earlier."

I told her how Richard hadn't come home early a single night this week to spend time with Mara.

"Yeah," said George. "That'd be right. Could be worse. *Very* irritating of course, but could be a lot worse. Like when I was in labor for the twins, Mossy missed the birth."

"He didn't get there on time?"

She gave a laugh. "He didn't get there *at all* because he was too busy shooting Kalashnikovs in Gdansk."

I laughed in disbelief. "Tell me you're joking."

"He couldn't possibly miss his brother's stag, now, could he?"

"Right," I said, mentally putting Mossy into my little black book, which, it had to be said, was not that little. "I think I'd have used the Kalashnikov on *him*." Then I realized what I'd just said. "Oh my God, sorry. That was a terrible thing to say."

"Nah, too obvious," George said without missing a beat. "You have to go for something that can't be traced back to you. That leaves no visible marks."

"Sounds like you've given this quite a bit of thought."

"Isn't that what everyone does when they're up at night feeding their babies? Plot their husband's demise?"

"You have to keep yourself awake somehow," I agreed.

"So anyway, when he got back from Gdansk, I hadn't slept in three nights and was pretty much hallucinating. Well, I really *went* for him. And I think it worked. He made sure to be there for the next baby anyway. Sometimes you need a good fight to clear the air."

"I'm not sure Richard and I necessarily...*fight*. We're really good at pushing at each other's buttons, but I've never really *gone for him*, so to speak. He's the more reactive one. But then he'll cool off and apologize and we'll forget about it."

"But doesn't he ever just...rile you up?"

"Oh, he does." I laughed. "I mean, I do voice my frustrations, but usually it's over email."

"Email?"

I nodded. "I read about it on the internet. This psychologist said if your spouse annoys you, you should put it all down in an email. You sleep on it for a night, and then you reread it. And if you still feel the same way, you send it. If not, hit Delete. That way, you don't let the primitive, vengeance-seeking part of your brain control your actions. Or something like that."

"Ah, Jesus, but you'd need a bit of vengeance sometimes, though, wouldn't you?"

"One time, Richard asked me why we always fought over email. And I said because research shows that he was statistically likely to disregard my concerns because of the high pitch of my voice."

George was laughing now. "Mossy can't stand my *tone*."

"Sometimes I even try to lower my voice so that he'll really listen to what I'm saying," I continued. "Which actually *does* work, but it hurts my vocal cords after a while. And it's sort of humiliating."

"Did you tell him all that?"

"Nah. I just put it in an email. And deleted it later."

She did that great laugh again, and the Chickadees' heads turned to us in unison.

"God, Mossy would love it if I just wrote things down instead of wrecking his head."

It struck me that we had been back in Ireland three months

now and George was the first person I'd had a real, proper conversation with. She didn't seem to worry what anyone thought of her. It was liberating.

Just then, the bell on the door tinkled and Mother Hen breezed in, gracefully shedding her pastel-pink rain jacket and shaking out her hair. George's eyes held mine and the corner of her mouth twitched.

As Mother Hen passed us, she said, "George," to which George replied in a flat voice, "Gina." Then Mother Hen turned to me with a bright smile and a super-friendly, "Well, are you feeling any better?"

She was talking about my swearing outburst the other day. I could tell by the voracious look in her eyes. No doubt she was the one who slipped Ms. Early's card under my coffee cup.

"Oh yeah. Totally fine. Never better."

She squeezed my wrist. "Good for you." And then she floated on to her posse.

I could feel George looking at me. Once Gina was out of earshot, I turned to her and said, "I was a bit upset the other day. Just some stuff going on at home... Anyway, Gina's *dying* to know what's wrong."

"Jesus, is there nowhere that woman won't stick her nose?" George paused, then said, "Not to pull a Gina, but...*are* you okay?"

"I, uh, actually went to someone to talk about it."

"Like, a..."

"Yeah, like a therapist."

"And it helped?"

I sighed. "Well. To be honest, it's all a bit excruciating, you know? I mean, *I* don't want to be psychoanalyzed. I just want Richard to stop being a dick."

I expected George to agree with me. She seemed the no-nonsense type. But instead, she said, "I actually get a free counseling session once a month. It's technically supposed to be for work-related stress, but I use it to have a nice long rant about Mossy. And you know what, the therapist's actually pretty sharp. No hippy-dippy stuff. She just kind of...helps you to see things in a different light. And you'd notice the difference. Like last week, Mossy was having a moan because I made him porridge when he wanted a fry, and so I flung the bowl of porridge at the wall."

I burst out laughing. "Sorry, but how is that good?"

"Normally, I'd have flung it at *Mossy*."

I laughed again. "Yeah. I just don't think therapy's for me."

"Fair enough. The *only* thing I'd say is that children pick up on everything, even if there isn't roaring and shouting going on." George paused, tidying the sugar packets on the table, then said, "Would it be worth giving the therapist another go, just to try and sort things out so Mara's not picking up vibes between the two of you?"

"Mara doesn't notice anything's off. I make sure of that."

George just stared off, lost in thought. "Because... I know it's desperate that my kids see me and Mossy fighting, but I kind of think, well, at least they see us dealing with it and moving on. Like, we fight, but we're able to make up and laugh about it after, do you know what I mean?"

"It's fine. Mara's fine."

"Of course," George said. "Sure, you know her best."

6

That night, after Mara and I watched *Return of the Jedi*—by ourselves—and she'd gone to bed, I settled myself down by the window in the living room overlooking the front steps. I was determined to wait up for Richard no matter how late he came back. It was half past eleven and he still wasn't home.

As I waited, I mulled over what George had said about therapy. Maybe she was right about it, but on the other hand, there were few things more mortifying than sharing your innermost thoughts with a slightly intimidating stranger. Surely I could figure things out myself. And, if not, then repressing it all and becoming a functioning alcoholic was always another option to explore.

I pulled my laptop onto my knee, opened the browser and typed in, "How to make your husband—"

Google gave me several endings to choose from:

...*happy*
...*jealous*
...*attracted to you while pregnant*
...*love you again*
...*stop drinking*
...*stop verbal abuse*
...*stop snoring*

None of those were quite right. But *how to make my husband stop going out to expensive hotels with other women, keep his word, and also, while we're at it, have the slightest desire to spend time with his family, without me turning into a hateful shrewish nagging harridan?* That would have just about nailed it.

An alarming number of articles were written by women who described themselves as "a child of God," or something similar, and suggested shedding your desire to control others, and instead devoting yourself solely to the happiness of your husband and children. Only in selflessness would women find true fulfilment.

But then I spotted another website, relationshipguru.com, that offered online advice. You didn't even have to speak to the relationship expert unless you wanted to. It could all be done through online messaging. This website offered a free trial consultation; all you had to do was take a brief "personality profiler." I clicked into it.

First were the multiple-choice questions.

Are you:
   a) Straight
   b) Gay
   c) Bisexual
   d) Questioning
   e) Pansexual
   f) Asexual
   g) None of the above

Boring old (a) it is.

What are you looking for from your coach?
   a) Actionable advice
   b) Clarity on what to think or feel
   c) Self-discovery
   d) Help developing empathy for your partner

Definitely not (d). If anything I wanted *less* empathy for Richard. So (a), again.

Next came the scoring questions. You had to pick a number from one to five to indicate whether a statement accurately reflected your personality, one being "completely untrue," five being "describes me perfectly."

Do you feel your needs are ignored or unmet in your relationship?

Definitely a five. This wasn't too bad. I was actually starting to feel pleasantly validated.

Do you feel lonely when you spend time with your partner?

Oooh, interesting. I had never considered this before, but now that I thought about it…five.

Now the site crunched the numbers, worked its magic and matched me up with my guru. She popped up on the screen, slightly unhinged-looking, like she lived off-grid and survived on berries and the occasional speared fish. But who was I to judge? Her name was Anya. Apparently, she was a matchmaker and *qualified life coach*. She had previously worked as a teaching assistant and hotel caretaker.

Oh, Jesus, she was typing: I've reviewed your responses…

Just then, a taxi drew up on the street outside our house. In the backseat, I made out Richard, fumbling around for coins again.

…and believe our Strategy Session will be a great opportunity for me to meet you and develop an action plan for you and your husband…

Sorry, meet? As in, IRL? Not unless it's in a crowded public place with a SWAT team on a nearby roof.

I heard the taxi door closing and Richard's footsteps climbing up the front steps to the house.

…ask you to please sign the following waiver: I agree not to hold Relationship Guru or its coaches liable for any decisions that I make as a result of coaching…

I flicked through her profile some more. Anya believes true contentment comes from plural marriage, with one man sharing love with several wives. She is a committed member of a Mormon community in Utah.

Right.

The door to the study abruptly opened and I slammed the laptop shut. Richard hesitated a moment, glanced at the laptop, then came in and threw himself onto the sofa.

"I was just doing the Tesco shop," I said, sounding a tad more defensive than I had meant to.

He closed his eyes and let his head sink back against the cushions. "Can we not? For once, can we just not?"

"Fine, I'll switch to Supervalu." But I knew that wasn't what he meant. He thought my comment was a passive-aggressive opening gambit designed to get a rise out of him. It wasn't, but my *next* one was.

"I must say, those original *Star Wars* movies really stand up to rewatching. I'm pretty sure I could recite most of *Return of the Jedi* at this point."

He nodded to himself slowly. "Here we go."

I almost lost my nerve then and gave up, but this needed saying. "You can't keep letting her down, Richard."

"Fuck's sake, Eliza, I'm only in the door."

He looked done in. And pissed off. I didn't care. I *did* care that Mara had kept watch by the front window for three hours straight hoping I was mistaken, and that Richard actually would make it home to her like he'd promised.

"I'm not going to let it slide just because you're getting annoyed with me."

"I'm not annoyed," he said.

"You *clearly* are."

He gestured in my direction. "You see what's happening right now? This is exactly what I was talking about. You're doing it again."

"What? What am I doing?"

"You're taking your own frustrations out on me."

"I'm frustrated because you let our daughter down. *Again.*"

His eyes settled on me with the same hard look I'd seen him give actors in auditions just before he crossed them off his list. I wondered if he'd been drinking again. "What did you do today, while I was at work? While Mara was at school?"

What was he getting at? Had he been monitoring my bank transactions again? I shrugged. "Nothing special. Same as every day."

"And what's that?"

"Like I said the other night, I've started practicing. In case some concert work comes up."

"Eliza, your piano's still wrapped in its cover. You haven't played once since we got to Dublin."

So he hadn't believed me. "I've been a tiny bit busy?"

"Busy with what?" he pressed.

Had he totally forgotten everything he'd said in his note? "Eh, orchestrating moving our entire lives from one country to another? And settling Mara into the new school?"

"We've been back three months. What do you do now? Every day?"

Oh, so we were going to go there, were we? "Who do you think does your expenses? Files your tax returns? Sorts out all the paperwork for your business accounts? And who does all the school runs, playdates, laundry, cleaning, cooking and dog care?"

He shook his head and simply said, "No." Like, all of that could not possibly account for my time.

"*And* I do all the paperwork for the theater accounts."

"Yeah…about that." He left me hanging for a moment then said, "I've been meaning to tell you. Turns out I should have interviewed external candidates for the role. According to Majella, we'll be in breach of regulations unless we switch to doing it in-house."

The *role* pretty much involved digging crumpled receipts out of Richard's pockets, the bottom of his briefcase and the floor of his car, trying to put them in order for the theater's accounts. And helping with the box office paperwork where I could. High-glamour stuff. But I liked the excuse to drop into the theater a few mornings a week, bring coffees for the office girls, hear all the backstage news.

The work itself wasn't particularly interesting but it was only now, when Richard said I wasn't wanted anymore, that I realized just how much I looked forward to the company, the sense of being part of a team. Even if it was only in a small way.

"Oh, right," I said. "That's a relief."

He watched me, waiting to see if I'd come back fighting. When I fell silent, he kicked off his shoes and reached for the remote. "Now you'll have time to practice."

7

"So, you came back."

I shifted awkwardly in my chair. "Yes."

This time I'd been careful not to make a big withdrawal at the train station ATM to pay for the session. Instead, I'd gotten a little bit of extra cash back every time I did a grocery shop. Just in case Richard was still "keeping an eye."

"It took you a while." Ms. Early's hair was combed straight back off her face and she had the air of someone long used to drawing attention, like a retired model. Or a prison warden. Today she was wearing a beautiful gray cashmere sweater with pearls running down the sleeves.

"I've been very busy," I said. *Busy losing my mind.*

Ms. Early took off her glasses and considered me. After a long pause, she said, "Maybe you don't believe I can help you."

Maybe I didn't. I'd been promised miraculous results by experts before—play therapists, occupational therapists, speech therapists and art therapists, each of them equally certain they understood the root cause of Mara's "issues" and swearing that, after a slew of shockingly expensive sessions with them, I'd quickly see the positive effects. And each time, they had made no appreciable difference. So although a younger me would have been swept up by someone like Ms. Early, the current me had reservations.

"It's not that. It's just... I've never done marriage therapy before."

"No. I don't suppose you have. I would imagine that up until this point, you have avoided tackling the problems in your marriage despite the fact that they occupy a great deal of your thoughts and energy. But your system of coping is no longer working. That's why you're here with me now."

I gave a tentative nod.

"Eliza, I want you to think back to the first day you came here. Do you remember? I made you sit out there on the landing for fifteen minutes after your appointment was due to start and you just took it. You said nothing about it to me. You didn't say, 'You know, I'm not paying for that quarter of an hour that you made me sit out there without even a *Hello!* magazine to read.' Instead, you just came in and were polite. You didn't want to offend."

"I'm not going to start World War Three because I had to wait a few minutes."

She gave a noncommittal tilt of her head. "And when you entered, I watched you take a full look around my office. Did you not wonder why my certificates, my diplomas and degrees, my qualifications weren't—*aren't*—plastered on any of the walls? You asked nothing about whether I'm qualified to give counsel at this crucial moment in your life. Why is this? You think that avoiding conflict makes you a good person? You pride yourself on being a people pleaser? No. This kind of behavior doesn't please. Eliza, what you are is *inoffensive*."

"So you're saying I'm like a vegan cheese?"

Ms. Early tutted, writing something down. "Humor is a comfort blanket for you, isn't it? If I can joke about it, things can't be too bad, right? And yes, it may help you cope temporarily, but it is not fixing anything."

I was on the brink of making a joke about *fixing* Richard but held it in. I'd save it for George.

When Ms. Early saw that I wasn't going to reply, she pushed herself back in her chair and gazed at me. "Your daughter, Mara. Tell me…is *she* a doormat, too?"

Was this woman for real? I actually wished at that moment that Mara was with me. She might be an introvert by nature, but she could be fearless. Lord knows she had sent tougher therapists than Ms. Early packing in her time. She was like a goddamn tiny Will Hunting.

"Wow. That's a pretty shit way to talk about a child."

To my surprise, the therapist gave a burst of laughter and clapped her hands together. "Finally! *Finally*, I get to see the real Eliza. I knew you were in there somewhere. Nice to meet you. So you do have limits after all. Now I see your daughter is the no-go area. Everything else is fair game—you, your husband, your marriage—but this is the one thing you never joke about. I get it. I respect it."

I realized Ms. Early had not been truly engaged in the session until this point. Now she was switched on, leaning forward, focusing all her energy and attention on me. "I have no doubt that she is a wonderful child, Eliza, and of course you are right in defending her from unfair attacks. But the strength of your reaction just now suggests something more… It suggests to me that *any* criticism of your child you'd take on board as criticism of you. It hits a very raw nerve. You believe that any fault in your child has been caused by you, by a mistake you made, by a flaw in your parenting."

Of course I believed it. Because it was true.

"I imagine you are raising your daughter in the modern way, to be strong and independent, all of these things? I suppose you buy her all those books about inspiring women, yes?"

"*Raising Rebel Girls, Volumes 1, 2* and *3*," I admitted.

"And you read to her about Cleopatra and Granuaile and Hatshepsut?"

"Guilty as charged."

"Pardon my bluntness, but you're wasting your breath. These are just fairy tales to her. Myths. Those stories make no difference. *You* are teaching her every day what it is to be a woman, what it is to be a wife, by how you live your life. *You* are teaching her what marriage looks like, what is acceptable, what to expect, what to tolerate. Just as your parents taught you. And as Richard's parents taught him."

"No wonder we're so messed up."

"What do you mean by that?" She was watching me closely.

I'd really just said it to break the tension, but I could see now that she wasn't going to let it go. "Let's just say I didn't exactly have a *typical* childhood."

"Go on."

Where to even start? I gave her the abridged version. My father had been a very promising musician as a young man, on track for an excellent orchestral career until he fell hard for my mother who was—he always made sure to tell people—"exceptionally beautiful." That was him all over: you were either exceptional or you weren't worth his time. They got married at twenty-one and the babies started coming, me first and then one a year like clockwork. After half a decade of marriage, they had a brood of five children, nobody spoke of my mother's exceptional beauty anymore and my father was grinding away as a lowly piano teacher to pay the ever-mounting bills. It was around this time that he spotted my talent. It became his obsession. If *he* couldn't make it as a world-class musician, then by God his daughter would.

From then on, it was all about me. Family photos and shots of my mother in her modeling days were pushed aside to make room for my trophies and framed reviews praising my performances. He became busier than ever as a piano teacher as word spread that his daughter was a prodigy. I had to rise at five every morning so he could fit my lessons in before school. As a teenager, weekends were dedicated entirely to practicing and performing. Perfection was expected and if it was not delivered, a black cloud of silence would hang over the house for days. My little brothers and sisters, along with my mother, would all bear the brunt of my mistakes.

"And then?" Ms. Early prompted.

What did she want to know? That I started having panic attacks then? That I began lashing back Rescue Remedy, not because of the calming flower essences but because of the 27 percent alcohol solution in each little bottle? And that I soon ditched those in favor of straight vodka concealed in water bottles?

"That's it."

"And your mother. Did she see the pressure you were under?"

My mother kept the show running at home and over the years developed a sort of fixation with making money stretch as far as it could. Maybe she wanted to impress my father. But she had become almost invisible to him. "Even if she had noticed something was wrong, my father wouldn't have listened to her."

"He didn't respect her?"

"No."

"No wonder you're so angry with Richard."

Not so fast, Ms. Early. You're not putting this on me. "I'm angry with Richard because he's extremely irritating. And quite possibly having an affair."

She jotted something down, then said, "And Richard's parents? What were they like?"

"His mother died when he was young and his father was so devastated that he sent Richard off to boarding school. When he was eight."

I expected to hear her say something like, *Ah! That explains everything: he exhibits all the traits of Boarding School Syndrome. None of this is your fault, Eliza. He is clinically incapable of being sound!*

But instead, she said, "Let me ask you something. If Mara ended up in a marriage like yours, how would it make you feel?" *How would it make me feel? Like taking out a hit on my undeserving little shit of a hypothetical son-in-law, that's how.*

Ms. Early smiled as she watched my expression. "We better make sure you set a good example, then." She picked up a notebook and pen. "Now that I know what you want, we're going to make sure it's not already too late. There are three essential questions that will tell me whether there is hope for your marriage. Are you ready?"

I nodded.

"First question. Do you argue a lot?"

"No," I lied. "Except for the occasional email here and there. And in my head."

I thought this would be a point in our favor, but she made a disapproving clicking sound and jotted something down. I tried to see what she had written but she had tilted her notebook so it was hidden from me.

"Surely fighting is bad?" I said. "Especially if you have a child?"

"Disagreements are natural. Inevitable. If there are fights, it means someone is still fighting for the relationship. Next question. Do you ever fantasize about living by yourself? I mean, you and Mara without Richard?"

"No," I said again. "I mean, only when he snores. Or comes home late, or drunk, and wakes me up. Or turns Mara upside down when she's eating, so that she ends up getting sick or choking. Or loses my car keys when I need to bring Mara to school. Or—"

"So that's a *yes*," Ms. Early said, making another note. "And the third question." She looked up from her notebook. "How did you and Richard meet?"

I hesitated. How should I play this? What was the "right" answer?

"Stop overthinking it," she said. "Just tell me how you remember it."

"Umm... Okay. So I met him in London. Our fathers were friends. Richard had just graduated from Harrow and was back living at home for the summer."

"And you felt a connection with Richard? An instant chemistry?"

I shook my head. "Not exactly, no. My father became too busy with his stream of rich pupils to go with me to all my performances, so sometimes his friend Matthews would stand in for him. And Matthews became a sort of unofficial manager. The problem was that he *also* became a sort of unofficial sex pest."

"I see. How old were you?"

"Twenty, but I was very sheltered. Inexperienced. I didn't know how to handle it. To be honest, I *still* wouldn't know how to handle it."

I proceeded to divulge how I'd put Matthews off as much as I could, but he acted like that was part of some game we were playing, which it definitely wasn't. I told my mother, but she seemed to think it was no big deal, and her only advice was to make sure I wasn't leading him on. She didn't want to tell my father because she was afraid of annoying him—and so was I.

My concerts had become bigger and more stressful, my schedule was increasingly hectic and I began to dread going to bed because of the recurring nightmares I was having about Matthews. By the time I got to know Richard, I was in a bad place. I had started controlling what I ate—because it felt good to be in control of *something*—and my clothes were hanging off me. I was barely sleeping. I was jumpy, nervous, startled easily.

One particular day, when Richard called to the house, it all spilled out in a big, messy, tearful confession. He was so kind and understanding. He wanted to help me. He said he was going to fix everything. I remember him saying that if he couldn't fix this, no one could. And then he came up with a plan. One night I sneaked out of my house and got into the taxi that was waiting for me at the bottom of my street, with Richard in it.

"He was right," I said. "He really did fix everything. Because then—"

Ms. Early held her hand up to stop me from continuing. "I don't need to hear more. This tells me enough."

"In a good way or a bad way?"

"It's not so much *how* you met that interests me, but the way you tell the story. If you were to say, 'Oh, looking back I can see all these red flags, I should have known there would be problems, I shouldn't have let him treat me like that,' then I can be fairly sure the relationship will not make it. But the way you smiled while you were talking about him, the warmth in your voice, the fact that it clearly makes you feel good to think about those early days... This tells me there is hope."

She set her pen down to study me. "Now I'd like you to do one more thing for me. I'd like you to think of a time when he did something that upset you. I mean something that *really* hurt you."

I immediately had my answer. "Well, one morning—when Mara was still a baby—I asked Richard to get her dressed and he put her clothes on over her pajamas. And that evening before bed, he just put on *another* pair of pajamas. So now she was wearing pajamas over clothes over pajamas. And I realized that if I died, he might just keep putting on more and more layers until she became a little round baby mille-feuille. The Baby of a Thousand Layers."

"Eliza..."

"I'm not trying to be funny. It really did bother me."

She gave me a disappointed look, then looked down at her notebook. "I suppose the photo you showed me in our first session will serve our purposes."

I wondered if she was going to get me to do that mind trick where you pictured someone you didn't like and then made their image spin round and round and then shot them out into the universe in order to trick your mind into thinking they were inconsequential. Or had died from some fluke humiliating accident. Like locking themselves into a walk-in freezer.

But instead, she said, "Over the next few weeks, whenever you're starting to think, 'Is therapy worth it?' or 'Should I keep going?' I want you to open up that photo on your phone and take a long, hard look at it. I want you to let all your anger and hurt come to the surface, and then use it as motivation to see this through."

It seemed like quite an unhealthy approach. I loved it. Nothing like being given permission to nurture a grudge.

"All right. Now we can get started," she said, clasping her hands together. "What we need to achieve is to simply, how can I put this, *adjust* the focus of your husband's energy."

"God, Richard's not going to like that very much. Especially if it means redirecting his focus from himself."

"Richard's not going to know."

I gave her a puzzled look. "But how will that work?"

"He won't be coming to any sessions."

"Okay…"

But if Richard didn't come with me, he wouldn't get to see that a professional marriage expert was taking my side. Wasn't that the whole point of marriage therapy? And if Ms. Early only wanted me to come, did that mean *I* was the one who was going to have to change?

Ms. Early leaned back in her chair and crossed her legs. She didn't look particularly pleased. "Look, Eliza, if you would prefer to go down the route of traditional couples counseling, that's fine. Go right ahead. But I can tell you, with over twenty years of experience, that it simply doesn't work. You'll spend months going to sessions together and the only thing you'll take away will be 'better' ways of complaining about each other's behavior."

I laughed. She did not.

"And," she added, "you'll constantly be encouraged to be honest with each other, to tell each other what you're really thinking. But all that does is systematically kill off any remaining traces of love, of desire, of mystery, of curiosity in the other person. It will drive you further apart. Let me tell you—'honest' communication is one of the single most damaging pieces of advice propagated by modern marriage therapists."

Right on, Ms. Early. If Richard knew half of what I was thinking, we'd be divorced by morning.

"What I offer is an alternative approach," she continued. "We are going to make use of the fact that the male brain has a greater degree of neuroplasticity than the female. It is malleable. In fact, it is exquisitely receptive to modification. In other words, Eliza, we will train, or retrain, your husband."

Was she joking? The words of Bertie Wooster came back to me, when his aunt praised a prospective fiancée who would *mold* him: *I don't want to be molded. I'm not a jelly.* To which his aunt replied, *that is a matter of opinion.*

"Are you saying Richard's like a jelly?" I asked.

"No. What I'm saying is we can switch your husband's empathy back on."

We can switch your husband's empathy back on.

I wanted to ask her to repeat that so I could record it this time and play it to myself on a loop while I cleaned the house. I wanted to embroider it on a cushion that I could hug to myself as I went to sleep on the floor beside Mara's bed whenever she got bouts of nervous vomiting.

She stared at me intently. "I should tell you, Eliza, I am extremely selective about the clients I take on."

Wasn't I already a client? Or was all this just a test run?

"If I am to work with you, then you must agree to one condition," she said. "You cannot—and I mean, *cannot*—tell your husband that you're seeing me. And you absolutely must not tell him about the methods we're using. If he finds out, not only will this therapy not work, but it will cause irreparable damage to your marriage."

I slowly nodded, not quite sure what I was agreeing to.

She set down her notebook and peered at me over her glasses. "So, Eliza. Shall we begin?"

8

Yeah, this was a mistake all right. I knew it as soon as we came out of the Fleet Street car parking lot and Mara said, nice and loud, "Mom, why is that man urinating on a window?" There had been an Indian summer feeling in the air and people had evidently started drinking early. The man in question was part of an English stag party and was, indeed, relieving himself on the window of an all-you-can-eat Chinese restaurant. Oh, and now he was wandering in for dinner. Lovely.

"He must have had too many fizzy drinks. Now, on we go."

Mara was traveling light; just a backpack containing her second-best magnifying glass, a camera and her volcanic rock collection. She also had a small cardboard box wedged on her head as a helmet and was wearing camo gear. I put my arm round her, pulling her close as we weaved our way down the streets of Temple Bar, trying to avoid the crowds. She'd gone quiet. When we finally hit the quays, she didn't even ask to lean over the too-low wall to look at the trolleys in the riverbed.

This trip seemed like a ballsy course of action. It was Saturday and I had decided that a little visit to the theater was in order. When Richard got home the previous night—*five hours later* than he'd promised Mara that morning—and I gave him a pointed look, he just brushed me off. *I have the whole weekend to make things up to her*, he'd said. But when I got up on Saturday morning, he was already out the door, saying something about extra rehearsals and how he'd be back in the afternoon. The afternoon had come, and Richard was still nowhere to be seen. So much for family time.

Well, if he wouldn't come to us, we'd go to him.

The front entrance of Blind Alley was shuttered, so we went round to the stage door. Once we stepped out of the sunshine into the velvety gloom of the theater, Mara's excitement returned. I was keen to head straight up to the administration floor, but she had different ideas.

"Please, please, please can we take a look through the Danger Door?"

I knew which door she meant. It was backstage and it separated the relatively modern part of the theater from the original, crumbling wing.

"Did you know that sometimes the handle locks and unlocks all by itself? And people say there's a ghost down there?"

"Mara, you know that's not true."

"Daddy told me! Can we just take the teeniest, tiniest peep through the door? I promise I'll only put one tip of one toe through."

So off we went and she did indeed just take the teeniest, tiniest peep through the door. And after that, she just had to have the teeniest, tiniest peep into the auditorium.

"Fine. One peep," I said. "But after that we're going straight up to find your father."

The auditorium was cavernous, but the acoustics were off because of all the scaffolding and building materials cluttering up the space. Richard was getting the ceilings repainted, new rich red embossed wallpaper put up in the boxes, an iron fire curtain installed and the gilt work repointed. It was going to be stunning but the scaffolding alone was costing five grand a week.

Mara was dying to clamber onto the stage, but I stopped her. Some of the cast was up there already, each and every one of them striking—even in their ripped jeans, sweatpants and hoodies. The lead male was dragging on a cigarette while leaning against a piece of scaffolding that bore a no-smoking sign. On a battered chaise longue, a soap star was half-heartedly trying to chat up a young woman scrolling on her phone.

I watched them while Mara entertained herself by crawling along the rows of seats. After a few minutes, the lead actor stubbed out his cigarette with unnecessary force and said, to no one in particular, "Fuck this. I'm off," and stalked off the stage. The others looked at each other and began gathering up their things.

Where was Richard?

I called Mara and we made our way to the office level. There wasn't a soul around. We looked into the general office, where I sometimes called in to chat with the staff who ran marketing and production. The lights were still on but there was a definite "weekend" feel to the place. Everyone had somewhere better to be.

We knocked on Richard's door, but no answer. We entered to find his office was empty, too. Just the portraits of former patrons of Blind Alley looking down on us. There was a lighter patch on the wall behind Richard's desk where the portrait of his predecessor used to hang. The painting was stashed away somewhere in the eaves now. The previous manager had driven the theater to new heights, but he was also a raging creep and when his mistreatment of actresses came to light, he was shown the exit and Richard's big chance had arrived.

Richard had several things going for him: first, he was a big deal in London; second, he was a hustler, a street-smart, bullied-at-Harrow Irish workaholic with a chip on his shoulder and a point to prove—in other words, he would make things happen;

third, and perhaps most importantly, he didn't have a lechy reputation.

Yet.

Mara skipped around, opening and closing everything, peering behind curtains, into cupboards and cubbies. Hmm, maybe she was on to something. I checked the corridor again. No one in sight. Right ho. Well, since we came all this way, we'd be remiss not to have a quick snoop…

Desk first. Top drawer: nothing of interest. Bottom drawer: locked. On to the computer. I tried to figure out his login. I tried "Richard" and "12345" and "BlindAlley." No dice.

I looked up from his desk to find Majella standing in the doorway. I had no idea how long she'd been there watching me. Majella, it's important to remember, took no shit. However, this had to be weighed against the fact that I was female, which gave me an immediate advantage. I had once heard her comment that when things went wrong, it was almost always a man's fault.

Majella lived the cause. She had an aggressive fringe and wore men's tailoring. She was the coolest person I knew. I also had a sneaking suspicion she was a genius, or at the very least, had been a champion debater at college.

"Hey, Mara, love the helmet," she said. Mara put a hand to the cardboard box on her head without saying a word, transfixed by the silver brogues Majella was wearing.

"We thought we'd drop by and surprise Richard," I said. Why was I explaining myself? I wasn't doing anything wrong. Not *very* wrong anyway, apart from snooping around my husband's office and trying to hack into his computer. But what loving wife *wouldn't* do that?

Richard said Majella was too serious for her age. *We weren't that serious, were we?* he'd asked. She was only four years younger than us, for God's sake. Way to make me feel like an old hag.

See also: referring to the women in the office as the "younger generation."

"Richard left about an hour ago," Majella said. "Said he was heading home."

Did he now? The lying sneak. "We must have just missed each other. That's the trouble with surprises, isn't it?"

She agreed, then turned to Mara. "Do you like the theater?"

Mara nodded at Majella's silver shoes.

"Do you like my shoes?"

Mara nodded again. In a quiet voice, she said, "Do you think fungi are plants or animals?" This was her favorite trick question.

"Mara," I said. "I don't think Majella has time for—"

"I think...neither," Majella interjected. "I think fungi are something else entirely." She walked toward Mara and squatted down next to her until she was at her eye level. "I think they're their own unique and separate life form."

Mara finally dragged her eyes from the silver shoes to meet her gaze. "Yes," she said. "So do I."

"Table quiz nerd," Majella said to me by way of explanation. Then she gestured toward Richard's PC. "Did you need help with something?" We both knew I shouldn't be on his private computer.

"No," I said. "No. We'd better be getting home."

She nodded. "The girls in the office are going to miss having you around, by the way. We all are."

"Oh. Yeah. I'm going to miss it, too, actually."

"I'd try to convince you to stay on, but I don't want to pressure you. I totally understand."

"You do?"

"Of course. I can't imagine how busy you are with Mara and then volunteering with the school..." She paused. "I honestly feel bad for imposing on you for this long. I should have realized it was too much to ask."

"I'm not volunteering with the school."

"Oh. Richard said... Sorry, I must have got my wires crossed."

"I really hope I didn't cause you hassle," I said. "I had no idea I was breaking regulations by helping—"

"Breaking regulations?" Majella gave me an unblinking stare.

"Wasn't I?"

"No, not at all." And I realized then there was no way Majella would have made a mistake like that.

We looked at each other. She knew, and I knew, that I'd been served another Richard Sheridan special. I forced a smile.

"Hopefully we'll see you around anyway," Majella said in a kind tone, making to leave.

"Wait," I said. "There is something I could use your help with actually."

She paused at the doorway.

I had to think on my feet. "Richard got sent a fine for not paying an M50 toll but I'm pretty sure it's a mix-up." I had heard the radio presenter talking about this exact situation on the drive in. "They won't drop it unless I send them proof that it couldn't have been Richard."

Who knew I could lie so easily?

Majella didn't say anything. She was not a person who felt the need to fill a silence, which I admired and envied.

"Is there any chance," I continued, "that you could get into his diary? I just wanted to double-check where he was on July twenty-fifth."

I was glad it was dark in the office. I could feel telltale blotches spreading up my neck to my face.

There was a pause. Then Majella said, "Sure." She quickly logged in and tapped a few things and said, "Here we go, his diary."

When she saw me hesitate, she said to Mara, "I don't suppose you'd like me to show you the thunder run?"

Mara gave a solemn nod, though I knew she had no idea

what the thunder run was. This was a first. Mara never wanted to go anywhere with anyone other than me.

"Oh no," I said. "You don't have to, Majella. I'm sure you have plans of your own." Also, the thunder run was an ancient contraption that involved rolling iron balls down a wooden trough to produce the sound of thunder. If Mara was going, then I was, too. I mean, *someone* needed to hover and keep asking whether it was safe or not.

"It would give you a bit of time to find what you're looking for." Majella looked me dead in the eye. She was my willing accomplice. "I'll take good care of Mara, don't worry," she added.

Once they were gone, I did a deep dive into the weird and wonderful world of my husband. Unfortunately, he wasn't *amazing* at filling in his diary, but there were some very interesting entries. For example: a note marking a phone call with a researcher for *The Late Late Show*. Seriously, he hadn't thought to mention *that*?

Ah, and here it was. Saturday, July twenty-fifth. A single entry: *Drinks with Lady Languish.*

I scrolled back farther through his diary to find the same exact entry dotted throughout the weeks leading up to July twenty-fifth.

Who the hell was Lady Languish?

I was about to shut the computer when a reminder pinged up on the screen. A reminder for an event that was happening in fifteen minutes: *Drinks with Lady Languish.*

In the distance, I heard peals of thunder rumbling throughout the theater.

9

Richard was home when Mara and I returned. I watched him moseying round the kitchen, staring long and deep into the fridge, opening all the drawers, not closing them. I knew he wanted to ask if there was anything for dinner but he had enough of a sense of self-preservation not to.

He had not commented on the yellow Post-it notes stuck to the wall. Or along the front of the oven, the clock and the toaster. They all read pretty much the same thing: some version of *Get a python* or the pithier, *Snake!*

They'd appeared around the house that afternoon. On the hall mirror. The screen of my laptop. The fireplace. The cistern of the toilet.

I was waiting for Richard to notice them, to be amused by Mara's funny little attempt at subliminal messaging. But he'd been home for seventeen minutes and still had not noticed any of the Post-its. Or he'd noticed but wasn't interested enough to ask about them. Too busy thinking about the theater. Or what to eat. Or mulling over the ethical quandaries of carrying out an extramarital affair. Or—quite possibly—he was thinking of nothing at all.

Here was a list of other questions he had not asked since

coming home: if Mara had found anyone to play with in the yard yet; how her homework went; if she was still awake and if maybe he should pop upstairs to say good-night.

And here's what *I* had not asked Richard since he got home: if he remembered that time we drove to the maternity hospital and I stayed there a couple of days and we came home with a—what do you call them again?—oh, yeah, a *daughter*, and did he know we still had one?

What I did instead was this: I pushed all of those thoughts deep, deep down until they were buried right around the place where I was working on my first ulcer and forced myself to say, "You must be tired. Why don't you sit down and relax? Dinner's almost ready. And I put a beer in the freezer to chill."

I actually had to turn away just then and breathe through my nose. If I made eye contact it would be game over. This was not only mortifying, but also very obviously a charade. He was sure to think I was mocking him.

This week you'll be entering phase one of the treatment plan, Ms. Early had said at the end of our last session. *We will trigger Richard's softer side by first modifying your own behavior.*

In other words, kill him with kindness.

There was silence. I glanced at him. There was not just shock, but *alarm* in his eyes. "Jesus, I haven't put cyanide in it," I said.

He laughed awkwardly. In fairness, I *was* acting weird. Maybe he thought I wanted to have a "talk."

"Why? Did I look scared?"

It was my turn to laugh then. "Yeah, you did, actually."

He sat down at the table, and I served him the first course. *Without* giving an ironic curtsy. It was his favorite—homemade French onion soup. With croutons.

Then I brought over the chilled bottle of Peroni.

"Wow," he said. "Why are you being so nice to me?"

Oh, please. It wasn't like I hadn't cooked dinner for him 1,785 times before. Not that I kept count. Apparently, you weren't supposed to. It was unhealthy or something. But I always found that the people who gave that advice were the ones who never cooked.

"Maybe you deserve it."

He didn't.

Once he'd finished the starter, I whisked it away and served the main course: rare fillet steak with all the trimmings—garlic-infused mash, sautéed onions, peppercorn sauce. And a dash of swallowed pride.

Again, that nervous smile. He knew something was up, but more importantly, he was hungry.

I opened a Peroni for myself. I was going to need it. "I just wanted to say…" *Deep breath. You can do this.* "I know you've been under a lot of pressure at the theater. And I know it sometimes feels like I don't give you any credit for how hard you work." *…at seducing women who aren't your wife.* "But I do notice, and I do appreciate it. I know work's going to be intense, with rehearsals and everything. But…you don't need to feel guilty if you have to put in long hours for the next few weeks." *Even though you've always worked long hours and have never felt guilty about it.* "And you don't need to worry about checking in." *Which should be easy for you—it's not like you've ever bothered to check in before.* "I've got things under control here. So, just…do what you need to do."

His chewing slowed down and he looked at me, again with that slightly stunned expression. "That is really nice of you, Eliza. Thank you."

I took away his empty plate and slid a large slice of chocolate cake and an espresso in front of him. *Was I at risk of larding it on too thick?* No, turns out the lard could literally never be too thick. It was not possible to over-gild this lily. This was not a man who would ever, *ever* wonder if he was deserving of something.

After a few minutes of devoting himself to the cake, he raised his eyes and said, "So. How are *you*?"

There was a time, back when Mara was a baby, when he used to ask this on the daily. At first, I was touched by the gesture, by the fact he was considerate enough to think about my well-being after a tough day at the theater. Then I found a book in his study titled *What to Expect When Your Wife is Expecting*. One of the pages was turned down, and the advice was to ask your wife how she was, every day, even if she was acting like a screaming she-devil. *Especially* if she was acting like a screaming she-devil. I was still pretty touched that he was making some sort of an effort to be caring, even if it wasn't entirely genuine.

But then I began to notice that no matter how I answered the question, he never responded. Not even a nod to show he had heard me. I began formulating a hypothesis that he was not, in fact, listening at all. I tested this theory by saying things like, "How am I? I'd say I'm about one more night feed away from a psychotic break. I'm also pretty sure I felt my soul leave my body for a minute earlier today."

Never the slightest flicker of reaction from Richard. Maybe he thought I was joking, so he didn't want to dignify it with an answer. But I found myself going further each time, pushing it to see. It became a sort of game, albeit a one-sided, self-destructive game that inevitably eviscerated my sense of self-worth.

And here he was now, reviving that old question. "How are *you*?" The emphasis on the *you*, as if we had at some point—unknown to me—agreed that, apart from this one-minute interval, our time and energies would be focused all on him.

"How am I?" I started. "Hmm, well, today I stuck my head in the oven to see if Sylvia Plath was on to something. But our oven is electric, so I just singed my eyebrows."

He looked at me with concern. "Why would you say that?"

Wow, he was actually listening.

"I'm joking," I said. "I'm fine. I mean, what do I even have to be stressed about?" I caught myself, then pivoted. "Anyway, enough about me. How are things coming along at work?"

His face closed over and he swirled the dregs of his beer around in the bottle. "Richard, what is it?"

He stared at the bottle for a long while as if working up to something, then said, "I'm letting everyone down. Everyone at the theater. And you. Mara." There was a break in his voice. Here it was, his big confession.

"What do you mean?" I said, even though I suddenly realized I didn't want to know.

He seemed unable to look me in the eye. "The last act... I still haven't finished it."

I bit my lip, wondering how best to respond. "Ah."

"We still need to raise a lot more funding. But any investors who are interested need to see the full script before they make a decision." He paused, then said, "But I'm stuck. I'm *stuck*," he repeated, as if admitting this to himself for the first time. "I just... I can't do it."

I looked at Richard, his head in his hands. I have to admit, part of me really just wanted to load the dishwasher. But because I'm not a *completely* hardened psychopath, I said, "You want my advice?"

He gave a nod.

"Obviously, I'm not a writer so I don't really know what I'm talking about, but when you boil it down, pretty much every story is about the cost of human connection, right?" I think I read that once on a flyer for a French film festival.

Richard looked up at me in surprise. "Well, yes, actually. I suppose so."

I forced a soft smile. "So maybe try to figure out an ending that shows your main character finally realizing that the price of human connection is worth it after all."

Richard went quiet for a long time, considering. As I watched him, I saw the tension in his jaw gradually ease. Finally, he gave a wry half laugh and said, "I wish I'd talked to you about this a long time ago."

"What can I tell you? I've got hidden shallows," I said, breaking eye contact. His affectionate gaze made me uneasy.

He was about to speak but his attention settled on my hands. I realized I'd been mock-playing the first few bars of a Chopin piece on the table. It was a habit I'd had back in my performing days. Even when I was away from the piano, my hands would still be practicing and I'd drift away to the music playing in my mind. It was a largely involuntary thing. In fact, I'd often be unaware I was even doing it. As habits went, I thought it was pretty innocuous. And I found it calming. But Richard had always considered it an unpleasant tic, like biting your nails. It had been years since it last flared up. I self-consciously withdrew my hands from the table.

There was a crackle on the intercom and then the sound of Mara crying out. Another nightmare. Instinctively, I got to my feet, but Richard said, "No, I'll go. You relax."

Well, blow me down. In all six years of Mara's existence on this earth, this had never, *ever* happened before.

One-nil to Ms. Early.

Obviously, I sneaked up after him and hovered outside Mara's bedroom door. Richard, when he was under pressure, had a short fuse and I didn't want her bearing the brunt of it.

"Not you. I want Mama," I heard Mara say.

This was usually enough to provoke Richard's frustration, but tonight he just said, "Yep, she'll be up in a minute now. I just needed to ask you something before you fell asleep. It's been bugging me all day…was the Chickenosaurus like a giant chicken with teeth? Or was it a tiny dinosaur with feathers?"

Her tone immediately changed to one of excitement as she filled him in—at length—on her thoughts. After a pause, I heard him say, "So were you having a bad dream? Before I came up?"

A long silence, then in a small voice, she said, "It was the same dream. About the mold."

What mold?

"What mold?" Richard said.

"The mold in the corner of my classroom."

"Oh. Is there a lot of it or something?"

"No, only a little but...*you know.*"

"What?"

"That fungus thing."

What fungus thing?

"What fungus thing?"

She lowered her voice so I could barely hear: "The zombie fungus."

"Ah now, Mara. There's no such thing as a zombie fungus."

Well played, Richard. When in doubt, follow the golden rule: deny, deny, deny.

"There is! It infects foraging ants in tropical forests. It penetrates the ant's exoskeleton and slowly takes over its behavior, controlling its every move. And then it feeds on its innards before sprouting through the ant's head!"

"Jesus," Richard said.

"That's why I hate going to school. Because of the mold."

There was a pause, then his voice changed. "Right. First thing tomorrow, I'm going to have a word with your teacher. I'll tell him there'll be free movie tickets for your whole class if he'll let me send a professional in to remove every single bit of that mold. How does that sound?"

There was a catch in Mara's voice when she answered, "Thank you, Daddy." It had been a long time since I heard her say that to him.

When he came out, he saw me standing on the landing and smiled, nodding toward her bedroom. "You're doing a great job with her."

And despite myself, I felt the little Pavlovian rush that always accompanied a compliment from Richard, even when I was fully aware that the compliment was really an admission not just of shirking his parental responsibilities, but of dumping them on me. Maybe Ms. Early was right. Maybe at my core, I was desperate to please. Like a pathetic lapdog frantic for a pat on the head.

"I mean it," he said when I didn't respond. "If it wasn't for you…" He broke off. *Sorry, was that a crack of genuine emotion?* "You're keeping the whole show on the road. And I'm sorry for what I said about your career. It'll be your time. After this play is finished. I promise."

This wasn't just a pat on the head. This was a milk bone, a tummy rub and letting me climb into the dishwasher to lick the plates. My traitorous pituitary gland was going into overdrive.

What happened next was just as shocking. I stayed there on the landing without speaking for a fraction too long and something shifted in the air between us. Neither of us made eye contact in the gloomy glow of the plug-in night-light, me propped against the jamb of our bedroom door, Richard with his back against the overflowing hot-press.

I knew what was coming, just as surely as you can tell at the end of an awkward first date that the other person is weighing up whether or not to lean in. And I could see all the various ways this might play out. When it came to Richard, I was a grand master. Most likely, I'd say I was tired and was going to turn in early, but instead of retreating to his study to watch CNN or Bear Grylls, he would appear in our room.

Plan B was deciding whether or not to pretend to be asleep.

Of course, pretending to be asleep didn't fool anyone. It was a rejection, and according to every agony aunt column I had ever read, rejection was deeply damaging to a man's self-esteem, so it would undo all the progress made this evening. And if he *had* betrayed me with another woman, or even if he was on the brink of an affair, wouldn't a rejection just drive him straight into her arms?

What would Ms. Early say? The key principle of her approach was to create positive associations. To heap praise and reward upon Richard *quickly*, so that he subconsciously began to associate certain actions with pleasurable outcomes, and those actions would then become habit. His kindness to Mara was definitely an action I wanted to encourage, and according to Ms. Early, timing was everything. It was now or never.

"Eliza," he said, in a low voice.

Here we go.

"I was wondering… I know you're tired, but would you stay up and help me with the script?"

Well, fuck. This was going to be harder than I thought.

Weekly Spouse Tracker

Rate the following spousal behaviors from 1 to 5:

1=non-existent,   2=poor/rare,   3=adequate/sometimes,
4=satisfactory/frequent,   5=excellent/always

BEHAVIORS	WEEKLY SCORE
Physical affection	2
Spontaneous acts of kindness	2
Gratitude for Service	3
General attentiveness	3
Reliability	1
Self-Absorption	4
Helps out around the house	1
Attentiveness to offspring	3
Answers texts/phone calls	1
Unaccounted-for disappearances	2

*To be completed in between sessions and returned to Ms. Early

10

My plan was to brush past the receptionist in a display of uncharacteristic chutzpah and march straight into Ms. Early's office. Possibly without even knocking. I was about to work some serious Main Character Energy, storm on in there and ask for her credentials. What *did* I even know about this woman?

That was the plan. But when I sashayed into the reception area, it was empty. Turns out it's hard to ignore a snooty receptionist when they're not there. And Ms. Early's door stood open. So that ruled out any barging. The therapist was sitting beneath the big sash window, sunlight falling on her as she sorted through documents on her desk. She looked up. "Eliza," she said, not in the least surprised to see me. I did my best to storm in, but that was also hard to do when someone is smiling and beckoning you.

"Come," she said. "Sit."

My initial plan had been to stand until I'd gotten some answers. But I'd had to walk quite a long way from the car park. Plus, I'd taken the four flights of stairs at an unwise pace. And—it had to be said—I was hungover.

So I sat.

Maybe it was her silk shirt or the cool way she combed her

hair straight back off her face, but I was suddenly aware of how disheveled and, dare I say, clammy, I was. Never mind, scratch that. It was time to unleash the New Me.

But just as I was about to begin my line of questioning, Ms. Early said, "Here you are," and handed me a sheet of stiff, creamy paper, which certified that Ms. Ellen Early had earned a master's degree in psychotherapy from Oxford.

I looked at her and she gave me a sly smile, like we were in on some secret joke. "This is what you wanted to know, yes? If I am...legitimate? Qualified?"

What could I say? Well, obviously, I could have said yes. But it turns out it was much easier to be rude to someone in your head. When you don't know they're an Oxford graduate.

"Eliza," she said again, touching the tips of her fingers to my hand. "It's completely normal to admit you have doubts. If you didn't have doubts, I'd be worried."

I cleared my throat. "Yes, I suppose I do have a few doubts. About the treatment."

"What part of the treatment are you unsure about?" Her expression remained neutral. Was she sympathetic or secretly seething? I just couldn't tell. But she was paying very close attention to me.

"Well...the whole 'Stepford Wife' act." It *was* demeaning.

"Stepford Wife?"

"You know, pandering to Richard's every need? Responding with delight to his every comment? Suppressing all my irritation, which, in all honesty, is quite considerable?"

"You've not noticed any improvement in his mood?"

"Oh, he's in great form. He's *lapping* it up," I said. "But I don't think I can keep this up. I'm exhausted."

"Why?"

"Why? Because *along* with pandering to his every need, I'm up every night helping him finish his play."

Ms. Early leaned forward in her chair, her hands clasped. "Tell me, what is the play about?"

I'd first learned the details of the play's plot that pivotal night on the landing, when Richard had asked me to help with the script—which, in all fairness, was actually quite good. Strange, but good. It was easy to lose sight of your husband's talents when you're too busy stewing in resentment.

"It's about a young woman who sets her sights on an older married man, and when he tries to end the affair, the young woman becomes more and more disturbed," I said.

Ms. Early raised an eyebrow. "I see."

"I'm not describing it very well. It's more nuanced than that."

"I'm glad," she replied, "because from what you just said, it sounds like it perpetuates a misogynistic narrative that absolves abusive men from any blame in a toxic relationship by labeling the woman as *crazy*."

"I didn't say the male character was abusive."

"Is he not?"

I considered the scenes Richard had shared with me. *Was* the protagonist abusive? I hadn't really thought of that. But even if he was, it's all a work of fiction, so that shouldn't be relevant here. Right?

"I'm sure it's a perfectly fine play, Eliza," Ms. Early added, reading my expression. "All I am trying to do is help you see that sometimes, when women are in relationships that have an uneven power dynamic—whether it be money, age or status—it becomes easier for that man to undermine the woman's confidence. To convince her that she's the cause of any problems in the relationships, that she's the *crazy* one."

"So you're saying my marriage has an uneven power dynamic?"

She cocked her head at me in a way that too closely bordered on pity. Then she flipped open my file. "So. How has Richard's behavior been?"

I sighed. "That's the problem. At first, he paid me a little more attention. And he made all sorts of promises—"

"And did he follow through on them?"

"Nope. He arranged to meet me for a nice lunch in town as a sort of thank-you for my help with the script, but then couldn't make it last minute." I shook my head and laughed despite myself.

"What did he say when he called to cancel?"

"Oh, Richard doesn't *call* to cancel. He just doesn't show up. But in all fairness, about a half an hour later, I received a text from one of the theater's office girls who let me know he wasn't coming."

"He was too busy to send you a message himself?"

"Masters of the universe don't have time for texting."

"How did you feel after that?" she asked, unfazed by my deflections.

I considered this for a moment, then answered in the most honest way I could. "Like slipping a smidge of arsenic into his truffle-oil risotto," I said.

There was the tiniest flicker of a muscle at the corner of her mouth. Was it the start of a smile?

This was my moment. I took a deep breath. "Ms. Early, I can't go on with the Stepford Wife act. I'm sorry, I do trust you, but I don't think changing *my* behavior is going to change *his*."

She didn't say anything. I tentatively stole a glance at her, waiting for her reaction. "Congratulations," she said finally with a smile. "You've passed the first test."

I frowned. "Test?"

"I'm sorry that you had to demean yourself, Eliza. But I had to let you figure out for yourself that no matter how you behave— whether you tie yourself up in knots for him, suppress all your needs, be the prototypical 'perfect' wife—it will not fix your marriage. The problem is not with you. The problem is with the recalcitrant domestic male in your life."

I slowly nodded, unsure where she was going with this.

Ms. Early leaned forward in her seat. "People say that it takes two to make a relationship fail. But in fact, the opposite is true. It takes two people to make a relationship *work*. Do you see?"

I tried my best to follow. "Kind of?"

"There are three types of people in relationships," she continued. "The first have no boundaries. They let their partner walk all over them and don't realize there's anything wrong with the situation. We'll call this category the *unconscious doormat*. You have now woken up from this state."

"So I'm a *conscious* doormat now?"

"Sure, if you like. You are now in the second category—people who have boundaries but don't know how to enforce them. They feel resentful, they know they're being wronged, but they are powerless to fix the situation. So they bemoan their fate, they vent, and over time, they become cynical. Embittered. This is where you are now."

Finally, someone truly understood me!

"And last," she went on, "there are those people who know what their boundaries are *and* know how to enforce them. If they don't want to do something, they don't do it. If they have needs, they satisfy them—without guilt, without worrying about offending anyone else."

"Let me guess, they're called *men*?"

Ms. Early smiled to herself—she liked this, I could tell. "What we must do now, Eliza, is move you from category two to category three. Yes?"

"By all means, sign me up."

"But we will never achieve that unless you believe you are Richard's equal," Ms. Early said. "That *both* of you are equally entitled to happiness, fulfillment, transcendence. But you don't believe that, do you?"

"Of course I do. Okay, well maybe not the transcendence bit."

"You're lying," she said. "To me, and possibly to yourself. He's got a hold over you."

"I wouldn't say *that*..."

"It's obvious. And that is what is blocking this whole situation." She paused, making sure I was listening. "Why do you put up with him?"

"Umm, well..." *Think, Eliza, think.* "I can't get into the Netflix app without him? We have this new smart TV and it's ridiculously overcomplicated. Seriously."

Ms. Early shook her head and flipped open a slim folder that lay on her desk. Joke time was over, apparently.

"He's got a hold over you," she repeated. "And to find out why that is, I need to dig deeper. I need to know more about your early days. Tell me more about running away together. What was that like?"

"What was it *like*?"

"Was it exciting? Frightening? Did it feel like you were being rescued?"

"Well, the papers did make it out to be some kind of real-life Romeo and Juliet situation."

"Wasn't it?"

"I mean...he was no Romeo. Trust me. He pretty much had a mullet back then."

"And the rescue part?"

I hesitated, mulling this over. "Yes," I finally said. "I suppose it did feel like he was rescuing me."

After the session, I walked to the train station in a daze. I hadn't opened up about our "honeymoon" era to, well, *anyone* before. But the past hour had just changed that.

I'd divulged it all to Ms. Early, starting with the fact that, once I told Richard about Matthews, he became dead set on bringing me to a convent academy where they took in female boarders with musical ability. But by the time we got off the ferry in Calais, I was sick. Really sick. It was probably a combination of months of stress, weeks of barely eating and then severe seasickness on the crossing. Richard wanted to bring me to a hospital, but I had refused. I was twenty years old, alone and seriously ill in a foreign country with a twenty-one-year-old man I barely knew. They'd definitely alert the authorities. Or worse—my father would be on the next flight over.

And so Richard, with nothing but his schoolboy French and charm, found a young doctor who ran a medical center in the docklands of Calais, who just so happened to be married to a nurse. Richard spun the couple a story of forbidden love and tyrannical parents—that part was true, at least. The doctor and nurse lived above the clinic, and it turned out they, too, had defied their families to live together before getting married. Long story short, Richard persuaded them not only to treat me, but also to let me stay with them while I recovered. He found a dirt-cheap hotel for himself around the corner and called to the clinic every day, asking to see me. And each day the doctor said no, insisting I was too weak for visitors, too weak even to talk on the phone. Richard settled for spending all day sitting on a bench below my window to show he was thinking of me. When I was well enough to sit up, I'd look out for him. He was almost always there, sometimes reading, other times writing in a notebook. On the rare occasion when he wasn't there, I would feel a lurch of disappointment.

He came every single day for two weeks until I was strong enough to leave. But by then, my father had sent word that he knew where I was, and that he was on his way to take me home. When I told Richard that my father was coming, instead of immediately accepting defeat, which I'd anticipated, he just went very still. Then he looked me in the eye and said, "Eliza, you are not going back with your father. I won't let that happen." It was moving, how protective he was over me. No one had ever been on my side like that before.

But Richard didn't know the man he was dealing with.

By the time my father turned up in Calais and summoned me to his hotel, I was a wreck again. The anxiety attacks had come back full force, and the night terrors were once again wrenching me from my sleep. It felt like I was allergic to him, and the closer he was to me, the more my body entered panic mode.

Richard told me not to go to the hotel, that he'd confront my father on my behalf. I knew it was pointless but acquiesced. Anything to postpone the inevitable. He was gone three hours total. And when he finally returned, the first thing he said to me was, "It's done." My father was taking the next ferry back to England.

Without me.

Richard had used his legal knowledge to convince my father that should this "dispute" end up in court, a judge would take a very dim view of the punitive terms of the contract I'd been coerced into signing while still a minor. He'd *also* pointed out to him how damaging it would be if my father's treatment of me appeared in the papers—which it undoubtedly would if we wound up in a high conflict court case. Unbeknownst to me, Richard had prepared and offered my father settlement terms that would avoid court altogether.

Terms that allowed me to buy my way out of the management contract.

Under the settlement, I still had to fulfill my remaining concert obligations and sign over the full earnings from those to my father. I also had to give him a bigger cut of my recorded music royalties and a percentage of my trust fund. But apart from that, I could do whatever I wanted. Get a new manager, change careers, start a new life. And in a year, when I turned twenty-one, I'd be able to access the remains of my trust fund.

I was finally free. Richard had worked a miracle.

Dublin had changed since my days of coming up on the train from Mullingar as a teenager every weekend to train at the

Royal Irish Academy of Music. The secondhand store where I used to buy vintage jeans was gone, replaced by a barista school. My favorite music shop had closed down, too, the windows whitewashed and a handwritten sign announcing a pop-up supper club coming soon.

Even the train station was different. The scruffy café that used to sell Easi-single sandwiches wrapped in cling film had been jazzed up with fake-library wallpaper and blinding Edison lightbulbs. Also, there was a piano. In the station. A bit battered, hand-painted in bright, street-art colors. But still, an actual piano, just sitting right there, waiting to be played. Was this a thing now? I stood looking at it, people bumping into me as they walked past, staring down at their phones. I'll just sit down on the stool. Nothing wrong with having a rest in front of a piano.

I'll just see if it's in tune. It was.

A passer-by, hearing a few notes, paused while they were walking past. I instantly stood up and headed toward my platform. It was time to get home. But just as I was about to push through the turnstile, I heard the rippling opening of a sonata. I recognized the piece, having performed it several times myself—Beethoven's *Les Adieux*. It was one of his most difficult sonatas from a technical point of view, and it also required an emotional depth that not many pianists managed to achieve. I couldn't see through the crowds but whoever was playing it now was doing so exquisitely.

I threaded my way back toward the piano. A circle had formed around it and people had their phones out, recording the performance. I squeezed my way to the front. A small, elderly man was playing with his eyes closed, a serene smile on his face. Next to him was a woman, her hands resting on the arms of an empty wheelchair. She was smiling, too, as she watched him.

I stood there for the full seventeen minutes of the sonata,

and when the man finished, I realized that my train had come and gone.

And that my face was wet with silent tears.

I had never heard the piece performed so well, with such depth of feeling. The man sat, not moving, until the woman helped him into his wheelchair. It was a slow process. His movements were fumbling and uncertain. I went over to help and his minder thanked me.

"That was incredible," I said to the man. "You must be a professional?"

He blinked at me several times, then gave the woman a worried glance. She placed a hand on his shoulder. "It's okay, Dad." He nodded and began pulling at the threads of the blanket she had placed over his knees.

"He played professionally for thirty years," the woman said to me. "He was a concert pianist."

"I thought so," I said. "I'm... I'm actually a concert pianist myself."

She had been tucking the blanket around her father more snugly, but now she paused to look at me properly. "Really?"

"I mean, I *used* to be. I... I don't..." I heard a quiver in my voice so I stopped.

She waited for me to go on and when I didn't, she gave me a kind smile and said, "It's a stressful career."

I wanted to tell her it wasn't the stress. But I just nodded.

"You must miss it all the same, though." The woman nodded toward the man in the wheelchair, smiling down at him. "I know Dad does."

She stepped away from him, toward me, and whispered, "He has dementia. Sometimes he can't even remember who I am, but he has perfect recall of the pieces he used to perform. It's uncanny. And it still gives him so much joy."

I glanced at him again. I realized he wasn't playing with the threads of the blanket. He was moving his fingers, still prac- ticing, still playing. Just like me.

"Every morning after breakfast, he gets restless, and nothing can settle him except playing the piano. It's because he played at that time every day for decades, you see. It's in his body. He *has* to play. He said to me once, 'The day I stop playing, Maura, is the day you call Flanagan's Funerals.'"

To my embarrassment, I found I couldn't reply. I just stood there and nodded in empathy. And deep understanding.

"We come once a week. Every Thursday," she added. "He won't remember that we've been here, but while he's playing, he's in heaven."

She seemed to sense that what she was saying had a particu- lar resonance for me, because she gave me another kind smile and put a hand on my arm. Then she was gone, wheeling her father away through the crowds, leaning forward to chat with him as they went.

11

It was midterm and Mara and I were visiting George. Mossy was in Connemara on a team-building work retreat.

"They're doing axe-throwing today," George said. "Mossy's team, not the children."

"Pity it's on during midterm," I said. George had had to take a week's annual leave to mind the four children.

"Oh no," she said. "It's not a coincidence. He volunteered to organize the retreat so he could rig the dates. Says he can't take the racket when they're all at home."

The children—Mossy Jr., the twins Tim and Seamie, and baby Frankie—were all buzzing around the kitchen. *Racket* was indeed an accurate description. George put two fingers in the corners of her mouth and did a sudden, sharp two-note whistle and the noise levels dropped away. When she had their attention, she grabbed a handful of sweets from a jar. She opened the back door and flung them onto the lawn. The three oldest children shot out, and baby Frankie made a decent attempt to escape by bum-shuffling at top speed toward the door before George scooped him off the ground.

Since arriving, Mara had stayed glued to my side, avoiding all eye contact, even when Mossy Jr. offered her first choice from their weapon box. *Even* when he generously said she could have first dibs on the motorized Nerf blaster.

"You don't want to go outside with them, Mara?" George asked. Which meant: *If you were my child, you'd be out there with the door locked behind you. Also, I'd like a proper chat with your mammy.*

Mara buried her head farther into my sweater. I gave her a little squeeze. She was grand where she was.

"I don't blame you," George said to her. "Look at them, little savages." Mara peeped out just as the twins grabbed a handful of each other's curls in a fight over a purple-wrapped sweet.

They wrestled free of each other's grip but weren't done yet. "Three, two, four, eight, you're a potato face," Tim roared at Seamus.

"You're a potato *butt*," Seamus roared back.

"Potatoes don't have butts."

I saw Mara's mouth twitch.

George shook her head. "Can you tell *butt* is their new favorite word?" Then she abruptly jumped up, rapped on the window and shouted to Mossy Jr., "Here. Stop ripping that. That's Daddy's good T-shirt."

She turned back to me and laughed. "The other night, right, Mossy said to me, 'Why do you put piles of my clean clothes on the bed? Don't you know I'll just knock them on the floor?' So *I* said, 'Fine, I'll put them somewhere better,' and I opened the window and I fuc—" She stopped and glanced at Mara. "I threw them out onto the lawn. He was mortified in case the neighbors saw and assumed I'd finally come to my senses and kicked him out."

"She's only joking, Mara," I said. "She didn't really throw his clothes out the window."

"No, I did," George said.

Mara wasn't really listening anyway. Her eyes were fixed on the garden. The sweets had all been pocketed, and now the twins were playing gladiators, with mixing bowls on their heads and mop-jousts in their hands. Mara peeled away from me and hesitantly stepped toward the door.

Mossy Jr. had shinned up a tree and was sitting on a slightly too high branch, his legs dangling. "Does Mara want to see the wasp nest?" he called to George.

"Ask her yourself."

"Mara, want to come up and see?"

She ducked her head away, shy of this ten-year-old boy she hardly knew, but then sneaked a glance up at him. She slunk back into the kitchen and I put out my hand to her, but she picked up her backpack and stiffly walked back out to the garden, over to the tree and began to climb.

"A wasp nest," I said to George. "What could possibly go wrong?"

"Relax," George said. "The wasps abandoned it last autumn. So, tell me all."

"All what?"

"You know what. The—" she lowered her voice, even though we were alone "—*photograph*. What did Richard say when you showed it to him?"

"I haven't exactly asked him about it."

"Ah, Jesus, Eliza."

"I'm biding my time. I need to do more snooping first. If I confront him now, he'll start covering his tracks and I'll never find out the truth. And besides, I took your advice and went back to that therapist. And she says that even if there *is* someone else, it's just a symptom of our problems, and that we need to treat the root cause."

"I know how *I'd* treat the root cause," George muttered, making a snipping motion with two fingers.

"I'm a week into her treatment plan, and I think she might be on to something."

George didn't say anything, just raised an eyebrow. "So what do you have to do?"

"Okay. So the first step was to stop criticizing him. No snarky comments when he comes home late, no cold shoulder even if he's being extremely irritating, no hounding him about where he's been. Instead, I have to act pleased when he comes home, ask about his day. Give him a hug."

George grimaced like I'd said I cut Richard's toenails for him. "Jesus."

"I know, I know. But I managed to force myself."

"Sorry, but what's the point of all this, exactly? Apart from setting feminism back fifty years?"

"The idea is to flood him with oxytocin every time he sees me."

"Ah, here. Oxytocin? Are you trying to send him into labor?"

"Oxytocin triggers a bonding urge in men. The therapist explained it all. There's science behind it. It's supposed to create a *subconscious positive association* whenever he thinks of me."

George jiggled baby Frankie on her knee and said nothing.

"Honestly," I continued, "we're getting on better than we have in ages. He's even asked me to help him with the script."

"It's not finished yet?"

"It just needs some last-minute tweaks. Anyway, all I'm trying to say is that it feels good to be working with him again. It's nice that he values my opinion."

"What do you mean, *again*?"

"Just that I used to help him with his articles, back in the day. When we first got married and we were stone broke. It felt like we were a team, you know?"

George sighed. "Let me guess, the team is—you feed him, he falls asleep on the sofa, you type up his script?"

I laughed along at this, even though it really *had* felt like the "good ole days" the other night. After we got married, a friend of Richard's offered us a cottage in the Cotswolds. We could stay as long as we liked. It was simple and quiet with no shower or central heating, but to me, after growing up in a small house crammed with seven inhabitants, it was heaven. Sometimes we did nothing more than read all day in front of the big open fireplace, or cozied up in the creaky old brass bed. Other times I messed around with compositions on the parlor piano while Richard tinkered with his play. The neighbors—hearing that a young couple was on honeymoon in their quaint village—took pride in dropping off chicken pies and bottles of homemade cider and garden vegetables. Richard, being Richard, always managed to charm them so that we were often invited to supper.

Most days, we sat on that little pier and talked about our future—where we would live when Richard's play was a roaring success, the music I could perform now that my father wasn't in charge anymore. We talked about how great it would be to travel together, to see Paris, Rome, New York, the world. But there was one day in particular I'll never forget. Richard and I were sitting out on the jetty, going through a composition I'd been working on, and I was explaining to him that it was still in the early stages, but if I spent a few weeks polishing it, it might be something special—when all of a sudden a gust of wind blew the score sheets from my grasp and scattered them across the surface of the pond. Without a moment's hesitation, Richard dived into the water, which, I should point out, boasted an impressive leech population, and didn't come back out until he'd recovered each and every page for me. He laid them out on the windowsills and pegged them to the clothesline. He saved my composition.

When money ran low, we would write articles together for obscure trade publications and advertorial pieces for women's magazines—the only work we could get. We'd spend mornings and evenings at the kitchen table, passing finished pieces between us to get the other's opinion. I *technically* had money at the time, but I wouldn't be able to access my trust for another year.

Then, right at the end of the trip, Richard broke the news—he had sold his play. "No more slaving over articles in a poky cottage in the middle of nowhere," he'd said. "We can go back to London." In that moment, I remember feeling a mixture of excitement and dread. I didn't want the honeymoon to end. I just wanted to stay right there, in that tiny cottage, to be woken every morning by the dawn chorus and breathe in the scent of honeysuckle coming through the open sash window, with Richard sleeping right next to me. It was heaven.

And it couldn't last.

"I'm guessing," George said, bringing me back to the present, "that there was only one byline on those articles you *helped* him with. And it wasn't Eliza Sheridan, am I right?"

She was right. But Richard was the one who got the commissions, so of course they used his byline. "Neither of us cared about that. We just needed the money."

She gave a slow nod but didn't say anything.

"Anyway..." I said, realizing the conversation was veering off course. "The point is he's in a much better mood. And you know what they say, 'Happy husband, less homicidal wife!'"

She remained unconvinced. "Of course he's in a much better mood. I bet he's lapping it up. He has it every way he wants now. He even has you doing his work for him. I'm surprised this therapist doesn't have you 'servicing' him before breakfast every day."

I thought about the moment on the landing. "It's not like that. Anyway, this is just the first step in the quote unquote 'behavior modification process.'"

George sighed. "Listen, Eliza, I'm as keen on manipulation as anyone, but it sounds like the only one modifying their behavior here is *you*. Shouldn't this be about getting Richard to change?"

I remembered what Ms. Early had said in our last session. *This is not about letting him win. This is about playing him. You are going to play him for the narcissistic egoist that he is.*

George bounced Frankie on her knee and watched me. Finally, she said, "So you're staying for dinner, right? I've got wine, I've got Magnums."

Mara was now climbing a rope ladder to join Mossy on the slightly too high branch.

"I'd love to stay, but—"

"You have to go home and cook a three-course meal for your husband."

Actually, I did.

Mara was now perched on the branch, legs swinging, listening to Mossy Jr., who was talking animatedly while he poked at the nest with a stick.

"Careful, Mara!" I called out. She was edging forward on the branch toward the nest.

"She'll be grand. Kids know their own limits," George reasoned. "If you want my opinion, the only thing Richard needs is a good kick up the ass. No offense, Eliza. It takes two to make a doormat."

I felt my face grow hot. "Says the woman whose—"

"Whose what?"

Whose husband went to Poland to shoot heavy weaponry while she was giving birth to twins. And was using axe-throwing as a valid excuse to avoid his own children.

I was about to say just that but was cut off by a cry from the garden. I looked out the window and spotted Mara, arms flailing. She had been trying to get closer to the nest, and she must have lost her balance and fallen.

I screamed her name and was out the door before I saw what had even happened—she had safely landed on the trampoline underneath the tree. When I got closer to her, she emerged, shaky but beaming.

"That. Was. *Awesome!*" Mossy Jr. shouted, as his siblings started chanting, "Mara! Mara! Mara!"

George came and stood next to me. "See? They're always grand."

They're not *always grand*, I wanted to say. *If they're always grand, why are there six pediatric orthopedic surgeons in the greater Dublin area alone?*

"Eliza," George said, turning to face me as her kids begged Mara to do her "trick" again. "All I'm saying is to be careful."

"But you're the one who encouraged me to go back to her."

"I know, but therapists usually just listen. And maybe help you see things in a different light. It's not normal for them to tell their clients exactly what to do."

"So what are you saying I should do? Just quit?"

"I'm not trying to rain on your parade, Eliza. Really, I'm not. But maybe just make sure she's legit before you take any more of her advice. I mean, what do you even know about this woman?"

Weekly Spouse Tracker

Rate the following spousal behaviors from 1 to 5:

1=non-existent,   2=poor/rare,   3=adequate/sometimes,
    4=satisfactory/frequent,   5=excellent/always

BEHAVIORS	WEEKLY SCORE
Physical affection	5
Spontaneous acts of kindness	4
Gratitude for Service	2
General attentiveness	5
Reliability	1
Self-Absorption	5
Helps out around the house	1
Attentiveness to offspring	2
Answers texts/phone calls	2
Unaccounted-for disappearances	2

*To be completed in between sessions and returned to Ms. Early

12

"Now, Eliza," Ms. Early said once we were both settled in session. "Where were we?"

"You'd asked about my—" I paused to do air quotes "'—love story' with Richard. But once I'd finished telling it, time was up. And I had to get back home for Mara."

"Ah, yes," Ms. Early said, nodding. "That's right. But you didn't finish the story, did you?"

"What do you mean?"

"It ended with Richard *working a miracle*, as you put it. But what happened after? Were there any consequences?"

I hesitated, feeling the palms of my hands begin to tingle. "Yes," I admitted. "There were."

She gestured for me to continue.

I took a deep breath in and finished the story. "It was only once we were back in London that Richard told me he'd missed his final exams at Middle Temple because of helping me in France. And not just that, but that he'd also been informed he wasn't eligible to sit them at a later date. Missing finals meant automatic expulsion. And he'd risked it all to help me—to save me from Matthews, from my father, from my past life. But when Richard's father found out, he pretty much disowned him. After all these years, he still doesn't talk to his father, but he never once made me feel guilty about it." I paused and looked up self-consciously, hyperaware of how long I'd been talking.

Ms. Early's expression remained unreadable.

"And he hates that Richard went into theater," I added. "He wanted his son to have a profession. He doesn't speak to me, and he *barely* communicates with Richard, even though Richard's tried to make peace so many times."

She still didn't say anything, just looked at me intently.

So I kept rambling. "He did all that for me, without expecting anything in return," I repeated. "Richard has a good heart. I think I've lost sight of that. His father still barely speaks to him, but he's never made me feel guilty about it or anything."

I took another moment to pause and looked at Ms. Early again, expectantly. I didn't anticipate a *gushing* response from her, per se, but I was surprised that the story didn't seem to move her at all.

Finally, after what felt like a lifetime, she spoke. "Has it ever occurred to you, Eliza, that Richard would not be a successful playwright if he hadn't run away with you?"

I laughed despite myself and waved the idea away. "Richard would have made it regardless. He's the most ambitious person I've ever met."

"But he was going into law to please his father, right?" she countered. "Perhaps, in a way, you freed Richard to do what he really wanted."

"No, that's not true. Richard was the one who decided to go into law."

Ms. Early leaned forward in her chair and said, "Let's assume, for a minute, that he *did* feel drawn toward the theater, toward writing. That he had no interest in becoming a barrister."

"But—"

She held up a hand to stop me from interrupting. "Maybe he realized he needed to do something to make a name for himself, to generate some publicity. Perhaps some big, dramatic gesture?" She paused for emphasis, letting her words sink in. "Or maybe he realized he needed to live a little, to get some life experience so he'd have something to write about?"

"We're talking about a man who has literally worn odd shoes to work without noticing. Trust me, he is not the Machiavellian genius you're imagining."

Ms. Early sighed. "*This* is what is blocking everything. You need to let this go. Richard wanted to run away as much as you did."

No. That wasn't how it was. And why was she questioning me on this so much? "I don't understand what you're trying to get at here," I said with annoyance.

She gazed at me. "Tell me this, Eliza. Who decided that you would live in London?"

"Well, Richard, but only because it was easier for him to get journalism work if we lived in a big city."

"And whose decision was it to move to Dublin?"

"He couldn't turn down the chance to run a theater. It's the opportunity of a lifetime."

Ms. Early threw up her hands in exasperation. "Can't you see the pattern, Eliza? *He* decided that you were going to run away. *He* decided you should live in London. And *he* decided you should move to Dublin for his career." She paused a moment, then said in a softer tone, "Eliza, what I want to know is where was *your* voice in all of this?"

I felt my chest tighten and cheeks grow hot. "Oh, so you're saying this whole situation was my fault?"

"I'm simply asking where your voice was."

I was beginning to regret coming here. I thought she understood the situation. I thought she was on my side, dammit.

Nevertheless, I answered honestly. "What's the point in having a voice if no one's listening?"

Ms. Early's eyes grew wide in excitement. "Yes! That is *pre-*

cisely my point. Well done. You're now beginning to perceive things in the right way." She suddenly stood from her chair and pulled a necklace from under her gray silk shirt. On the end of the necklace was a key. And with that key she unlocked a cabinet in the corner of the room. From my vantage point, I could make out rows and rows of boxes, vials and containers of different shapes and sizes. She examined the labels before finally selecting a squat blue bottle with a tiny handle, then relocked the cabinet.

She walked back over and placed the bottle down on the table. "And now for the *real* treatment. It's quite strong, so I'd suggest using it sparingly. Two shots will be more than sufficient for the time being. Having said that, don't worry too much about dosage. The worst that could happen is a bad hangover."

I hesitantly picked up the bottle. "What is this? Alcohol?"

Ms. Early nodded. "It's brewed with a very particular formulation of herbal yeast that proves extremely beneficial in these types of cases of ingrained behavior. You, Eliza, can safely drink it. In fact, I recommend that you do. It will help you to loosen up and say the things that need to be said. But it should have a marked effect on Richard. Now be prepared—its primary purpose is to reignite connection, but it also reduces inhibitions. He may tell you things you never knew." She paused, then added, "Or things you may not want to hear."

I raised an eyebrow at her, unable to hide my skepticism. *What was this, some kind of underground apothecary disguised as a therapy practice?*

"I have never had a case yet where this did not work," Ms. Early declared, clearly reading my expression. "I've had clients who had *already* separated but ended up reconciling with their husbands after following this treatment. Others even went on to have another child."

Another child.

A little brother or sister for Mara. A built-in best friend.

I took the bottle from her, pulled the cork out and sniffed, then quickly recoiled. It smelled like paint stripper. Was George right? Could I really trust this woman? This stranger?

But then my own words came back to me: *What's the point in having a voice if no one's listening?*

Maybe it's time I *made* him listen.

Richard was deep in thought that night when he entered the study. It was late, nearly midnight. It took him a few moments to spot me on the sofa but when he did, he looked as if he was about to retreat. But then his eyes moved about the room, sensing something was different. I'd switched off the overhead light, lit the corner lamps, set a log fire burning and put some Jamie Duffy piano music playing in the background.

"What's *that*?" Richard asked. He was pointing at the coffee table, upon which sat Ms. Early's blue bottle. I reminded myself what she'd said—she had never known this treatment to fail.

"Poitín," I ad-libbed.

"Poitín, Eliza?" He was smiling now. "What on earth are you doing with poitín?"

I shrugged, playing into it. "It's not illegal. Not anymore. Besides, Michael Fassbender loves this brand. Calls it the Irish ayahuasca. Always has it for his poker nights in LA with, uh, Paul Mescal and…" *Think, think. Who else was Irish?* "Barry Keoghan."

"Yeah, right." He laughed, but I could tell he wanted to believe it. He loved that shit.

"It's true. Gina was telling me. Her daughter Aurora's agent knows everyone in the business."

He took the bottle, examined it, took the stopper out, sniffed it and quickly recoiled. "Fuck it. If it's good enough for Fassbender…"

I poured us a shot each and we downed them together.

Whatever it was, it was *strong* but I felt immediately better.

Calmer. Like I could see everything more clearly. Such as this very man in front of me.

It quickly started loosening him up. He began chatting about his day while I just listened and nodded.

And observed. The way he talked, talked, talked. About his casting problem. His Majella problem. His script problem. His *no one appreciating the genius in their midst* problem.

I poured two more shots for us.

"This is good hooch," he said. Then he looked at me, *really* looked at me. "You know, after all these years, I still never quite know what to expect from you."

We started chatting more easily after that, and not just about Richard. About Mara, and the places around Dublin that we should take her to see. I told him that Mara was doing her best to bring the tone down at her posh school with the ill-timed biological facts she regularly dispensed. A few days earlier, I'd received a call from the school letting me know that Mara had caused an upset. Apparently, she'd informed the class that eyelash mites don't have anuses and that's why they inevitably explode. Parents, the teacher informed me, had complained.

Richard laughed long and hard at this. Then he made *me* laugh even harder by doing an impression of Mother Hen reacting to news of the eyelash mite fiasco. I had forgotten what an excellent mimic he was.

I realized we were both enjoying ourselves, enjoying each other's company. It was a foreign feeling.

When Richard leaned toward me, I flinched, watching as a look of surprise and something else—regret?—passed over his face. I was jumpier than usual these days. Slowly, he reached out his hand and tucked a piece of hair behind my ear.

"Eliza..." he said breathily.

His hand was still by my face. With the smallest movement, he brushed his thumb across my lips. So gently that my skin tingled. I forgot what that felt like—what *he* felt like.

Our eyes met.

He stood up, went to the study door and locked it, then slowly walked back to me.

Later that night in bed, Richard stroked my hair until he realized I was silently crying. "What is it? Did I do something?"

I pretended it was nothing, but I knew what it was. I had thought we'd never be this close again, that this was gone forever. But it was still here. Underneath it all, he was still the old Richard.

We were still *us*.

13

Richard, Mara and I stood at the front door of Mother Hen's sensitively upgraded, standing-on-its-own-grounds period residence, a pink helium balloon in the shape of the number six bumping against us. Richard was not speaking to Mara, who was in her shark costume, and I was not speaking to Richard. The love bubble had not taken long to pop.

It all started because Richard voluntarily brought Mara to the playground the day before. Entirely unprompted. Which was a tiny miracle in its own right. But upon their return, Richard told me he'd bumped into and *hit it off* with Mother Hen's husband, Johnny. This was also a surprising but welcome development. Richard had never knowingly befriended a parent before. But then, like a cat dropping a dead mouse on its owner's pillow, Richard had presented me with the news that he had wangled an invitation for Mara to Aurora's birthday party. *Ah, Richard, sweet, innocent Richard. How little you know of the world of women.*

We were not invited. On purpose.

Alexis Junior School had very strict rules about the distribution of party invites; they were not to be handed out in class, in the line, or anywhere on the school grounds so that no child felt excluded—which is ironic, considering the administration turned a blind eye when Mara was repeatedly excluded "on school grounds" at recess. A staunch rule-follower, Mother Hen abided by loudly handing out the printed, embossed, beglittered invitations in the Honey Café—to the few Chickadees whose offspring were deemed photogenic enough to populate the celebrations, that is. It was to be a select gathering and I knew that an off-the-cuff, unapproved comment such as, "sure come along, the more the merrier," *wangled* from Aurora's father, did not constitute an invite.

Richard and I disagreed on this point. And we went on disagreeing about it all evening and into the morning until he finally hit me with a low blow: *You keep saying Mara needs to make friends, and this is the perfect chance. But you're going to turn it down because you're pissed off with me.*

I thought of Mara sitting on the gravel of the windblown schoolyard, a small figure in a purple coat, all by herself. I had tried talking to her teacher, Mr. Mellon, about what could be done to help her. Maybe the school could introduce a buddy bench for children who felt too shy to ask others to play, or maybe even a buddy system for new kids? But he'd just dismissed my ideas and said these options weren't possible at Alexis. No explanation as to why. Just no. And to make matters worse, he'd added, "Maybe you could try a few playdates?"

I was a suburban educated mother in the Western hemisphere with a tendency toward overparenting. Did he really think this was new information to me? I was the goddamn queen of playdates. Well, sort of. In fairness, I did try to resist them at first. But once Mara started at Alexis and the predicted connections failed to materialize, I had to reassess my stance on the issue. There was not, it seemed, enough friendship to go around, and if you opted out of the playdate system, you were willfully choosing to warp your child's social life. And so I dived in and invited child after child to our house. But for some reason, those interactions never blossomed into friendship. And we'd now worked our way through all the girls in the class. Except for Aurora, Mother Hen's daughter.

But Aurora already had a best friend by the name of Amelia in the class next door. "Twinnie," they called each other. And so I'd decided against inviting Aurora over, as I was now well-versed in the Chickadee Playdate Rulebook, in which Rule Number 3, subsection 4, stated that you must never try to oar in on a BFF situation. And if word got back that you were trying to poach a bestie, there would be Consequences.

"We're basically gate-crashing. Just so you know," I'd reminded Richard when I reluctantly got dressed for the party that morning. I chose my casual-yet-put-together weekend look. A.k.a. the same black leggings I wore almost every day.

"You're really wearing *that*?" Richard asked, running his eyes over me.

"Well, now I'm not. When you've said it like that."

Mara's outfit was another matter altogether. The fact of the matter was that there were two choices for girls' birthday parties: a Disney princess dress with clickety-clack plastic heels that left red welts on soft little feet, or a frothy tulle-skirt ballerina number. Or, at a pinch, you might get away with a floral dress.

So obviously, Mara wore a shark costume. And that was that.

Except that wasn't that. Because Richard had suddenly, out of nowhere, become finely attuned to social niceties, aside from no gate-crashing, of course, and insisted she put on a dress. But in a standoff with Mara over a dress, there was only going to be one winner. Richard had yet to learn that. I should have set a timer, because it only took Mara a mere thirty seconds to put an end to his nonsense. It went a little something like this:

RICHARD: Mara, you are going to wear a dress.

ME: You forgot to add *young lady*.

MARA: I can't wear a dress.

RICHARD: You're going to go upstairs and change into a dress. *Now.*

MARA: I don't have any dresses.

RICHARD: Yes you do, that red thing with the bow—

MARA: I wore that when I was three. I've grown eleven centimeters since then. I. Have. No. Dresses.

RICHARD [*looking at me*]: Why does she have no dresses?

ME: Because this isn't the Middle Ages? My mistake.

[*Long pause.*]

RICHARD: Fine! Let's bloody go so.

MARA: Let's bloody go! Let's bloody go!

Just one big, happy family.

And now here we were, waiting at Mother Hen's front door. Richard seemed to be waiting for me to press the doorbell.
So I didn't.
And neither did he.
Fine, I thought, after Mara's hand began to tug on mine. *Guess I'll be the grown-up here.* I reached for the illuminated button with the camera eye above it, but just then the door swung open to reveal Mother Hen, wearing an electric blue jumpsuit and hair so volumized I had an urge to check if there was some kind of miniature scaffolding structure going on under there. She blinked her "real" mink lashes and said nothing. I braced myself for the worst.
"Oh my God, Mara, you are adorable!" Mother Hen surprised us all by saying. She then ushered us in without (a) ask-

ing what the hell we were doing there or (b) pretending there was no party on so we'd have to leave.

We followed Mother Hen into the kitchen, which was almost as beautiful as its Instagram incarnation. It ran the length of the house and had three sets of arched French doors opening onto the gardens. A small old woman was working at pace setting up silver chafing dishes over heaters on the island, but her progress was impeded because she had to keep stepping around two of Mother Hen's closest Chickadee confidantes, who were chatting and casting glances at a bottle of rosé chilling in an ice bucket. A girl of about twenty, dressed in black, was lounging by the sink, texting with one hand and holding a tray with the other.

This, I then realized, was a drop-and-go party. Parents were not supposed to stay.

Shit.

We had two choices. Option one, leave Mara alone there, knowing she would curl up in the coat press until her chance came to escape out the front door, after which she would run down the graveled drive to the street, almost get knocked over by a car reversing out of a neighbor's electronic gateway and then hide behind a bush, refusing to budge until I returned to coax her out.

Or option two, we could stay, like the unwelcome spare tools that we were, even though it meant inflicting two hours of mutually excruciating small talk on Mother Hen's inner circle. We chose the latter.

Aurora suddenly came running in from the garden, resplendent in a highly flammable turquoise princess gown. "Hi, Mara," she said. "Look what my dress does." She twirled around and LED lights turned on and illuminated the skirts, playing a tinny version of the song "Let it Go," from the movie *Frozen*. "It's motion activated."

Mara held out the book she'd picked out for her and Aurora ripped open the wrapping. "Nature's Deadliest Creatures through the Ages," she read aloud. Mother Hen placed a hand on Aurora's shoulder and squeezed, and the little girl said *thank you* so robotically I realized the hand-on-shoulder move was a manners-training cue.

After a long pause, Aurora said to Mara, "I've got some new makeup. Want to put some on?"

The two girls looked at each other. I knew what Mara was thinking. Only if the makeup doesn't contain squalene because it's often derived from sharks. Thankfully, she kept it to herself. "Or we could jump on my bed?" Aurora suggested.

Now she was talking Mara's language.

Mara glanced at me and when I nodded, she followed Aurora out of the room. I felt Richard give me a nudge. *"See?"* his elbow said. *"See the way she just made a friend? Entirely thanks to my intervention?"*

I resisted the urge to communicate via *my* elbow, albeit harder, that the *wangled invite* was his first ever parental intervention, so the initial signs of success counted as beginner's luck. Plus, we'd only been here five minutes. A lot could still happen.

"You're staying?" Mother Hen asked.

"Do you mind?"

"Mind? I'm delighted." She took my wrist—and Richard's—as if we were the only two people she really wanted to talk to. "I just wanted to make sure," she said, looking from me to Richard, "that Johnny didn't offend you. Blurting out the invitation like that. I was so embarrassed when he told me, in case you'd think I'd... I don't know...excluded Mara or something. Because *you* know me, Eliza, I'm all about bringing people together, including them. That's just who I am."

She still had a grip on our wrists and our arms waved like puppets as she gesticulated. I wondered if she'd been doing tequila shots before we'd arrived. Or if her benzodiazepine supply had run out. "When Johnny said it to me," she continued,

"I suddenly realized I never got the chance to give you Mara's invitation, what with all those silly school rules, and so *I* said we'd better drop it over to your house, and *Johnny* said I was being completely ridiculous, he'd already told Richard the details and I was completely overthinking it."

Richard smiled and said, "In fairness, we'd probably have lost the invitation anyway so it's just as well the way it worked out."

Because we're such a disorganized, flaky family. Hilarious, Richard.

Mother Hen did indeed find it hilarious. Then she said to him, "The boys are in the garden if you'd like to join them. And do me a favor? Keep an eye on the burgers. Johnny always cremates them."

There were four men standing around a barbecue, in different versions of the same off-duty alpha male outfit—battered utility shorts, loafers with no socks and sweaters draped around their shoulders. The golden hairs on their tanned legs caught the Indian summer sun. The sleeves of their linen-blend shirts were rolled up to flaunt their watches.

The oldest man in the group was holding forth, gesticulating with barbecue tongs. Was that *Johnny*? Richard hadn't mentioned that he was a good twenty years older than Mother Hen. I watched as Richard walked out alone into the garden, dressed all wrong in a corporate-blue shirt. He paused for a moment, assessing the group, and then I saw the shift, something no one else would have noticed. He tilted his chin up, slid his hands into his pockets, rolled his shoulders back. He had decided in that moment which version of himself he was going to be—a man who didn't need a drink in his hand, or an introduction, to be relaxed among strangers. He stayed right where he was, rocked on his heels, surveyed the scene. He would make *them* notice *him* and wonder, just for a moment, if maybe they should have ironed their shirts.

According to plan, Johnny finally saw Richard and I watched him hesitate as he tried to place him. The other men glanced over their shoulders to follow his gaze. Richard strolled toward the group, hand straight out to Johnny. As the older man took it, Richard said something that made the whole group laugh as one. Johnny gave him an appraising look before flashing him a Gillette ad smile and handing him a spare set of tongs. I'd forgotten just how good Richard was at this. Not for nothing had he spent six years at a British boarding school.

I realized Mother Hen had been watching this interaction, too. She seemed relieved that the men had accepted Richard so easily. Now she turned away and called over to one of the Chickadees, "Nikki, open the rosé, will you, and bring Eliza a glass?" *We were about to celebrate a child's sixth birthday by getting drunk at two in the afternoon? Count me in.*

"So," Gina said, steering me over to an enormous L-shaped sofa. I recognized it from one of her Insta reels: *You've been getting scatter cushion styling wrong your whole life and here's why...* "You and Richard seem to be getting on well?"

"Well, I haven't killed him in his sleep yet. So that's something."

She laughed too loudly. "You're gas, Eliza. But that's not what I wanted to talk to you about..."

I raised an eyebrow at her.

"Johnny told me you're a concert pianist. I can't believe you never said!"

"Oh. Well, *used* to be. Not anymore."

"But you're professionally trained?" she asked.

I slowly nodded, unsure where she was going with this.

"I knew it! I mean, Nikki thought it was most likely just a hobby because, you know, you've only got one child and she's at school now and how do you fill your hours, blah, blah, blah..." *Gee thanks, Nikki.* "But I said, no, I was sure you were a professional." Her hand was back on my wrist again. "This is fantastic."

I wasn't sure why exactly it was *fantastic*, but before I could ask, I got distracted by the sight of all the children, including Mara, being shooed out into the garden toward an entertainer— some young woman in Lycra who had apparently been hired to do a Taylor Swift cardio jam workout. Mara was definitely not the Taylor-Swift-cardio-jam-workout type. I kept an eye on her while trying to figure out where Mother Hen was going with this line of inquiry. On one hand, her proposition seemed to bode well for a possible friendship between Mara and Aurora. On the other hand, maybe she was just trying to sell me some Tupperware. Or an at-home tooth bleaching kit. You never knew with her.

"Did you study at the Royal Irish Academy?" she asked.

I was once again distracted by the scene going on outside. Mara was opting out of the nonoptional cardio jam and had wandered off down the garden. She had taken out her magnifying glass from her backpack and was now lying flat out on the ground underneath a bush, examining something. Richard was still in the group of men by the barbecue. He was speaking and I noticed they were all leaning in to catch what he was saying.

"Yes," I replied absentmindedly. "For a few years. But really, I studied with my father."

"Amazing," she said. And she didn't even sound sarcastic. Nikki was calling to her, asking her something, but Mother Hen waved her off, then turned back conspiratorially to me. "I love Nikki to bits. But watch she doesn't corner you. After a glass or two of wine, the woman can talk about air fryers for literally hours."

I must have looked surprised at this little show of claws toward a fellow Chickadee because she said, "What?" followed by, "Listen, I've been meaning to say this for a while. I'm sorry if we've maybe seemed a bit...standoffish."

"Oh. Not at all." *One hundred percent.*

"And also, you always seem so...so fine by yourself, you know?"

In the garden, Aurora had left all the others to see what Mara was doing. Aurora really was a likeable child, despite all the makeup and the heels and the robotic politeness. She was kneeling down beside Mara, not minding that her princess dress would get soil on it as the two girls bent their heads close, fascinated by whatever game they were playing.

"So I was wondering…" Mother Hen continued with a mock-nervous expression. I braced myself for questions about how therapy was going. "Have you ever taught?"

I suddenly checked in to the conversation. "Taught? Oh, you mean the piano? No. *God*, no."

Undeterred, Gina said, "Because we were thinking, wouldn't it be the perfect way for you to make use of your talents? You could put it on your… I don't know, portfolio, or whatever. As experience. We'd cover any little costs, of course. And it could be here in my house once a week. Handy for everyone."

"Everyone?"

"Well, for Aurora, of course, and Nikki's girls. And Other Nicki's kids. And if it goes well, we'd be more than happy to put the word out. Get you some more little customers. What do you think?"

Just then, Nikki walked up to us carrying huge wineglasses. "Will these do? They're the only ones I could find."

Mother Hen pressed a finger to her temple and said, "*Red*-wine glasses? For rosé?" Then she called over to the girl by the counter, "Stephanie? Would you mind bringing in some white-wine glasses from the pantry?"

Stephanie didn't look up from her phone. "In a minute."

Mother Hen pressed her lips together and took a few breaths through her nose. Then she said to me, "She's Johnny's daughter. From his first marriage. *Completely* takes after the mother."

"Don't worry. I'll get the glasses," I said, glad of the excuse to get away.

Their pantry was so obsessively organized it bordered on

alarming. I could imagine Mother Hen coming in here when she got stressed, calming herself by gazing at the little glass spice jars and the canisters of nuts, each one spaced exactly one hand's width apart, and repeating, *I am so grateful* over and over. There were champagne flutes and brandy balloons and punch cups and whiskey snifters, all on appropriately labeled shelves, but I could not for the life of me find the white-wine glasses. In my search, I couldn't help but notice the huge whiteboard, with a timetable written out, evidently a rundown of today's, and probably every day's, proceedings. The first few points had been ticked off: flower delivery, Johnny to collect cake, take hair rollers out, light barbecue coals, get emergency contact details from parents. But the one below that gave me pause. All she'd written was: *Eliza?*

Before I could give the note a second thought, I was suddenly aware that something was going on outside.

A child was screaming.

14

When I returned—glassless—to the kitchen, I looked through the open doors and saw Mother Hen hurrying down the garden past the circle of men. I quickly followed suit, right as the entertainer pulled the plug on Taylor Swift.

Everyone was crowded around Aurora and Mara.

Aurora, tears streaming down her face, was holding a beautiful enameled box in her hands. "She put...she put a..."

"What? What did she put?" Mother Hen pressed.

Aurora turned her now puffy red face to her mother. "She put a baby bobbit worm in my new jewelry box!"

And then the wailing, my Jesus, the wailing.

"A *what*?" Her mother took the box from her and examined it. "It's just a worm, Aurora."

"It's not! It's a baby bobbit worm. They're carnivorous. Mara told me!"

I took Mara's hand in mine and squeezed. I knew what had happened. She had recently developed a pretty intense fascination with bobbit worms and had a strong suspicion that they might also live on land, as well as in the seabeds surrounding Indonesia. She must have been testing out this hypothesis in Mother Hen's garden.

"Aurora," Mother Hen said. "Listen to me. Bobbit worms aren't real."

I felt Mara's hot little hand tighten in mine. *Oh, God, here we go. Three, two, one...*

"Bobbit worms *are* real," Mara insisted. "They're ferocious underwater worms that can grow up to a meter long and they strike from under the seabed and snatch passing fish and drag them into their underground larder and they're named after Lorena Bobbit who cut off her husband's—"

Mother Hen gave out a little yelp and put her hands over Aurora's ears.

"Mara!" I scolded. Bloody David Attenborough and his feckless obsession with encouraging children's natural curiosity in the world around them.

"I was just going to say—"

"No, Mara, that's *enough*."

"It's fine," Mother Hen kept saying while trying to soothe Aurora, who was, by the way, *loving* the attention.

"I was just going to say that it was a silly name anyway," Mara whispered sadly to me. "Because worms are hermaphrodites."

"Tell you what, Richie," a voice said from behind us. "You'd want to keep the kitchen knives locked away in your house." Johnny and the other men had gathered nearby and seemed intent on defusing the situation.

"And have a few ice packs handy just in case," Richard—sorry, *Richie*—joshed back, his voice a good two postcodes posher than usual.

"Right!" Johnny said, clapping his hands together. "Time for your present, I think, Aurora."

"But the photographer, Johnny," Mother Hen said tightly. "I told her three o'clock."

He looked at Mother Hen and sucked on his lip. She looked back at him. Some impenetrable communication passed between them, and then Mother Hen kneeled down in front of

Aurora, kissed her on the forehead and said, "Ready for your present?"

With a flourish, Mother Hen produced a big pink envelope with *Aurora* written on it in swirly writing. But as she was about to hand it to her daughter, Johnny told her to hold on and signaled to Stephanie, who—sullenly—carried over a giant rectangular box wrapped in gold paper with a giant bow.

Aurora stopped crying. She took the lid off the giant box. Inside was a smaller one, and then another smaller one, and so on and so on like a matrushka doll, which made everyone laugh, until finally she found the little gold cushion with a key on it.

"This way," Johnny said, leading Aurora through the gate at the bottom of their garden that led into the lane running behind all the houses on the street. We all trooped after them. Johnny motioned to a green metal gate set into the back wall of their neighbor's garden. "Go on," he said to Aurora. "Try the key."

She did so, then pushed the gate open and peered through. Then she turned and threw herself at Johnny, squeezing him tight. "Oh, thank you, Daddy. Thank you, thank you."

Inside was a full-size, pristine tennis court with vivid green synthetic grass, freshly painted white lines and high cedar fencing all around. A super-tanned woman in tennis whites stood smiling by the net, and now she came over and presented Aurora with a tennis racket. "Hi, Aurora, I'm Amy. Your daddy's asked me to give you some tennis lessons. Would you like that?"

Aurora, now mute with happiness, nodded.

No one else seemed to notice that Mother Hen had been lagging at the back of the crowd, her mouth shut tight. Now she pinned on a smile, strolled over to Johnny and slipped her arm round his waist. "Johnny, this is just so special. You've made her so happy."

"She does look happy, doesn't she?" Johnny watched as Aurora managed to lob a ball back over the net, a self-satisfied smirk on his face.

"She's a natural, Johnny. There's your retirement fund sorted," one of the men said.

Johnny nodded toward the instructor. "I hope so. Amy Johnson doesn't come cheap."

"*I'd* rank her pretty highly," Nikki's husband chimed in. "Can I come over for lessons, too?"

"Behave, you," Johnny said.

"Highest ranked female player in Ireland, isn't she?" came Richard's voice from beside me. He looked unruffled and cool. He also wasn't ogling the tennis coach like the other men. All his energy was trained on Johnny.

Johnny turned to face him, an impressed look on his face. "You know your stuff."

Richard shrugged. "Bit of a tennis nut."

He hated all sport. I couldn't believe he had even heard of Amy Johnson. He must have quickly googled her.

"We'll have to get together for a game sometime."

"Love to," Richard said. I raised my eyebrow at him, but he ignored me.

After a little more chitchat, everyone drifted back toward the house.

Everyone except for Richard, that is. I spotted him loitering on the tennis court, speaking to someone on the phone. Although he seemed to be doing more listening than talking, nodding every few seconds. When he hung up, he didn't move, just stood there, lost in thought. Though I would rather have stayed to spy on him, Nikki, who was now rather tipsy, linked my arm through hers and I had no choice but to follow the crowd.

"Where'd you go?" I asked him twenty minutes later when he eventually appeared back in the garden.

"Nowhere. Jesus. Anything else you want to grill me about?" *Yes, actually, Richard. How much time you got?*

After the drop-and-go parents arrived to collect their children, and just the inner circle was left—Nikki and Nicki and their "hubbies" who, I had finally twigged, both worked for Johnny—it started pouring. We ran inside and somehow all ended up in the music room.

I sat at the piano with Mara and Aurora as they messed about with the keys. I was glad for an excuse to observe, rather than join with the others who were crowded onto the two low sofas getting drunk. Mother Hen was holding forth on one sofa, talking to Richard about his appearance on the *Late Late Show* to promote the theater. "Kielty is a pet, isn't he?" she gushed, and before Richard had a chance to reply she continued, "I've a feeling this might be our year." She dropped her voice above a whisper, just loud enough for me to hear. "You know, for the *Toy Show.*"

"Getting tickets, do you mean?" Richard asked.

This made her laugh. "God, no. I mean for Aurora to be picked as one of the dancers. She's up to grade three in ballet already. Her agent couldn't believe she wasn't picked last year. *Soooo*...if you happen to see Kielty again, you might put in a word?" She played it off like she was joking but her tone said otherwise.

"Aurora has an *agent?*" Richard laughed.

"She was scouted," Mother Hen said, a little defensively. "She just loves performing. She's always picked for the leads in the Christmas concerts, isn't she, girls?" She tried to lower her voice, but because she was now drunk, it didn't really work. "Just between us, Mr. Mellon already gave me the nod that she'll be Dorothy in the school summer production."

Aurora overheard this and said, "But, Mom, I don't want to. I just want to practice my tennis."

"Plenty of hours in the day, my darling."

"Ballet, acting...if she played an instrument, too, she'd be a triple threat," Richard said to skate over the slight awkwardness.

Mother Hen leaned forward and put a hand on his knee.

"Yes, exactly! That's why I was asking Eliza earlier about giving her piano lessons."

Then everyone looked at me. It was unfortunate that I was, at that exact moment, sitting between Mara and Aurora, helping them to pick out a few little tunes on the piano.

"That's a great idea," Richard said, giving me a look that said, *Isn't it, Eliza?*

"You know what? I'd love to? But I'm just so *busy.*" I paused to catch Richard's eye. "You know, between doing Richard's accounts, and the theater paperwork, I'm flat out."

"Good man, Richie," Johnny said. "Always get the wife on the books. Don't want to miss that extra employee credit, am I right?"

"Like you need it, Johnny," one of the men jested.

"Only a fool turns down free money," Johnny replied sharply.

"But, Eliza, remember what Majella had said to me about the regulations?" Richard asked. His tone was lighthearted, but there was a hint of warning in it. "We can't have you in the office anymore."

"Oh yeah," I said breezily. "I actually chatted with Majella about it."

"You did? When?"

"That Saturday you had to go in for the extra rehearsal session."

The extra rehearsal he hadn't turned up for. Because of being out on the town with Lady Languish. "And we sorted it all out," I added nonchalantly. "There must have been crossed wires or something, because Majella said there's absolutely no problem with me working in the office! Problem solved." I gave him a tight-lipped smile.

The chatter in the room fell away as everyone surreptitiously took notice of our conversation. "That's great news," he said in the end. "Really great."

After the conversation moved on, Johnny sat next to me and

handed me a glass of champagne. We watched as our spouses entertained the others, Mother Hen keeping the banter going and Richard sending everyone into gales of laughter with his anecdotes about famous actors. They could have been old friends.

"All that energy," Johnny mumbled, looking at his wife. For the first time that day, he sounded tired. He nodded toward Richard. "Man of the moment, isn't he?"

"Yep."

He glanced sideways at me, picking up on my tone. He was silent for a moment, then said, "Of course, behind every successful man—"

"Is a woman with a kitchen knife?" I really hadn't meant to say it out loud.

But Johnny laughed. "I have to confess," he said, "these sorts of parties aren't really my thing. I just go along with it for Gina."

"They're not really my sort of thing, either."

There was a pause, then he lowered his voice. "What *is* your thing?" It was the way he asked the question, just a shade too interested. And I also realized he was sitting just a shade too *close*. My whole left side prickled to attention.

"*That's* my thing." I gestured toward Mara, who was now playing on the window seat with Aurora.

"Yeah, kids are great," he said and nodded toward Stephanie. "Only problem is they grow up. That's why you've got to have your own life." He pulled a bottle of champagne from a nearby ice bucket and went to top up my glass but I put my hand over the top.

"Thanks, but I've had more than enough already."

He took the glass from me and filled it anyway. As he passed it back to me, his fingers brushed against mine. "I've a feeling you're just getting started."

15

"Overall," Richard said, using the edge of the counter to pop the lid off a beer bottle, "I'd say that went pretty well."

I was busy looking at a video of a baby panda going down a slide, something I liked to do as a reward for getting Mara to sleep. Not just pandas, I should add. I'm not totally vapid. Sometimes I mix it up with, say, baby hedgehog montages.

"Don't you think?" Richard pressed.

I made a sort of noncommittal hum just as my phone pinged. It was George.

George: Eh, wtf??? You're literally all over MH's Insta stories

George: Thought Mara didn't get the nod to Aurora's party?

I flicked over to Instagram and tapped into Mother Hen's profile. George was not wrong. There I was in the background of several photos, Mara in a few others, and as for Richard? Well, my Jesus, if he wasn't up front and center stage, guest of honor and *delighted* to be there. We were all bathed in a sort of golden-hour glow that softened and mellowed everything.

She'd also posted a reel, taken from the garden. The video looked sun-dappled and grainy, like a 1950s home movie, giving it a heartstring-tugging nostalgic quality. It was, of course, filtered to within an inch of its life. In reality, the day had been dull and heavy with the threat of thunder, and the low yellow-gray sky had given everyone's complexion a dengue-feverish tinge.

Underneath the post, Mother Hen had written: *Gotta make those memories. #blessed*

"You have to admit," Richard said. "It was not entirely horrendous."

"Fine. It was not entirely horrendous." I looked down at my phone to shoot a quick text off to George:

Eliza: It was from the bowels of hell

"You seemed to be getting on well with Johnny. Impressive guy, isn't he? Serious smarts. But cultured, too, you know? Very well-read."

"Yep. Very impressive. Very cultured," I said, not looking up at him.

Eliza: MH's hubbie got stuck with me.

George: PLEASE tell me Jude didn't get too handsy.

Eliza: Jude? Do you mean Johnny?

George: Nickname is Jude...

George: Cuz he did a Jude Law?

Eliza: ???

"Very interested in the arts," Richard continued. "Told me he's a silent investor in the Dublin International Film Festival."

George: MH was the nanny. Did u not know?

George: That's why she's never had a nanny for Aurora

George: Anyway, hope you left before "keys in a bowl" time

"And Gina's good craic, isn't she?" he went on. "I mean, a little OTT maybe, but she's got a good heart. And you can tell everything she does is for Aurora."

I paused from typing out a response to George.

There was one point during the party when I'd escaped to the garden to get a break from the crowd in the front drawing room. I found the big pink envelope that Mother Hen had been holding out to Aurora earlier. It had been ripped carelessly open and was being blown around by the breeze. Lying in a puddle nearby were two pieces of white paper. I pulled them out: they were premium tickets for a special mother-and-daughter viewing of *Swan Lake* at the Bord Gáis Energy Theatre. On one of the tickets, she'd written: *To Aurora, with all my love, Mom.*

I thought of Mother Hen's face when Johnny upstaged her with the whole *I bought you a tennis court* spectacle. I had brought the tickets back inside and placed them on the rack above the cast-iron range to dry. I was about to return to the drawing room when I heard male voices. Two men were standing just outside the French doors of the kitchen, the tips of their cigars flaring every so often in the dusk.

"Still a mess, if I'm honest," one of the men said. It was Johnny. "After a decade you'd think she could be civil. But no. And cost me a fucking fortune. I'd probably have stayed with her if I'd known that. And it all goes the same way after a while anyway."

"You can say that again." It was Richard. I should have retreated from the kitchen but I was afraid they'd notice me if I moved.

Also, I didn't want to.

I heard Johnny say my name then. He was asking something about me.

"Yeah, yeah," Richard said. "She was the real thing. Could have been one of the greats."

"Any money in it?"

"*Serious* money."

"Shit."

"Because it's not just the concerts. It's album sales, master classes, endorsement deals, all that. And she won a piano worth six figures. Sometimes I think that maybe she likes that thing more than me."

Ha! At least there's something we can agree on, Richie.

"And would you not just, I don't know, put the feet up, be her manager, sit back and let her bring home the money?" Johnny asked incredulously.

"Would *you*?"

There was a pause, then, "Fuck no."

And they laughed together.

"It's beside the point anyway," Richard had said. "Those days are over. She's left it too long. Lost her edge."

"Why'd she quit?"

Richard puffed away on his cigar, then finally said, "She wasn't able to keep up the pace. The international concert circuit, it's grueling. And cutthroat, you know? Always some new prodigy snapping at your heels. She couldn't hack the pressure."

You've got to be fucking kidding me.

"And let me guess. Somehow, it's 'all your fault'?" Johnny asked.

"*All* my fault."

"She must miss it, though."

"She says she doesn't, but you're right. I mean, pianists are all a bit…"

All a bit what, *Richard? Let's hear it.*

"A bit odd, you know?" I shot him daggers from my hidden vantage point. "I mean, they spend ten hours a day on their own with an instrument for company," he said with a sarcastic laugh. "But since she's stopped playing, it's like she's just… gone inward or something. She's not herself anymore. That's why she's let herself go."

The fucking nerve. *How dare he?* I so badly wanted this to roll off me, but the truth was, it hurt even more because of how close I'd felt to him the night before.

Johnny glanced up at Richard. In surprise, I hoped. "You should be grateful she's not out blowing all your cash on laser peels and personal trainers and girls' spa trips to fucking Marrakech. I've had to chop up Gina's credit card *three times*. In the last year."

"At least Gina makes an effort," Richard replied. "I mean, look at her tonight. Life and soul of the party."

"It's all for show," Johnny said dismissively. "At least Eliza's genuine."

"Yeah. Genuinely *miserable*."

I realized I'd never responded to Richard's comment about Gina and looked up to see him tapping away on his phone. "Just texting Johnny to say thanks. It really was sound of him to invite us. Mara got on great guns with Aurora."

A moment later his phone pinged, and he smiled to himself as he read it and typed out a reply.

He looked at me with a glint in his eye, as if he had exceedingly good tidings indeed to impart. "They want to take us to lunch. Gina and Johnny. Friday at one. Somewhere in town. He'll organize it and send on the details. How nice is that?"

Lost her edge. My throat tightened. "And what did you say?"

"I said we'd love to. I don't have anything on that I can't put off. No one really works on Friday afternoons anyway."

His phone pinged again. "Johnny says Nikki's going to collect Aurora and she'll take Mara home with them, too. Can I say yes?"

"You want to go?"

"Why wouldn't I?"

"Ha. I don't even know where to start."

He glanced up from his phone and gave me a searching look. "Sounds like you do."

Here goes. "First, how is it that you're never able to spend time with us as a family, but you can make lunch plans at a moment's notice with another couple? Practically strangers?"

"And we're off," Richard muttered, shaking his head.

"Second, Mara said she would run away and live in the wild if I ever made her go to Amelia's house."

He sighed dramatically. "Eliza. *Normal* people go out. *Normal* people leave their children with other people. One of the girls in the office? She has six-month-old twins, and she's back at work. *And* she's out every weekend."

"Well, sorry, but I can't agree to that arrangement. And if that makes me abnormal, fine."

"What is your problem, Eliza?"

Let herself go. My cheeks grew hot. "Have you ever considered that *I'm* not the one with the problem?"

He picked up his phone, tapped something into it, then put it back in his pocket. "Done. You win. I told Johnny you don't want to go."

"What did you do that for? Now they're going to hate me."

Richard sighed in exasperation. "I didn't put it in those words, obviously. The lunch is canceled. You got what you wanted. As usual. But this time it isn't just *me* who's affected. It's Mara, too. If you're trying to stop her becoming friends with Aurora, you're going about it perfectly."

Yeah, genuinely miserable. I took in a deep breath. "We both know you're not doing this for Mara."

"What's that supposed to mean?"

That he had never met a rich person he wasn't compelled to impress? That furthering his glorious career was all he really cared about? But I couldn't say any of that. Instead, I said, "Who were you talking to on the phone? At the tennis court, when the rest of us were walking back to the house?"

He ran a hand through his hair in frustration. "Seriously, this again?" But this time, he wasn't denying the phone call.

"Why did you lie about it?"

"Why do you think?"

Because you don't want me to know you're a philandering cheat? "I have no idea. Hence why I'm asking."

"Because it was a work thing, Eliza, Jesus. Just Majella complaining about the script. *Again.* And you apparently go crazy when I take work calls at the weekend. So I lied. Because I couldn't take another mood. But it seems we've ended up here anyway."

I didn't say anything.

"It never even occurred to you that Johnny might invest in the theater, did it?" he spat out. "I'm trying to keep the lights on here, Eliza. That's why I wanted us to go for lunch with them. I *need* to get him onside. You have to build a relationship with these people first, a connection. They have to feel like you're one of them. But once again, you just had to make it all about you."

Weekly Spouse Tracker

Rate the following spousal behaviors from 1 to 5:

1=non-existent,   2=poor/rare,   3=adequate/sometimes,
            4=satisfactory/frequent,   5=excellent/always

BEHAVIORS	WEEKLY SCORE
Physical affection	1
Spontaneous acts of kindness	1
Gratitude for Service	1
General attentiveness	1
Reliability	1
Self-Absorption	5
Helps out around the house	1
Attentiveness to offspring	1
Answers texts/phone calls	1
Unaccounted-for disappearances	3

*To be completed in between sessions and returned to Ms. Early

16

Ms. Early sat up in her chair, giving me a thoughtful, assessing look. She flicked a gold lighter on and off.

I had just brought her up-to-date on the fight(s) with Richard. I told her everything—the shark costume debacle, Richard's hurtful comments to Johnny, the lunch invite, how we were barely speaking now. "I don't think the treatment is a good idea," I summed up. "Things have actually got a lot worse."

She remained silent a long time, then leaned toward me. Her expression told me she'd just come to some conclusion. "When I became a therapist, Eliza, I made a rule of never talking to my patients about my personal life. I have always thought it unprofessional to cross that divide." She paused for a moment, then added, "But yours is not a typical case."

I was intrigued by this shift in her attitude—this openness—because in all our previous sessions, Ms. Early seemed so restrained, so unreadable.

"I grew up in a tiny village in the west," she began. "We were poor but my parents loved me and I always knew they were proud of me. I was at the top of my class, the smartest child in school. But when I was sixteen, my mother died from a rare disorder and a year later, my father died of a heart at-

Pause

tack. I think it was a broken heart, really." She stopped there for a moment, then continued. "And so at age seventeen, I was pretty much alone in the world. When I found out I'd been accepted into a pharmacy degree in London, there was nothing to keep me here. So I went."

I learned that, while in London, Ms. Early tried to get by on the small insurance payout she'd received when her father passed, but it wasn't nearly enough, so she took extra jobs wherever she could. While working as a till girl in a shop, she caught the eye of the owner, a recently widowed man who was taken by her serious nature. She, in turn, was drawn by his own solemnity. She felt compelled at the time to ease his pain.

One thing led to another, and he started taking her out for day trips with his son—boating on the Thames, visiting Anmer House, even going to the opera. She somehow managed to balance all this with her studies.

However, she then began spending more and more time at his house to help with cooking, cleaning, everything. Because the man was so busy with his businesses, little by little, Ms. Early found herself running the household by herself.

When she first met the widower, she was on track to graduate with a first-class degree. But now she was so exhausted from all the demands in her life—running the house, trying to parent a troubled motherless boy, still working mornings in the shop. All while grieving the deaths of her own parents.

It was too much for her, and she soon dropped out of college.

That was when the widower asked her to marry him, to move in with him and his son.

"You know that old quote?" Ms. Early asked then. "Marriage is a bribe to make a housekeeper think she's a householder?"

Her new husband assured her she'd want for nothing. And this was true—as long as she was prepared to go cap in hand to him. And then it became less true. And then it became impossible to get money for anything but the most basic household purchases.

But their house was always full of visitors, friends of the widower's, businessmen and their wives. And gradually, Ms. Early began to make a little pin money by helping the women with problems that had been dismissed as trivial, or imagined, by their male doctors. They brought up their problems with Ms. Early because they knew she had trained as a pharmacist, even if she hadn't technically qualified. And perhaps most importantly, because she was a woman. She discreetly passed them treatments for cystitis and cramps, helping more than a few of them diagnose STDs their husbands had brought home to them. She started developing her own balms and lotions, mainly herbal, but very occasionally—in cases of extreme need—pharmacological. Word spread of the effectiveness of her treatments.

For reasons she could never understand, her husband had only grown colder and colder toward her over the years, treating her like an unpaid servant. And when he found out that she'd been treating his friends' wives, he was livid. She tried to explain that she'd only wanted to help, but he insisted that she'd somehow humiliated him, brought him into disrepute. In an act of staggering vindictiveness, he reported her to the authorities for dispensing pharmaceuticals without being a licensed practitioner.

Now, leaning back in her office chair, Ms. Early fiddled with her lighter again, and flicked it on a full ten times without saying another word.

"I'm so sorry," I said. "What happened to you?"

"I was fined a very large sum of money. And he turned me out of the house."

It took her years to get back on her feet. But she did it. She worked two jobs to get by, and studied at night to be a psychotherapist. "And that is what I've been doing ever since."

"I'm sorry," I said again.

"I've told very few people about this."

"You think I'm like you? Is that why you told me?"

She paused for a moment, considering. "I do see myself in you, yes. You deferred your own dreams for your husband's sake, and for your daughter. I know how natural this type of sacrifice is for women, who are socialized from birth to subjugate their own hopes and needs for the good of the family. I did it myself. I set aside my academic studies because I felt so sorry for my husband and his little motherless boy. Very noble, yes?"

I tentatively nodded, not sure if this was meant to be rhetorical.

"The problem is this," she continued. "My sacrifices, made out of love, earned me nothing but disdain. The more I gave up, the less he respected me. All it did was confirm to him that his needs were more important than a woman's—and further, that a woman shouldn't even *have* needs."

She folded her hands in her lap. "But it's not just that I see myself in you—Richard also reminds me of my husband. Charming on the surface, but so much self-pity and entitlement underneath. My husband enjoyed having power over a woman, and believe me, Eliza, so does Richard. In any event, it took me a decade to rebuild my life. I certainly needed help, but there was no one to turn to, no one to lean on. So I did it alone. But when I had finally created a future for myself, I swore I would devote my life to helping other women put into difficult circumstances by the men in their lives. Women who could have really been something, who could *still* really be something."

She looked up at me then, a wistful look in her eyes. "Women like you, Eliza."

"I would never have guessed you went through something like that," I said. "You're so strong."

"I am *now*." She gazed out the window as if caught up in her thoughts, then snapped back to the present. "Tell me this,

Eliza. Have you ever, in your whole marriage, told Richard to fuck off?"

I laughed. She had such a refined way of speaking that she made this sound like the most reasonable thing in the world.

"It's a serious question," she said. "They're very powerful words. Especially for a woman to say."

"I say it all the time."

"You do?"

"I mean, not out loud, really. Not to his face."

"Even when he deserves it?"

I deliberated over this. "I snap back in my own ways, but I've never specifically directed those *exact* words at him. I mean, does anyone ever deserve to be spoken to like that, no matter who they are?"

She gave a despairing laugh. "Of course they do, Eliza."

"What about compassion? What about keeping things civil?"

Ms. Early clicked her tongue. "You see, this is the problem right here. Yes, there are times in life for compassion, but there are times in life when you must defend yourself. When you are under attack, it is right, *necessary*, to get angry. To fight. And if you, Eliza, are incapable of doing a simple thing like telling someone to go fuck themselves when they deserve it, then you are incapable of fighting for yourself." She stood up and came around from behind her desk. With an impatient movement, she motioned for me to get up out of my chair, which I dutifully did.

"All right," she said, when we were standing facing each other. "Now say it to me. Imagine I'm Richard. Tell me to fuck off."

"This is ridiculous."

"Let me hear you say it."

"No. This isn't me."

"Do it, Eliza!"

Those days are over. She's left it too long.

"Fuck you, Richard fucking Sheridan," I burst out.

This was clearly making Ms. Early's day. "Good. *Very* good. Louder this time."

And this time I obliged without any problem. In fact, I got so into the exercise that the secretary popped her head around the door to check that everything was okay and I wasn't having a psychotic break from reality.

"Everything is more than okay, thank you," Ms. Early said, smiling at me like a proud teacher would with an A-student.

When we were seated again, she told me that my homework for the week was to manage to say this to Richard himself when, not if, he did something that merited it. I agreed, really just to get her off my back. There was no way I was going to throw that in Richard's face. But I had to admit that the exercise itself had been therapeutic. My body was fizzing with adrenaline. My hands were even trembling a little. But I felt good, elated even.

"Excellent," Ms. Early said. "*Now* you're ready to increase the dosage of our last treatment."

"*Increase* it? But I've just told you that it's only made things worse!"

"Eliza, I need you to remember that I have helped a great many women through this exact process. Trust me, things are exactly as they should be right now. Richard's behavior is coming along beautifully."

"Beautifully? He said I'd *let myself go*. He called me genuinely *miserable*."

"Yes. He did. But he also, without prompting, brought Mara to the park. Befriended another parent for her sake. Got her an invitation to a birthday party. Took an interest in her social life. And, from what you've told me, it seems you…reignited the romantic connection between you? You must agree that these things are not insignificant."

"Well, sure, when you put it like that. But—"

"And if we compare this to how distanced he was from you and Mara when you first came to me, it is undeniable that we have been making strides."

She said that the next step was to double the dosage. When I next administered the tincture—the *"poitín"*—I was to be sure that Richard consumed four shots. "Trust me, Eliza. We will soon begin to see even *greater* change."

17

In the train station on my way home, the old man was at the piano again. His daughter did say they came every week, and I realized I'd been subconsciously hoping to find them here.

He was not playing a classical piece this time but a traditional Irish song. I recognized it from when I was young. It was the type of music that naturally appealed to me, but that my father dismissed completely. *Classical was where the prestige was, and the money, so why waste time on folk tunes?* he'd always say.

Maybe this piece wasn't as showy as the last, but I loved watching him play it. The music was entirely in his hands. He made it look so effortless. There was a serene smile on his face. I knew that feeling all too well, when thoughts fell away, when the people and places around you disappeared.

When he finished the tune, I stepped forward. His daughter smiled in recognition.

"'King of the Fairies,'" I said. "I've always loved that piece."

Her father turned to look at me. "Do you remember when I kept making a mistake in the last bar? And Mrs. Murphy rapped me so hard on the fingers that I had welts?"

He was addressing me directly. I glanced at the daughter and she subtly nodded for me to go along with it. He appeared to be confusing me with someone else.

"Ah, yes. I remember," I replied. I may not have been there for the rapping incident, but I could guess how it had gone. Musicians often traded stories of teachers who'd used various forms of punishment in an effort to make them better performers. Or simply to take out their frustrations. Nobody "set out" to be a piano teacher, at least according to my father. He said it generally happened when talented musicians got married, had children and needed a steady income. He hadn't used a *ruler* on me per se, but he showed his anger in other ways, like throwing score sheets at me, slapping my hands, that kind of thing.

"My father almost slammed the piano lid on my fingers once," I found myself saying. "I think he only stopped himself because I had a concert the next day."

The man's face clouded over. "He should *never* have done that. I'll have words with him." His eyebrows narrowed and I could tell he was becoming agitated. I watched as his daughter tried to soothe him, gently rubbing his arm.

"Don't worry," I said. "It won't happen again. I don't even play anymore."

He reached out a hand to squeeze mine tight. "My dear, we never stop playing." Then he turned back to the piano and began another tune.

That night, Mara was tucked up in bed and Richard was—surprise, surprise—still at work. I slipped into the music room and rummaged through the boxes until I found the Chopin score again. Then, layer by layer, I peeled back the cover from my piano and lifted the lid. I sat down, laid my fingers on the keys, rested a foot upon the pedals. I closed my eyes and did the relaxation exercises I used to do before performances. I would imagine myself back on my cousin's dairy farm where I'd gone a few times during summer holidays. It was always so calm there compared to our pressure-cooker home. My cousin and I just had to do our daily chores and then we were free to roam the farm, to lie in the long grasses of the meadow reading and chatting. I imagined myself lying on my back, my cousin next to me, novels abandoned in the heat haze, both of us gazing up at the cloudless blue sky, eating tea cakes, drowsing off.

It was heaven.

I took a deep breath, opened my eyes and set my fingers upon the keys. Then I picked out a few notes, ran a few scales. I was surprised but delighted to find that the piano was still perfectly in tune. Often pianos went out of tune when they sat unused for a long period, even if you took all the precautions around heat and humidity.

I set the Chopin score upon the stand, opened it and slowly tried the first bar. And then again, even more slowly. I played it ten times, then moved on to the next bar. I noodled around like that for a while and was onto the third page when I heard the door creak open.

It was Mara in her dinosaur pajamas, hair rumpled.

"You're playing again, Mama." She sounded delighted.

Normally, I would have shut down the lid and brought Mara back up to bed. But I thought of the old man in the train station, and his daughter who looked at him with such love and pride. Their bond forever preserved within the keys of a piano. "Here," I said, scooting over on the stool to make room for her. "Come sit next to me."

I showed her how I warmed up before playing, starting with stretching my arms. She copied with little stretches of her own. Then I showed her how I did scales and arpeggios to warm up my fingers. I told her that the third step was to play a favorite piece of music. To warm up my heart. I showed her how to set the metronome ticking. She was delighted with herself; she'd never been allowed to touch it before.

Then I taught her middle C. And all the other notes. She

soaked it all up. I couldn't teach her fast enough. I showed her how to play a simple melody with three notes, and watched the glee on her face once she'd mastered it.

I'd had that once. The pure joy of playing, of creating a lovely sound, and nothing more. But I'd lost it along the way, bit by bit. With my father always watching, constantly critiquing me, the stress had begun to outweigh the joy of making music. Playing had become working. It was all about pleasing him, about perfection. In the months leading up to my escape to France, I had begun to feel something approaching hate for the piano, even though it was the only thing in the world that I was good at. And then, even after I broke away from my father and his fixation with the classical greats, I'd tried to please Richard by playing the kind of music he had decided would boost my career. He knew theater and he knew audiences, so I let myself be guided. I began to doubt my own taste and, little by little, my own ability to decide on *anything*. I'd gone straight from one man to another. I'd never given myself a chance to be on my own.

But the pleasure on Mara's face was moving, and I felt something inside me shift. I blinked back tears so she wouldn't think something was wrong. Until now, I'd resisted putting any kind of pressure on her to start learning the piano because I wanted her to find it for herself. Only then would I be sure I wasn't pushing her into it just to fill some need of my own. In all honesty, I'd been afraid she'd be good. Afraid I'd turn into my own father, unable to resist the glory of raising a prodigy. But I saw now that *denying* her the chance to learn wasn't right, either. She had music in her. Of course she did. Maybe I'd overcorrected.

"Now just you play," she said, taking my hands and putting them on the keys. "Play something, Mama."

I hesitated, then, very slowly, I began to play the opening chords to "King of the Fairies." And for the first time in a long time, I wasn't playing to impress anyone, to be perfect, to be "the best." I was playing for the sake of playing. And to make my little girl smile.

I told Mara that some pianists felt like their piano had a personality. She nodded and said she sometimes felt this way about her magnifying glass.

"Does *your* piano have a personality, Mama?" she asked.

"Yes. Yes, I think so." Some pianos were mellow and warm; others had a precise clarity. My piano had an otherworldly quality that added a haunting resonance to the sound.

"She has a name, too," I added. "I call her Delphina." I'd never told anyone this before, not even Richard.

"Delphina," Mara echoed, stretching out her arm and touching the lid, gently, as if the piano was a wild creature she was trying to befriend. She turned back to face me, her expression changed. "Are you crying, Mama?" Mara asked in concern.

I was thinking about the old man.

I was thinking about my father.

I wiped at the corners of my eyes and told Mara that the magical part of playing the piano was that you could transform sadness into something beautiful. And that on days when the world felt too hard, you could escape into music.

I explained to her that each pianist had their own favorite composers and styles, and that you had to figure this out if you wanted to truly reach your potential.

"What's your favorite, Mama? Your favorite piano music?"

I smiled at her. "I'm still figuring that out."

18

There was one slight problem in implementing Ms. Early's instructions: Richard was not speaking to me. All because he had to cancel lunch with Johnny, his new bestie. So persuading him to sit down and bond over *even greater quantities* of high-potency hooch of indeterminate origin was a non-runner. I had to get him back onside first. And it was going to take something big.

That is how Mara and I came to be sitting in a shiny black limo with Mother Hen, Johnny and Aurora on one side, and Nikki, Hubby—I had missed his name when first introduced and now it was too late to ask—and Amelia on the other. The adults were lashing into the champagne, and the two girls were knocking back sparkling juice. Someone had Taylor Swift's latest album playing on their iPhone and there was a party atmosphere. Even the two men looked buzzed. Mother Hen was off the charts. She had two layers of tan on and her nails were painted a glossy tangerine, her cheekbones so reflective I could have checked my teeth in them.

For a moment I hesitated, not one hundred percent able to breathe properly. What had I been thinking, orchestrating this unlikely, forced and deeply uncharacteristic scenario? But this shindig was necessary to thaw the frozen tundra between Richard and me. Ms. Early and I had formulated this plan together, and I was determined to see it through.

The advice a play therapist had given Mara on making new friends suddenly came to mind: 1. Smile. 2. Make eye contact. 3. Ask them what games they like to play. So that was what I did. Apart from step three. And step two, because I didn't want to send the wrong signal to Johnny. So basically, I just smiled a lot.

Majella was waiting for us at the main entrance of the theater. She welcomed us into the foyer where smooth jazz was being piped through the sound system and an intern was standing with a tray of champagne flutes and smoked salmon blinis.

As she gave me a welcoming hug, Majella murmured that she had asked the stage manager to distract Richard while she had gotten things set up.

"This is so cool!" Aurora said to Mara, pirouetting around to the music. "I can't believe your dad owns this. I can't believe you get to come here whenever you want. You are *so* lucky."

Mara was momentarily speechless. She had never before been the center of attention. Then she said, with a new confidence about her, "Wait till you see the thunder run."

The theater *did* look magnificent. Richard had poured frightening amounts of money into the upgrade—the ceiling moldings now glinted with fresh gilt paint, and the imported Parisian globe lights glowed in the dusk.

And then I saw Richard. He was standing on the curved stairs, surprised to see us all and not entirely...thrilled. I hurried up to him.

"Hey," I said. "Look, I messed up with the whole 'Johnny taking us to lunch' thing. I wanted to make it up to you so I organized a little get-together." I stalled here but gathered myself to look him in the eye and deliver the last excruciating line. "You were totally right."

At this point I was supposed to squeeze his hand or some

other equivalent show of physical affection, but I simply could not persuade the relevant neural impulses to fire.

He looked at me with confusion and a soupçon of suspicion, but I pressed a flute of champagne into his hand and all seemed to be forgiven.

Majella, in her admirable take-charge manner, had positioned herself in the center of the foyer and was dinging a spoon against her glass. "Girls," she announced to Mara, Aurora and Amelia, "your private ghost tour will begin in a few minutes, so why don't you get yourselves an ice cream to bring with you?" Aurora took Mara's hand and they raced over to the Ben & Jerry's cart I'd arranged.

"Mara's mum and I will be conducting the tour. The rest of the grown-ups can enjoy the champagne reception here, and there's also an open tab in the bar for anyone looking for further refreshments. Then Richard will show you around the theater. You will be the only people to see the newly refurbished auditorium before opening night. And once today's read-through is finished up, the actors are looking forward to meeting you and giving you a personal welcome."

Richard called this type of meet-and-greet event—where visitors had private introductions to the actors—the "Money Can't Buy" special. It was a big seller with corporate sponsors. He didn't seem to see the irony in the fact that these companies literally *did* buy this *exclusive bespoke access*—it was entirely based on a material transaction. But regardless, it worked. The executives liked to feel chosen.

"Pretty nice joint you've got here, Richie," Johnny called over to him. Richard drained the rest of his glass and set it aside. Then he greeted Johnny like an old friend, and they gave each other two-handed politician handclasps. A switch had flicked on in Richard and it was *showtime, baby.*

He was off, with a compelling tale of the ups and downs of restoring the theater to its former glory. This, I knew, was a key part of his investor sales pitch. "And then, just when we thought that was the worst of it," I heard him say to Johnny, "the engineer tells us the royal box is about to come down. The support beams were almost completely eaten away by wood-worm. Could have collapsed at any moment."

"Fucking nightmare," Johnny said, shaking his head. I agreed with him that this was indeed a nightmarish scenario. It was also one I had been completely unaware of until this moment.

"You just never know what you're going to get with these old structures," Richard said. "Not until you start opening them up."

"They're still worth it," Johnny said. "The character of a place like this? Priceless."

Richard looked at Johnny in the way that I imagine Paris of Troy once gazed at Helen. My plan was working.

It was decided that Johnny, Hubby and Nikki would stay with Richard, who said he'd bring them to the bar first. "Let's see if I can figure out how to pull you a pint," he joked. He was in his absolute element.

Mother Hen was torn for a solid few minutes about which group to go with. Then she gave herself a little shake and declared she would stay with the girls. "I wouldn't miss it for the…" She trailed off, her eyes widening.

Everyone turned to see a woman coming down the stairs, and it was obvious even from a distance that she bore an uncanny resemblance to Hollywood A-lister Sasha Jones. Then the penny dropped: she *was* Sasha Jones.

Sasha was wearing the uniform of the 1 percent, everything in various shades of neutral—flowy white trousers, a gossamer-thin ivory shirt, a cream cashmere coat draped over her shoulders. Clothes that would be irretrievably grubby after their first outing. I had an image of her shrugging the clothes off in a dressing room, letting them fall in a heap on the floor, saying to an assistant, "Oh, you like them? Take them, they're yours."

Richard was alternating between beaming at Sasha like she was his firstborn child graduating from Harvard, and glancing at Johnny and Hubby to check they were impressed. He needn't have worried on that front. They were mesmerized. *I* was mesmerized, for God's sake. It was like she was a different species, as if she sucked up all the light from us mere mortals and was shining it back at us from within.

"Gosh," she said in her famously breathy voice, "I hope the audience is this attentive on opening night."

Everyone laughed and relaxed a little as she glided toward us. She offered each person her hand and made sure to look each of them in the eyes with a smile, like they were the only interesting person in existence. "*So* nice to meet you. I'm Sasha... A pleasure, I'm Sasha..."

Like we didn't bloody know!

Then another penny dropped. What she had said about opening night—is it possible that Richard had cast *her* in the lead role? After Anna had to drop out, Richard had been under major pressure to attract another *name* to fill the role. Well, there weren't many *names* bigger than Sasha Jones.

Majella discreetly reminded us that it was time to get the children's ghost tour underway. Mother Hen and I looked at each other as we both did the same mental calculation. Would it be worse to: (a) backtrack out of the kiddie tour and reveal ourselves to be mistrustful, jealous hags *or* (b) play it cool and go on the tour, leaving our overexcited and not entirely trustworthy husbands with this smoldering-hot but also exceptionally talented actress?

"Come on, girls, let's have some fun," Mother Hen declared and that was that. And off we trooped, heads held high, not that the men noticed.

"They're like bloody Labradors, aren't they?" she whispered as we reached the costume department. "Was it just me or were they practically salivating?"

I was too distracted to reply. This whole situation raised so many questions. How had Richard pulled off this coup? Why didn't he tell me?

And most importantly…was Sasha Jones the kind of woman who might wear a backless dress so low it revealed her lack of underwear?

While the girls rummaged through children's costumes from pantos and historical productions, Gina sidled over and flicked me a coy Princess Di look. "By the way, I meant to ask… It's okay if I film some stuff, right? My Insta followers go nuts for this kind of 'authentic family time' content," she said, using air quotes. "I literally can't give them enough."

My mind was more than a little occupied now with imagining Richard and Sasha downing shots together back at the bar. I didn't have mental space or energy left for this. "Um, sure?" I said. "But would you mind not posting any footage of Mara?"

I really would have preferred if she just put the damn phone away altogether, but Mother Hen had 50,000 followers and counting. That meant free publicity for the theater. And if there was one thing Richard loved, it was free publicity. I needed to stay focused.

She gave me her trademark *smiling with her eyes* look and touched my arm, which I noticed she always did when she got what she wanted. "Of *course*," she assured me, rummaging in her giant tote bag and producing a selfie stick. With a practiced move, she extended the telescopic handle and fixed her oversize smartphone into place, then clicked something called a LuMee light around the phone's camera. "I would *never* post anything that someone wasn't comfortable with. I'm all about ethics."

Majella beckoned for us to follow her down the spiral stone steps into the crypt. She was an excellent guide and had a storyteller's knack for making the theater's history riveting. But I wondered if she needed to go into *quite* so much detail about the ghost who was said to haunt the theater's corridors, allegedly locking and unlocking door handles and making the lights go out, and playing pranks on the cast at dress rehearsals. At this rate, the tour would take forever.

As we moved through the underground passageways, the girls on the lookout for the signs of the ghost, Majella fell into step with me.

"So," I said. "Sasha Jones."

"Yep," she replied in a deadpan tone. "Sasha Jones."

"How can the theater afford her?"

Majella didn't say anything, just gave me a look.

We finished up in the auditorium and joined everyone on-stage with Sasha and a few other cast members. Richard was demonstrating the new high-tech revolving platform.

Mother Hen interrupted this love-in with a cry of, "Oh. My. God. *Brain*wave!"

Everyone turned to look at her in confusion. "Aurora, my darling, over here, hop up onto this platform," she called out to her. "We're going to do your *Toy Show* audition video, right here, right now. It *has* to have the X-factor or we can forget about it. You're up against contortionist twins who volunteer with a homeless charity. Hey, Richie? Do you think we could get some lights focusing on the platform?"

So *Richie* was officially a *thing* now, apparently. And did Gina really care this much about the *Toy Show* or was she just trying to divert some of the limelight from Sasha?

Probably both.

Richard radioed through the lighting instructions to a technician who was working late, and Mother Hen busied herself setting up a tripod. Then she angled the phone toward Aurora, who was standing alone on the giant turntable.

"But I don't wanna," Aurora whined, hopping off the platform.

Mother Hen bit her lip, then with forced kindness, said, "It'll take two minutes, darling, and then you can have another ice cream. Now *hop back up there.*"

"But I'm allowed as many ice creams as I want. Mara's dad said so. I've already had three."

Mother Hen held up a hand. "Don't even go there, missy."

"Fine." Aurora trudged back onto the platform, muttering under her breath, "But you can't force me to be any good."

"Okay, great, now we just need music. There's a piano right there. Eliza, darling, can you just play us something?"

"Oh. Sorry. I… I don't perform anymore."

"This isn't performing," she reasoned in the exact same tone she had just used with Aurora. "No one's even watching." *Right, apart from the two dozen people now onstage, one of whom is a Hollywood star.*

"Yeah. Sorry. I'd really rather not." I could hear my voice getting wobbly. It did not deter Mother Hen. She just wouldn't drop it. Now everyone was looking at me, probably thinking, *why won't she just play the damn piano? Isn't she supposed to be a pianist or something?*

"I can play if you like," came a silky voice. "Though I'm afraid it might not be very good."

Sasha Jones to the rescue. She shrugged her coat off her shoulders and handed it to Johnny. Then she sat down at the piano and began playing a simple, slow classical piece. Everyone stared. Was there nothing this goddess could not do?

All the while, Aurora had been rotating round and round on the platform. "Mom? I don't feel so good."

"We talked about this, Aurora, remember? Never complain, never explain, okay?"

Then Mother Hen did a "five, four, three, two, one" signal with her fingers and Aurora began her little ballet routine. I had to admit, it did look lovely. There was something very pretty about the way she pirouetted while revolving, like a tiny well-trained cog within a cog.

But then the tiny well-trained cog stopped dancing, turned pale and bent forward, hands on her stomach. Before any of the adults reacted, Mara jumped onto the platform. She ran over and put her arms round Aurora to steady her, just as Aurora's three ice creams made a reappearance. All over Richard's beloved state-of-the-art revolving platform.

"Aurora!" Mother Hen cried, appalled.

Aurora lifted her head and said triumphantly, "Told you I felt sick."

19

The next morning, Richard—who, for as long as I had known him, had been physically incapable of waking before 9:00 a.m. unless you carefully trickled a glass of water on him, and sometimes even that didn't work—*hopped* out of bed at daybreak and got Mara dressed and fed. Without asking me where we kept her socks. Or trousers. Or coat. After, he popped up to me with a frothy coffee and a lifestyle magazine, kissed me and said he was taking Mara to the playground so I could have a lie-in. And all of this: Without. Being. Asked.

It was literally everything I had ever wanted.

But how are you supposed to enjoy a lie-in when your husband was possibly/probably trying to sleep with/already sleeping with/in love with one of the most beautiful women in the world?

To distract myself from ruminating obsessively about Sasha Jones, I decided to tackle the worst job in the house, a.k.a. fixing the broken toilet in the horrible under-stairs bathroom. Obviously, when I say *fixing*, I mean duct-taping the lid closed and sticking on a sign that said, "Do not use! Remember, this does *not* flush! Use other toilet!"

And *then* I sat on the tiles and googled Sasha Jones. Turns out she not only possessed an unearthly beauty, but she was the real deal acting-wise, too. She had honed her craft in the theater before moving on to the big screen, and she always tried to squeeze in performances in artsy off-Broadway shows in between blockbusters. I also discovered she was married to a ludicrously good-looking film producer. Lately, though, there were rumors of trouble in paradise. Sasha had been pictured out and about without her wedding ring and had, according to the gossip sites, temporarily relocated to Ireland because she needed "space to figure things out." I put my phone away.

"Fancy a martini, Sir Pickly Popsicle?" I said to Mr. Pickles, who, barred from the park for inappropriate behavior with a cockapoo, had stayed behind and was observing my plumbing endeavors with interest. "Yes, I know it's still the morning but I won't judge you."

Sir Pickly Popsicle tilted his head to the side quizzically. Then, maintaining perfect eye contact, he cocked his leg and peed on the tiles.

And then, as I sat wedged between a blocked toilet and a puddle of dog wee, the doorbell rang. I trudged to the hall, stiff from crouching for so long. It was Mother Hen. She was wearing an extra layer of tan with a hint of glitter in it, and the hair, *dear God* the hair, was its own separate living entity at this stage. She clearly wanted to be invited in. I tried to steer her toward our never-used music room, which, although cold and uninviting, was at least clean.

"Don't be silly," she said. "We'll pop down to the kitchen for a cup of tea." There was no brooking this storm; she was a river that could not be dammed. I thought of the piles of dirty dishes in the sink and on the counter, the remains of breakfast all over the table. They were on my list of things to sort out after I'd tackled the toilet. If she'd called in advance and given me notice of, say, about two weeks, there was a chance that things would have been tidied.

Regardless, in she charged, down to the basement, positioning herself at the table for, in her words, *tea and biscuits and a good gossip*. You couldn't really talk, she argued, in the Honey Café. All those flapping ears.

"So look," she began, as I made her tea with a fork—no clean spoons. "I know you must be mad at me. And I deserve it—but I swear, Eliza, it was a complete mistake." *Sorry, what?* "It's actually a really positive thing? For all of us."

"Gina, what's going on?"

"Oh, my God. You haven't seen it." She made an "oopsie" face. "Right. So I know you wanted me to edit Mara out of my videos but the problem is… I did something really silly. I wasn't recording Aurora's performance. I was actually—by complete mistake—um, live streaming it."

Ah.

It had, according to Mother Hen, gone totally viral overnight. Like, *totally*. Instagram was lighting up with it. The internet was going wild for Sasha and Aurora's double act, but everyone was melting over Mara, too.

"Show me," I said.

She turned her phone to show me the video. Yep, there we all were at the impromptu performance. There was Mara bopping along in her T-Rex costume. And then I saw Johnny and Richard, both transfixed by Sasha at the piano. And there *I* was, transfixed by Richard.

I handed Gina's phone back to her, and as she took it, she caught my hand for a moment and held my gaze with a look that said *yes, our husbands have the absolute hots for her, but we're going to keep our chins up, Eliza, and we're going to put on a bloody good show of not giving a damn.*

We were interrupted by the creak and slam of the front door and the clatter of feet coming down to the basement. They were back. Richard was in the best of moods when he entered the kitchen, leaning close to kiss me and complimenting my perfume.

"It's anti–head lice shampoo," I said.

He didn't hear me. He had moved on to air-kissing Gina and admiring her "gorgeous glow." She all but purred with pleasure.

"I've just seen your video," he said to Gina. "The chairman of the theater's board forwarded it to me. Said there hasn't been such a buzz about the theater in decades, maybe ever." He shook his head in awe. "With one video, you've done what a team of PR professionals couldn't manage in six months."

Gina exhaled. "Oh my God, that's such a relief. I actually was a *teeny* bit nervous that you guys—" her eyes slid in my direction "—wouldn't be one hundred percent delighted about the video? Because Mara's in it?"

Then Gina and Richard both looked at me.

"Well," I said, "we've always said it would be best to keep Mara out of the limelight. Till she's old enough to decide for herself. Isn't that right, Richard?"

I waited for him to get defensive, to say that I was being overprotective, that lots of children Mara's age had their own *YouTube channels, for God's sake!*

But instead, he said, "It's your call, Eliza," without even a hint of sarcasm.

"I meant to say, Richard," Gina cut in smoothly, "Johnny's been thinking lately of, I don't know, diversifying his portfolio? And after last night, he's considering recommending Blind Alley to some of his investors…"

Richard whipped his head around to face her. "Wait. Are you serious?"

She nodded.

Richard was so delighted that he picked Mara up and spun her around by the arms, which she loved but I didn't because 75 percent of childhood shoulder dislocations happen in this exact way. Then I realized Richard's expression wasn't delight. It was intense relief.

"What about…if I left the video up and just blurred Mara's face?" Gina suggested.

Mara, a little dizzy, shrugged. "I don't mind."

Gina and Richard looked at me expectantly. "Sounds like a good compromise?" Richard prompted.

"Fine," I said.

"Excellent!" Richard clapped his hands together. "Now, what do you say I crack open some champagne?"

"Let me call Johnny," Mother Hen said. "See if he can come round."

It was the evening and our kitchen was littered with the detritus of our impromptu *intime soirée*. At some point Johnny had decided we should order in food, but Richard's suggestion of getting Thai food delivered was dismissed. Johnny said One Pico's on Stephen's Green was good.

"Hardly the kind of place to do delivery?" Richard laughed.

"They do for me," Johnny said.

When the food arrived, Richard—not Johnny—covered the bill. I also noticed it cost three times the amount of our weekly grocery shop. But I didn't say anything about it.

I also didn't say anything about what went down in the utility room.

There I was, on my tiptoes, struggling to reach a bottle of wine that was stashed on a high shelf, when I realized Johnny was leaning against the door frame. Watching me.

In theory, he should have been a very attractive man. But there was something about him. Maybe it was my sense that he probably hadn't cut his own fingernails for years. I imagined a small, young woman in a uniform silently buffing his nails for him and pushing back his cuticles while he talked into his phone. Or maybe it was the luxury hotel–spa smell that seemed to emanate from his very pores, as if he regularly marinated himself in a Jacuzzi filled with sacred lotus massage oil. Whatever it was, there was *something*.

In the end, he stepped toward me and reached up, effortlessly taking the wine down. He glanced at the label, then handed it to me. But when I took it, he didn't let go.

"If you were my wife, I'd never send you to fetch drinks for my guests, like a waitress," he said with too much eye contact.

What could I even say to that? *If I was your wife, I'd try very hard to persuade you to wear socks?* Johnny had a penchant for four-hundred-euro suede loafers that showed off a daring amount of bare upper foot and ankle. This raised so many questions. Did his feet not get sweaty and uncomfortable against the leather inner sole? Or did he in fact wear those little flesh-colored foot-sies they gave you in shops when you were trying on shoes? Would this be better or worse?

I really wanted to stop thinking about Johnny's feet. I really wanted to breathe air that wasn't thick with neroli and jujube. But he would not let go of the wine.

Then Richard suddenly appeared behind Johnny. I saw him notice the polite tug of war over the bottle of wine.

"There you are," he said, making his presence known. I wasn't sure if he was talking to me or to Johnny.

Johnny didn't immediately turn. He just gave me an assessing look as if trying to read me, or possibly communicate intent. Then he turned to Richard, palming the wine off on him. "We can't drink this. Give the French Paradox a shout. Get them to drop a few bottles around."

The rest of the evening went relatively well. Gina was mainly chatting nonstop, as if trying to reach some kind of daily word count. She was her usual touchy-feely self, putting a hand on Richard's arm every so often to emphasize a point. Richard, for his part, was doing that "mirroring" trick he'd picked up at some communication seminar or other, whereby he reflected a person's body language back to them in order to "forge a deeper connection"—the same thing he did at Aurora's birthday party with Johnny and company.

In other words, he was a master of manipulation.

I watched in amusement as he returned Gina's touches, leaned in when she did and threw his head back in laughter whenever she said anything even remotely funny.

Johnny, on the other hand, was largely quiet, happy to let his overeager wife and my overeager husband provide the entertainment. Occasionally, his eyes would drift toward me but Gina didn't seem to notice. Then again, she didn't even notice if the person she was talking to walked away to refill their wineglass, or, I don't know, scream into the void?

Mara and Aurora were in the snug, flicking through books and building forts with the sofa cushions.

In the end, it was Gina who called time because Aurora had an extra-early dance rehearsal the next morning. There was a lot of air-kissing and variations of *we must do this again*. Richard helped Gina carry the now sleeping Aurora out to the taxi he'd called for them. I'd assumed Johnny would follow them out, but no, there he still was, leaning against the island. If he was drunk, he hid it well.

"He sees the way I look at you," he said to me.

"I don't know what you're talking about," I lied, feeling my cheeks grow hot.

"He sees the way I look at you and still he gives me the hard sell," Johnny continued. "No way in hell I'd do business with someone if they looked at *my* wife like that."

"Maybe you could stop looking at me so." I was surprised at myself. My inbuilt pandering reflex had deserted me.

"Maybe I don't want to."

Richard came back in, rubbing his hands together, then stopped, sensing he had, yet again, walked into something.

"Good times, Richie," Johnny said. "Let's do this again, yeah? Give us a chance to drill down into the numbers."

Richard, to give him his due, hesitated at first, his eyes flicking between Johnny and me. We both watched him deliberating. "Just say the word, Johnny. I'll make it happen," Richard said.

I had gotten what I wanted. Ms. Early's plan had worked. Richard wasn't just regularly speaking to me again, but he seemed to genuinely enjoy it. For the past couple of days, he'd been in the best of moods. I used to love when he was like this, buzzing with ideas, able to laugh at himself, joking at how patient I was with his "freak-outs."

We stayed up after Gina and Johnny left. Richard was getting great pleasure from analyzing the night.

"Drill down into the numbers. That's what he said. He must have been talking about an investment, right? Is that how you read it?"

I smiled along, silently communicating, *sure, sure, definitely thinking of investing.* If Richard noticed something was off, he pretended not to. The wine had run out. If it wasn't for Ms. Early's voice in my head, I would have called it a night.

I walked toward the high shelf of the cleaning press and took out the blue bottle, pouring each of us some shots, each of which Richard immediately downed. I managed to discreetly tip mine into a pot plant. Then I poured again.

With each shot, Richard became looser, more at ease, more talkative. He seemed less affectionate than the first time I'd administered Ms. Early's hooch, but definitely more uninhibited. Was this wrong? It definitely felt a little wrong.

Just say the word, Johnny. I pressed a fourth shot on him.

"So," I said. "You didn't tell me about Sasha Jones."

"No." He didn't say it in a defensive way, just calmly stating the facts. Weird.

"Why not?"

"I wanted to, I really did. But they made me sign an NDA."

Let's see if I could push this a bit further. "Richard," I said softly, touching his arm. "Richard, who's Lady Languish?"

He gave me a confused look. "You know about her?"

"Umm, yeah. Yeah, I know about her."

"I tell you, she's a live wire. I feel like I'm twenty-one again when she's around."

"Oh. Um, okay. Well, who is she?"

He ignored me and I could see him fighting sleep. I still had other lines of inquiry, and this direction was starting to feel like a dead end. So I pivoted. "Why did you say it was against regulations for me to work in the theater? Why did you lie?"

"Because," he said, a casual smile on his face, "I didn't want you coming in to the theater."

Those were his actual words. "What's the problem? With me coming in to the theater?" I pressed.

"It's my workplace. I feel like you're looking over my shoulder when you're there."

That was actually pretty reasonable. I *did* look over his shoulder when I was in there.

"And…" he added, yawning. "I didn't want you finding out about the pianist."

"What pianist?"

He rested his head back against the cushions of the sofa and let his eyelids close. "That's strong stuff, Eliza."

"What pianist, Richard?"

"I wrote in a piano scene. Into the play. And I hired a professional pianist to play it."

"Okay…? So why wouldn't you tell me?"

"Because if I told you, then you might want to do it. Perform."

"And what would be so bad about that?"

"If you performed, that's all they'd write about."

"Who?"

"The reviewers. And I'm not going back to being the pianist's husband."

Weekly Spouse Tracker

Rate the following spousal behaviors from 1 to 5:

1=non-existent,   2=poor/rare,   3=adequate/sometimes,
4=satisfactory/frequent,   5=excellent/always

BEHAVIORS	WEEKLY SCORE
Physical affection	3
Spontaneous acts of kindness	2
Gratitude for Service	2
General attentiveness	3
Reliability	1
Self-Absorption	5
Helps out around the house	1
Attentiveness to offspring	1
Answers texts/phone calls	1
Unaccounted-for disappearances	4

*To be completed in between sessions and returned to Ms. Early

20

Ms. Early rose and came around from behind her desk. She drew a chair over to sit directly in front of me. I hadn't been this close to her before. She brought with her a scent of wood smoke that put me in mind of evenings closing in and candle-light and dark, damp soil.

I caught her up-to-date on the past week's events, specifi-cally my conversation with Richard where he said he wasn't going back to being *the pianist's husband* again. And I told her about the Lady Languish live wire comments, and that he had said she made him feel twenty-one again.

"This is good," she said once my update was over.

"Eh, not for my self-esteem, it's not. He pretty much admit-ted to having an affair."

"It's good because we have a much clearer idea of what we're dealing with. Now that we've diagnosed the problem, we can treat it."

"Treat it? This isn't bedbugs we're talking about."

"What I'm saying, Eliza, is that if it *is* an affair, we can nip it in the bud. But first we must return to the fundamental ques-tion. What do you want?"

"I want to nip *Richard* in the bud."

Her previous amused look disappeared, replaced by a flash of irritation. "Eliza," she said sharply. "I can see that the jokes, and this…this attitude is just a front. And I know exactly how you got here. Every time Richard hurt you, every time he lied to you, you built up this defensive shell, layer by layer, because you discovered that it protected you from the pain. I'm not criticizing. It is a natural reaction to your situation.

"And so you *pretend* that you don't care. But you need to know that if you keep going like this, there will come a point when you *really* don't care. It could be months, it could be a year. But once you reach that point, there is no saving your marriage. Because by then, your cynicism would have turned into bitterness. I have seen it many times with women who have come to me too late. And so I ask you the same question I asked you at our very first session together. What do you *want*?"

I gazed at the framed picture on the wall behind Ms. Early, the only decoration in her office. It was a beautiful sketch of a woman on a rocky bluff facing the sea, her hair tangling as she leaned into the wind. The sleek heads of three seals looked up at her from the water. And then I thought of those other women who sat or would sit in this same chair, staring at this sketch as Ms. Early tells them they had left it too late. That there was no hope for their marriage.

"I want the old Richard back," I heard myself say. And then it all came out. How I wished he would still put his arms around me and promise that everything was going to be all right, like he did all those years ago in the early days; that he would look at me the way he did in our honeymoon cottage, as if he couldn't quite believe his luck; that he would still sound proud when he introduced me to people. How foolish I was to think we were starting to find our way back to each other that wonderful night in the study when, all along, he'd been seeing someone else. Another woman whom he now had feelings for—feelings I thought he'd only ever feel for me.

"So to make a long story short, I'm just a pathetic little door-mat who wishes her husband still loved her," I said in summary, feeling much, *much* worse. "Is that what you wanted to hear?"

Ms. Early just stared at me without breaking eye contact. All her earlier frustration and annoyance was gone. "You are not pathetic, Eliza." Her tone was surprisingly gentle, almost motherly. "The move to Dublin, I don't imagine it's helped."

"No. It hasn't."

We'd moved to Dublin just when my mother had started making tentative contact with us again, mainly out of a desire to get to know Mara. My parents lived in Bath now and Mara and I had even been planning on traveling there to meet my mother. From what she'd said, I'd gotten the impression that my father was softening, too. That he might even meet us. Despite all the hard times, I missed my family. But with the move to Dublin, it felt like all the progress had been undone. I'd asked my mother if they'd like to fly over and visit us but I'd gotten a terse text back to say my father was too busy with work to travel. And that was that.

And at least in London, even though I wasn't a working musician anymore, there'd always been friends from the old days inviting me along to recitals and album launches, always someone crashing in our spare room on their way to perform at a concert or festival. I hadn't appreciated just how much it meant to be included, to feel like you were still part of a scene.

"I imagine you're on your own a lot. Since Richard prevented you from working," Ms. Early said.

"He didn't *prevent* me."

She gave me a pointed look.

"And I'm not on my own all the time. Mara's with me."

"Ah, yes, Mara. You've mentioned she's your top priority. That's a lot of pressure."

"I'm her parent. I signed up for it. I love her."

"No, I mean for Mara. That's a lot of pressure for one little girl."

Low blow, Ms. Early. Reading my hurt expression, she added, "I don't mean pressure to behave perfectly or be a prodigy or anything like that. What I'm saying is that Richard has isolated you from your family and friends and—"

"I wouldn't put it like *that*."

"Eliza, you're isolated from your friends and family. Your ability to earn a living is restricted because you're effectively parenting alone. And *now* your husband appears to have found comfort elsewhere. And so, if we're being honest, apart from your new friend, whom I presume is busy with her own life, all you have is Mara. And Mara is a perceptive child. She will sense that you have devoted yourself entirely to her. And she will begin to feel that she owes you a debt. That is a heavy burden to put on a child."

How dare she? "I *love* my daughter," I said in a warning tone. "I love being home with her. There's nothing wrong with that. I'm supposed to devote myself to her. I am her *mother*."

"Yes, you're correct. You are Mara's mother. And nothing else."

I felt as if she'd slapped me. I could feel the tears forming but I didn't care. "What do you want me to say? That the one thing that truly made me happy is gone? Forever, never coming back? Is that what you want me to say? That I used to earn thousands in an evening, but now I have to sneak money at the till at Tesco just to pay *you*? For sessions that only ever make me feel shittier? That I don't fit in here and never will, with all these perfect mothers with their perfect fucking lowlights, or that my husband keeps buying me fancy clothes because he's so embarrassed by how I look? That I feel like I've fallen off the edge of the planet and the *only* person who remembers that I exist—the *only* person who actually loves me—is my six-year-old daughter? Forgive me, Ms. Early. Forgive me for being so *weak* that I take comfort in my daughter's company."

I sat with my face in my hands and let the tears come. I cried and cried and cried, till there was nothing left.

Only then did Ms. Early speak. "You've been holding it together for a long time, Eliza. But you're not in this alone anymore. I'm in this with you now." She handed me a gray silk handkerchief with her initials in the corner, and I wiped my eyes, both embarrassed but also oddly lighter, cleansed.

She stood and walked over to the cabinet. She unlocked it but instead of choosing one of the blue bottles, she reached instead for a sealed brown pouch. Then she sat back down at the desk and set the pouch on the table between us. "You know what an aphrodisiac is, I assume?"

I laughed aloud at this unexpected, but not unwelcome, shift in conversation. "Yes, but—"

"Good. In this next step of the process, we're going to harness the power of *anaphrodisiacs*. These are compounds that… quell, or *blunt* the libido, if you will. They're sometimes used by people with an overly high sex drive. Oh, and sex offenders out on parole," she added. "Now, I know what you're thinking, but this isn't the same thing as chemical castration at all."

I most definitely had not been thinking that.

"All *we're* going to do is administer high dosages of unrefined, powdered chasteberry extract to your husband," she continued nonchalantly, as if what she just said made any sense. "Simple but highly effective."

"Chasteberry?" This was the most made-up thing I'd ever heard, and this says a lot, given Mara and her extremely…*vivid* imagination. "You're joking, right?"

"It's a recognized herbal remedy," she said blankly. "The ancient Greeks and Philistines knew its power."

"Oh, well, if the Philistines were into it…"

She was unimpressed with my reaction, but she handed the pouch to me anyway. The label read:

Chasteberry Extract

Vitus Agnes Powder

Non-GMO and Vegan

Herbal supplement for menstrual comfort

Menstrual *comfort? What the hell?* I examined the small print. "It specifically says here that it's only for women."

She gave an elegant wave of a hand, as if to say, pish posh. "They have to say that to cover themselves."

"Cover themselves against what?"

"Sometimes, and I mean very occasionally, chasteberry can have a few minor...side effects. Hot flashes, breast tenderness, that kind of thing."

"*Breast tenderness?* Even in people who don't, umm, have...?"

She drew breath, paused, then said, "It can—though this is *very* rare—cause temporary enlargement of the...well, the mammary glands. But none of that is important. What matters here is that it works. Chasteberry is also known as Monk's Pepper because monks used to chew it to reduce sexual urges. This has worked for centuries. And it will work on Richard. He will simply lose interest. And even if his interest is, shall we say, *piqued*, he will find himself physically unable to act upon it. We shall induce, if you will, a state of temporary impotence."

I laughed in disbelief. "Is that even *legal*?"

"Eliza," she said in the testy tone of a teacher trying to keep their patience with a particularly slow-witted student. "The only question of any importance here is this—are you willing to take the necessary steps to stop your husband's affair while you still can, or are you just going to sit there and watch as it gathers pace until it blows up into a full-blown love affair? Until he decides that he deserves to be happy and that he's going to leave you for this younger woman?"

"We don't know she's younger," I muttered under my breath.

"Oh my dear, they're never *older*. Anyway, the point is, you need to decide now if you're willing to do what it takes to get what you want. Which, from what you've told me, is to keep your family together."

I thought about the look on Richard's face the night before when he'd talked about Lady Languish. Excited, invigorated. Alive. Did I really think he was going to voluntarily give that up?

"All right," I caved. "I'm in."

Ms. Early gave a satisfied nod. "Good. Now for this to work, you must get at least two tablespoons of chasteberry extract into his diet each and every day without him noticing. As soon as he stops taking it, the effects will disappear almost instantly and his performance abilities will return to normal."

I opened the pouch. Inside was a brownish powder. I sniffed. It had a pepper-ish aroma.

"If you see...*evidence* that this dosage isn't strong enough, then you may increase it up to a maximum of three tablespoons," she added.

"But won't he be suspicious? That he suddenly can't...*you know*."

She laughed at this. "I'll tell you how it's going to play out. Once Richard notices his *problem*, let's call it, he's going to do some research on it. Then he's going to go to his doctor. Because this is the one problem that men take seriously. And the doctor is going to tell him that it is often caused by work stress. Or drinking. So if Richard suddenly starts cutting back his hours, or switches to nonalcoholic beer, you'll know why."

Only minutes before, I was wishing I'd never set foot in Ms. Early's office. But I had to admit I was *really* starting to warm to her. And to this new plan.

"Think of it like a circuit breaker. Richard is blinded by his..." Ms. Early cleared her throat. "He's blinded right now.

This treatment will wake him from his reverie and help him see clearly again. To see what's actually important. And to realize all he has to lose."

21

Richard was sitting at the kitchen table, eyeing the banana, blueberry and strawberry smoothie in front of him. I'd lashed in a serious amount of sugar and honey to disguise the taste of the powdered anaphrodisiac.

"Just try it," I said. "I've added loads of superfoods. We need to build you up."

"We do?"

"With everything you have going on right now, we need to keep you in tip-top shape. I put in flaxseeds. And some chia seeds. Unbelievably nutritious. Packed full of zinc!"

He looked suspicious. "Why are you suddenly worried about my zinc levels?"

The smoothie sat there between us, beads of condensation gathering on the outside of the glass. Ms. Early had been very clear—I must ensure Richard consumed the correct dosage of powder *every single day*, or else this wouldn't work.

"Lady Gaga has one of these smoothies before every performance," I ad-libbed. "Swears by them for energy." Usually, a celebrity endorsement was all it took to pique Richard's interest.

He raised an eyebrow at me. "What's this sudden fixation

with my zinc levels *and* with Lady Gaga? When have you ever even mentioned her name before? Is everything okay?"

Everything would be *perfectly* okay if he would just be a nice obedient little spouse and bloody well drink his chaste-berry smoothie and be done with it. But no. Always with the questions.

"Fine," I relented, when I saw this was going nowhere. "Fine. It's…it's an aphrodisiac."

It was all I could think of in the moment.

His eyes met mine, widening in surprise. Not, it had to be said, altogether *delighted* surprise. And he just shook his head.

An uncomfortable silence grew between us.

"Let me see if I have this right," he said in the end. "What I'm hearing is that you think we have a problem…in that department. But instead of, I don't know, talking to me about it, your solution is to trick me into drinking…some kind of weird Viagra smoothie?"

Cholesterol! Why hadn't I just said I was worried about his cholesterol? It was the answer to all of life's unwanted questions. But it was too late now. The damage was done. I had thought he'd be pleased by the idea of an aphrodisiac. But of course, I'd just wounded his ego—which, in my defense, wasn't hard to do. I braced myself for the retaliation.

"And can I just point out," he said, "if *anyone* needs to be lashing back aphrodisiacs round here, it's certainly not me."

And there it was. "What's that supposed to mean?"

"You know what it means."

"Maybe I need it spelled out."

"Just that *you're* the one who's not interested. For the record."

For the record? Jeez, couldn't a wife surreptitiously try to render her husband impotent with some kind of medieval anti-Viagra without being made to feel like a subpoenaed witness at a state tribunal? "It's a bit hard to show interest in someone who's never here," I parried.

"I'm here right now, aren't I?"

"And I've never wanted you more," I deadpanned.

I felt him riling himself up. Taking aim. "You know, this happens to women around your age."

Excuse me? "Do enlighten me, Richard. What exactly is it that happens to women around my age?"

A more perceptive man, or really, any man who valued his life in the slightest, would have known by my tone to leave it there.

But not my husband. "They lose interest in…that side of things." I gave him a warning look. "Maybe you should get a checkup," he added.

"What kind of *checkup*?" I felt myself about to erupt.

"You know. Women's stuff."

"What women's stuff?"

"With a gynecologist."

"A gynecologist."

"That's what I think."

Until this moment, I had actually been feeling a little uneasy about Ms. Early's latest plan, wondering if I was crossing some kind of moral line. Not anymore. Now I wished I had a syringe of pure, concentrated Monk's Pepper to jab directly into Richard's carotid artery.

"Because the only possible explanation for a woman not wanting to sleep with you is that there must be something physically wrong with her," I clarified.

He just shrugged, like, *yeah*.

"You're not yourself, Eliza," he said in the end. "You haven't been yourself for a long time."

"And you very much *are* yourself, Richard," I shot back at him. I knew that if I didn't leave the kitchen right then, I'd say a lot more than I should. So I forced myself to turn and walk away. But before I left, I took the chocolate brownie I'd made earlier from the fridge and left it on the counter.

Which may not seem the most searing parting move ever. Except that I knew that Richard was (a) still hungry and (b) had never knowingly turned down dessert. So there was a high probability he would eat a very generous portion of said brownie.

A brownie, I should add, that was absolutely jammed to the gills with Philistine's Droop, as I liked to call Ms. Early's special powder.

Now we'd see who needed a gynecologist's appointment.

22

It was nine o'clock in the morning and a gaggle of mammies was lingering in the schoolyard, waiting for their kids to wave to them through the classroom window.

George, who—in flagrant contravention of school rules—always legged it the second she had deposited the twins in the yard, had beaten the rush in the Honey Café and nabbed our favorite window table.

"So," she said by way of greeting. "You had quite the time at the theater. With Gina and all the gang."

I assumed this was in reference to the "Money Can't Buy Special" night. There was something off about the way she said this, though. A bit prickly. "You saw Gina's video," I said.

"I showed it to Mossy Jr. He thought the theater looked really cool."

Ah. Now I got it. "I'm sorry. I should have asked if you and the kids would like to come. Honestly, I didn't think you'd want to spend the evening with the Chickadees. God knows I didn't."

I saw from George's face that she would have come regardless. That she thought I'd replaced her with Mother Hen. "It would have been a lot more craic with you," I overcompensated, even though it was true. "I haven't gone over to the Dark Side, I swear."

She glanced at me over her coffee. "You might at least have told me about Sasha Jones. You do know one of the main reasons I hang round with you is to get firsthand showbiz goss, right?" There was a glint in her eye now. The old George was resurfacing.

"I didn't know!"

"How could you *not* know?"

"It's very easy not to know if your DH doesn't tell you anything."

"Ah."

"Apparently, he had to keep it under wraps while negotiations were ongoing, blah, blah, blah."

"But surely he could have told *you*?"

"You'd think."

"So I take it the…" George leaned in closer and lowered her voice. "The therapy isn't really working?"

"No, no, it's working. It's definitely working."

I was now five days into the impotency treatment. There'd been a few days where Richard had been distracted and irritable. And then, miracle of miracles, he'd started coming home at a more reasonable hour. And avoiding alcohol. And there'd been zero *evidence* that he was currently capable of continuing an affair, even if the spirit was still willing.

"Is that why you sound so thrilled?" George asked.

I nodded. "It's weird. Richard's doing everything I wanted, but now he's being *so* docile that it's kind of…creepy? Do you know what I mean?"

"I can honestly say I have never experienced that problem with Mossy."

"It's hard to explain but it's like being married to… I don't know, Ned Flanders or something."

"Too good to be wholesome?"

"Exactly! When Richard was predictable—predictably self-ish—at least I knew where I stood. But this is unnerving. Like the other night, right, I went downstairs for a drink and I caught him watching—"

George put up a hand. "I do *not* want to know."

"Don't worry, it was nothing bad. Concerning, yes, but for other reasons. He was…" I looked around the café and lowered my voice to a whisper. "He was *snuggling* with Mr. Pickles, watching a Netflix documentary on Princess Diana."

"No."

"And he was—wait for it—*weeping.*"

George made a mock-horrified face. "Are you sure he's not pregnant?"

"I know, right?"

"You need to be careful, Eliza. Next he'll want to talk about his emotions."

I lowered my voice again. "He already *has.*"

"You've created a monster."

"Seriously, though, he really is creeping me out. It's something about his eyes."

"Does it look like he's hearing voices in his head?" George asked, amused.

"No. It's just the pupils…they're, like, madly dilated when he looks at me."

"Ha. Well, that's easily explained."

"It is?"

"Men's pupils dilate when they look at a woman they find attractive."

"Puke. You're joking, right?"

"*Puke?* How is it puke, Eliza? He's your husband!"

"No. He's a pregnant Ned Flanders masquerading as my husband."

We fell into silence for a minute. Then George said, "Is it still just the Stepford Wife kill-him-with-kindness stuff?"

"Uh-huh," I said vaguely.

Well, now I definitely could not tell George about the impotency treatment. Or the fake poitín.

She'd be horrified.

"So…" she said awkwardly, tracing a pattern through some spilled sugar on the tablecloth. She was avoiding eye contact. "You know that photo you showed me? Of Richard at a hotel with someone. Did you ever do anything about it? Was that not what you were trying to figure out in the first place?"

"I'm biding my time."

She looked up at me in surprise. I knew she was thinking, *still*?

"Ms. Early says we need to cure the root cause of our problems, not treat the symptoms," I said.

"Ah, here, Eliza."

"Okay, I *did* do a bit of investigating myself."

"And?"

"I'm not sure what it means, but I went into the theater one night he said he was working late. And he wasn't there. He was having drinks with a woman. And he lied about it. And then one night, when he was…when he was drunk, he started talking about some woman who made him feel like he was twenty-one again."

I watched as George tried—and failed—not to grimace. "Anything suspicious on his phone? Or in his email?"

"I don't know his passwords."

She looked mock-appalled, then shook her head. "Eliza. Sweet, innocent Eliza. You have so much to learn."

"You don't hack into Mossy's stuff, do you?"

"Please. It's not hacking if they're your spouse. I prefer to call it a *loving snoop*."

I wasn't sure I liked the way this was going.

"Right," George said resolutely. "Here's what we're going to do. I'm not in work till later. We're going to go to your house right now, and I'll show you how easy it is."

"I'm sorry but I can't. I have to—"

"Eliza, you need to get over this fixation with watching Mara in the yard. It's not healthy for you, or for her."

"It's not that," I said defensively. "I said I'd do yard duty today."

"How on earth did you get roped into that?"

I hadn't been roped into it at all. Mother Hen had dangled the chance to get onto the yard duty roster like a carrot. One of the main reasons Mara had agreed to set foot in Alexis Junior School was because I said I'd be able to see her in yard at lunchtimes. But until now, I hadn't been able to deliver on that promise. I had applied for yard duty, but it was oversubscribed. I was told to try again next term. Or hold out for a cancellation for the bake sale.

But when I'd offhandedly mentioned to Gina that I missed the cut for yard duty, she got straight on the WhatsApp and a few minutes later, informed me I was in. I only found out afterward that she'd *persuaded* her yard partner, Nicki-with-a-*c*, to step aside this term.

"Just unlucky," I lied.

George didn't say anything. I knew she was reassessing me: I was now officially a Joiner. "Rather you than me," she finally said. "Let's just hope you don't get partnered with one of the Chickadees, right?"

Just then, the door tinkled and in swanned Mother Hen. Her bracelets jangled as she waved to me. She was ready for action, wearing head-to-toe Sweaty Betty workout gear. She shook her head mock-scoldingly as she approached us. "Eliza! There you are. You're late for orientation."

I felt George's eyes on me. "Sorry, what orientation?"

"Eh, for yard duty?"

"Yeah, come on, Eliza," George chipped in. "How else are

you going to know what to do if someone trips over their shoelace?"

"Right?" Mother Hen said, missing the sarcasm.

George turned to me. "Word to the wise? If it all gets a bit Hunger Games with the twins, I find it best to just let them fight it out till there's blood."

Mother Hen's mouth dropped open. I fidgeted awkwardly and said to George, "My house tomorrow, then?"

She looked like she was about to say something more, but just gave a cursory, "I'll let you go."

"I'll call you later," I said.

She didn't reply.

23

Yard duty started off as yard duty. We monitored Aurora and Amelia as they played hopscotch, Mara hovering nearby.

But then Gina led me away to a small bench, shooed a kid off it and got down to business. "So..." she started. "I have some news."

I should have known she had an ulterior motive in my being here.

"I had a very interesting call..." she went on, a nervous look on her face. She seemed to be treading carefully. "From the *Late, Late Show*," she specified. "One of their researchers."

"Oh. Was it about Aurora's *Toy Show* audition?"

She nodded emphatically. "Yes, in a way. They want Aurora to come on *Toy Show* and perform the song."

"Wow. That's amazing." It really was. "You must be delighted."

"Yes, yes, of course. So delighted." She hesitated, then said, "And now this is *totally* optional of course, but the thing is... Well, they asked if Mara would go on, too."

"Mara? What do you mean, *Mara*?"

"They saw her in the video and thought she was just the cutest!"

I couldn't believe what I was hearing. "What did you say to them?"

"Well, I told them they could count on Aurora, naturally."

"Naturally."

"But then they said…" Mother Hen paused. "They said that they're only interested in Aurora if Mara will do it, too. It's a double-act or nothing." She bit her lip and looked at me expectantly.

"Oh."

Neither of us said anything for a few moments.

Then Gina said, "I know what you're thinking, Eliza. That I'm like one of those awful women off *Dance Moms* or some kind of crazy Kris Kardashian mom-ager."

"No, of course not." *One hundred percent.*

"But my big thing is—and I drum this into Aurora every day—that she should always, always make her own money. Any work she does as a child, whether it be ads, TV, modeling, whatever, I've been putting it into a trust fund for her that she'll get when she turns twenty-one. And who knows? It might even be enough for a deposit on a house. My mother raised me this way when *I* was little, but I didn't understand it at the time. Not until I had a child myself."

I looked at her in surprise. "But Gina, you have your own career. You're an influencer."

She gave a shrug. "If I had my own clothing line with a high street chain, maybe. Or signed with bigger sponsors. But even then, it would never pay the bills."

She paused to help a little boy who got a crayon stuck in his ear, then continued her spiel. "You see, my father left my mother when I was very little. He never gave her a penny. She had to scrimp and save to send me to ballet and drama and singing. I was actually good," she admitted with a small laugh. "When I graduated performance school, I started getting dance work and a few singing gigs, and then some really good panto parts. But even after a few years in the business, you never knew where the next job was coming from, so I had to do a lot of temping during the day to make ends meet. That's how I met Johnny, actually. I was temping as his secretary and then he hired me as their nanny." She paused and seemed to deliberate over how much to divulge. "He was married when we met."

"Oh. I had no idea," I lied.

She gave me an incredulous look. "Oh please. I'm sure George has filled you in."

I neither confirmed nor denied.

"Anyway," she said, "he seemed like a proper man, Johnny. You know what I mean? Not like the boys I'd been going out with back then. He had good taste, he looked after himself, he came to my flat and cooked me seafood linguine. And I remember thinking to myself, *well, this is it.* Can you imagine? Smitten over bloody seafood linguine. First and last time he ever made it, by the way."

I was surprised, and honestly impressed, by her candor.

She confessed that she knew he was married, but that he'd said his wife, Miriam, didn't even like him anymore. They were on two separate paths. She had her tennis and her interior decorating business and their daughter, Stephanie; he had his work.

"Which was all true," Mother Hen conceded. "But what I *didn't* know was how he treated her during the split."

The first Miriam knew about the impending divorce was when a Sherry FitzGerald agent turned up on their front doorstep to value the house. He was getting all their assets valued. Not surprisingly, Johnny hired the best divorce lawyer and managed to keep the family home, which was highly unusual. But running two households was incredibly expensive. There had to be cutbacks.

So Stephanie's private school fees were axed.

"She used to go here," Mother Hen told me. "To this school. But she had to switch to a non-fee-paying school after the divorce. Which is perfectly fine, don't get me wrong. Except all her friends dropped her." She paused. "What do you make of that?"

What did I *make* of that? Sounded to me like there was trouble in paradise. Mother Hen seemed to be siding with the discarded wife, not her own husband.

And also, why was she telling me all this?

"Johnny's the most generous man in the world," she said. "Until you get on the wrong side of him. Then he'll destroy you."

We did a circuit of the yard, and after a half lap she stopped walking and turned to me, counting on her fingers. "Samantha Mumba, Charlotte Church, Imelda May, that girl who played Luna Lovegood, the kidnapper guy from *Love/Hate*."

She waited for a reaction, and when none was forthcoming, she said, "They all started on the *Toy Show*. Eliza, this is Aurora's big break. This is her chance to make a career for herself, to make her own money…"

The little boy returned. He'd gotten the crayon stuck in the other ear now. "It's just going to have to stay there till you go back to your teacher, isn't it?" Mother Hen said to him tersely. He wandered off again.

She focused her attention back on me. "All Mara would have to do is dance in a costume, Eliza. No one will even know it's her, if that's what your concern is." Her tone was cooler now. She'd had enough of little Ralph Wiggum shoving crayons in his orifices.

And of me not giving in to her.

She waited, just looking at me, but when I made no move to respond, she glanced over at our daughters and said, "I mean, I suppose I could see if we could persuade them to let Amelia stand in for Mara. They might not even go for it. And even if they did, I'd hate for Mara to be left out of all the rehearsals and the excitement and everything. It would be *such* a bonding experience for the two girls. Can you imagine? And if we have to switch to Amelia, they'd be so busy, there wouldn't be time for playdates or any of that. And Johnny and I wouldn't have time to hang out with you guys like we've been doing lately..."

Don't worry, Gina, message received loud and clear. If I wanted Mara to keep her one and only friend in this entire world, and Richard to get his investment, then all I had to do was sign my highly introverted child up for a live entertainment show with an audience of a million people.

As I mulled this over, Mother Hen turned her attention to Mr. Mellon, who strolled by us with a cup of tea in his hands. "He's a little sweetie, isn't he?" she whispered to me.

Mr. Mellon was neither little nor a sweetie.

Her eyes followed him as he made his way across the yard. "I love having the chats with him. Of course, he has to be nice to me because Johnny's the school's biggest sponsor." She laughed despite herself. "We should say hi!"

Thanks, but no thanks. I'd had more than enough *chats* with Mr. Mellon. He'd taken to regularly grabbing me for *a quick word*, which, in Mr. Mellon speak, translated to: *I'm now going to update you on the ways in which your child's personality does not fit in with my world view.*

In fact, the latest *quick word* had happened only a few days earlier. Apparently, there had been a *situation* during Gaelic football practice that day; Mara had refused to participate. *It's her attitude, Mrs. Sheridan,* he'd said. *Alexis prides itself on being a very participatory school, but Mara doesn't seem to want to fit in. Sometimes I almost feel like...she doesn't respect my authority. Your daughter barely looks at me when I'm speaking to her.* This was the only thing we'd agreed on thus far. I knew for a fact she didn't respect him or his authority because, when a fuming Mara had returned from her first day of school, she covered Mr. Pickles's ears and reported that Mr. Mellon had said that animals didn't have personalities. Then she muttered, loud enough for me to hear, that he *probably didn't even believe in evolution*, which—in Mara's book—was the ultimate put-down. *And another thing,* Mr. Mellon had added, *she's unsettling the other children in the class by refusing to sit at any of the tables at the back of the room. She says she doesn't want to sit near the mold. She keeps talking about spores. Mrs. Sheridan, I can honestly say I've never had problems like this with any other child. Alexis has a code of conduct, Mrs. Sheridan. I have a duty to let you know that this is a formal warning.*

But before I could make up an excuse *not* to greet Mr. Mellon, Mother Hen had already jogged over to him. I reluctantly followed suit.

"Aurora told me she might be on the *Late, Late*," he was saying once I'd caught up to them. "Amazing, though I'm not surprised."

Gina noticed my presence and gave me a sideways glance. "It's almost a sure thing, but it just depends on whether her little friend Mara will do it with her. Eliza's unsure because Mara's a bit...*you know...*" I narrowed my eyes at her. "Shy."

"I'm just not sure it's right for her," I said, which wasn't true. I was *one hundred percent sure* that it wasn't right for her.

They gave me an assessing look, then Mr. Mellon cleared his throat. "We all want to protect our children... Sometimes, the hardest thing for a parent to do is give their child what I like to call *a loving push*. But it's almost always the right thing to do."

Can I give you a loving push, Mr. Mellon?

"God, that's *very* wise," Mother Hen said. I thought of what George said and looked at her pupils. They were, most certainly, dilated. "Can I put that on my Insta feed?"

"Only if you tag me," he replied flirtatiously, with—no lie—a wink. "And I think in Mara's case," he continued, returning his attention back to me, "it could be a real bonding experience with Aurora. In fact, I'd say it's exactly what's needed to help her settle in."

"Fine," I said tightly. *Fine, fine, fuckity fine.* "I'll think it over."

24

I was in Richard's study, waiting for him to come home so I could talk to him about the *Late Late Toy Show* quandary, when the doorbell rang. This was quickly followed up with furious knocking. I opened the door to find our neighbor Mrs. Overend on the doorstep, her fuzzy orange dog, Milly, cradled in her arms.

"I have a message for your husband," she said when I opened the door.

So we were skipping pleasantries, then.

"I'm sorry. He's not here."

"You tell him that because of his actions—which can only be described as *highly* irresponsible—Milly will have to miss Crufts this year. The very year she's tipped as favorite for Post Graduate Bitch."

The poor woman was close to tears. What on earth had Richard done?

"I *specifically* asked your husband if that creature had been fixed," she said. "He said, and I quote, 'Yes, of course. My wife took care of that.'"

"That creature?"

"Your dog."

"Mr. Pickles?"

"If I had known he wasn't neutered, I would never in a million years have let him within a mile of Milly," she continued, pacing back and forth in the doorway. "This is in breach of the Kennel Club breeding regulations. It's not even twelve months since Milly's last litter. I'm mortified. I can only pray the girls at the Pekingese Club don't get wind of this."

"Wait. Are you saying—"

"Milly's pregnant. By your *mongrel*." She pointed to Mr. Pickles, who had, right on cue, emerged from downstairs.

Oh, Sir Pickly Pie. Did he sneak his way into Mrs. Overend's garden or something?

"Now, I understand you're highly strung and apparently you're not able to cope with a child *and* a dog," Mrs. Overend went on angrily, "and I put up with all that piano racket and never said a *word*." She seemed to be drawing on deep reserves here. "But this is too much. I simply cannot continue with him. The money came in handy. And God knows the dog certainly needs my help. But it's not worth it. Not after this."

"Wait," I said. "Are you saying you've been training Mr. Pickles?"

She looked at me, surprised. "Where did you think your dog was every evening?"

Until lately, Richard had been getting home too late to help with dinner or to put Mara to bed, so he told me to leave the dog-walking to him. He needed to blow off steam and unwind after work anyway, and a really long walk in the fresh air allegedly helped.

"Walkies," I said to Mrs. Overend, straining a smile. "I thought he was gone for walkies."

It took Richard well into the following evening to notice that Mr. Pickles wasn't there. But eventually, the time came—

as it did every night—when he said, "Will I take Pickles out for you?"

I let the *for you* comment slide. I was playing the long game here. I watched as Richard tracked down the lead, then the unscented biodegradable poop bags, then the dog's tennis ball and ball launcher. Only when he was at the door did he realize Mr. Pickles was missing in action.

"He's at the vet," I said nonchalantly. "Overnight stay."

"The vet? Why, what happened?"

I made a snipping motion with my fingers and watched as Richard's look of surprise morphed into a grimace. "I didn't know we were doing that."

"I said I'd take care of it, remember?"

A light dawned in his eyes. He nodded and I nodded, both pretending to remember a conversation that never happened.

"Yeah, so the vet said there were two options for sterilization," I continued. "You could go for chemical neutering, which is basically a testicular injection…" I left a little pause there to let that sink in. "Which *would* work, in terms of making him sterile. But the vet said it wouldn't mellow any problematic male behavior. So we decided it was best to go for option two."

"Option two?" he asked uneasily.

"Complete castration."

Richard winced.

"That's where they give the dog a general anesthetic and surgically remove both testicles."

"Right."

"It went really well."

"You've already done it?"

I shrugged. "It's the responsible thing to do. We don't want litters of mini-Pickles popping up all over the neighborhood, do we?" I dunked my chocolate marshmallow tea cake into my tea and took a bite. "A few days wearing the cone of shame and he'll be fine. But the vet said definitely no walks for the next while. Just gentle exercise in the back garden. Till the sutures are removed and the incision on his scrotum heals. Want a tea cake?"

"I think I'll pop out for a bit of fresh air anyway," Richard said, then quickly added, "if you don't mind."

"I don't mind in the slightest."

And off he went. The second the door shut behind him, I dashed upstairs to Mara's room. "Mara, my darling, are you awake?"

She opened her eyes, confused.

"Want to go see some urban foxes?"

She yawned. "Can I go back to sleep? I was having a lovely dream about the cretaceous period."

"But the foxes only come out at night. It'll be so fun! You'll see."

She reluctantly sat up in bed and I helped her down the stairs. By that point, she was awake enough to walk out to the car with me.

We belted down the back lane and nudged out onto the main road. And there he was, walking at a good clip, seemingly deep in thought, his hands plunged into his pockets. He was walking down Merrion Road, heading out of town. Past the Royal Dublin Society building, and around the corner. Was he maybe going to Herbert Park? Was he actually just getting some *fresh air*?

But no, he wasn't. Instead, he walked right on through the entrance of the Five Seasons Hotel.

I pulled up on the curb opposite and watched as he crossed the forecourt, gave a salute to the doorman like they were old pals, then disappeared through the revolving door.

Just like the one in the photo.

25

George and I stood in the marble-clad bathrooms of the Five Seasons, psyching each other up for showtime. It was the evening after my discovery about Richard's late-night *walkies*. I had immediately rung George to tell her she'd been right: the time had come for a *loving snoop*. I gave her the facts and she instantly decided that the situation required a stakeout. She was right. No more messing around with bloody herbal smoothies; it was time to take action.

Mossy was home minding all the kids, and now here we were, in little black dresses and full makeup, going over our game plan. Which was, basically, to just wing it. We decided to take up position in a discreet corner of the Whiskey Bar, which was more Richard's style anyway. It was a good vantage point—we could see everyone in the room and we had views of the Lobby Lounge and the Garden Terrace, too.

"Jesus, this is good stuff," George said, sipping on her rosé Prosecco. She was chatting away, telling me about her day at the maternity hospital, and I appreciated the distraction from my own nerves. "Swear to God. You can tell from their suitcases when they arrive in to have the baby. You just know *exactly* what you're in for."

"Like if they have Louis Vuitton, they're going to expect five-star treatment?" I said, taking a quick glance around the room. So far there was no sign of Richard.

"Say for example, you see them coming in with one of those black Samsonite suitcases with a combination lock, right? You sure as hell better make note of every single thing you say and do, and that *they* say and do, because if the slightest thing goes wrong, you'll be slapped with a lawsuit faster than you can say *episiotomy*." She paused for another long sip of her drink. "And then there were the ones who arrive in with the pink sparkly cases. They'd have the tan done, the fake eyelashes, the permanent eyebrows for the obligatory *look-I-made-a-tiny-human-while-looking-hot* Facebook photo." Her eyes fell to my drink. "Are you not going to drink that?" she asked, gesturing to my glass. "Come on, Eliza. Nurse's orders."

I took a sip to keep her happy. "So which type of suitcase do you think I am?"

She laughed. "That's easy. You'd have had an enormous suitcase on wheels, packed to bursting for every eventuality. I bet when Mara was born, you had three sets of Ziploc bags marked *small*, *medium* and *large* on the labor ward with you, with a vest, nappy, Babygro and hat in each one, just in case the consultant's weight predictions were off."

"Nope," I said. George looked surprised. "I had *four* bags. I brought a preemie set, too, in case she was extra small."

George laughed, shaking her head in amusement. "Ha. Knew I had you pegged." Her eyes moved across the room and I watched her expression change. "Here," she said, suddenly alert. "Show me that picture again?" I pulled up the photo of Richard on my phone and she glanced from it to someone on the far side of the room. "Nope. Not him."

Just then, the bartender appeared in front of us and presented a bottle of champagne on ice. "From the gentlemen sitting behind you," he said with a twinkly smile. I not so subtly turned around to find two men in identical deal-maker uniforms—open-neck blue shirts and slightly too tight blazers. They raised their glasses to us.

George swiveled on her stool and raised a flute to them while I hissed at her not to encourage them, and not to drink their champagne. To send it back.

She turned to face me. "You know what your problem is?"

I was going to ask why we were working off the assumption that *I* had a problem, before remembering that we were in a bar stalking my husband.

"I'm just too fun?"

"You need to let your hair down. I mean literally." She reached forward and pulled my hair from its clip and sort of zhuzhed it up with her fingers. "There. Much better."

I heard one of the men behind us say, "Bravo," which was, let's be honest, intensely irritating. But on the other hand, the champagne they had sent over was a vintage Moet. It would be rude not to have a *little* sip.

"Right," George said. "Enough sitting around waiting. I'm going for a quick scout. You keep watch here." She shimmied off toward the lobby and did a decent impression of a sober person until she realized she was walking toward a mirror, at which point she casually diverted her path and was gone.

In the Lobby Lounge, a young woman in a black cocktail dress was playing the baby grand piano. So far, she'd been sticking to the usual background *soft bossa nova* that hotels always made pianists play, but then she moved on to something entirely different. It sounded like a jazz interpretation of something modern and popular, but I just couldn't place it.

I walked over to her once she was finished. "I loved that. Do you mind me asking what it was?"

She leaned toward me and whispered, "'Shake It Off.' Taylor Swift. My boss would kill me if he found out."

I laughed and tapped the side of my nose. "Your secret's safe with me."

"You seem to be enjoying it anyway," came a voice behind me. I turned and saw Blazer One, one half of the Gordon Gekko double act. He nodded to my glass.

The pianist went back to her bossa nova.

"It's lovely, thank you," I said, avoiding eye contact. I *told* George we shouldn't have accepted the bottle. These were the sort of guys who would want a return on their investment.

"You know, there's something about seeing a beautiful woman drinking champagne."

There it was: the cringe factor. And where the hell was George?

George, George, why hast thou forsaken me?

"I'm sorry," he said in a more normal tone. He must have sensed my internal eye rolling. "I didn't mean to make you uncomfortable. We're just celebrating. My friend over there had some good news." He gestured to his sandy-haired compatriot in the Whiskey Bar. "He sent the bottle over because he wanted to spread the good fortune around, that's all," he explained. "Think of it as…no-strings-attached champagne. How does that sound?"

"Pretty good, actually," I admitted, letting him refill my glass. "So what *is* your friend celebrating?"

"Sold his company today. For ten bar."

"I'm guessing bar doesn't mean a thousand."

"Try million."

The problem with someone trying to impress you is that it makes you immediately want to act really, really unimpressed. "So when does it all end, Gordon?" I said, quoting *Wall Street*. It was at that specific moment that I simultaneously discovered I was, in point of fact, drunk. Before the champagne, I'd also put away a couple of strong cocktails. "How many yachts can you water-ski behind? How much is enough?" I had gotten quite into character by that last line, doing my best Charlie Sheen eyebrow waggle.

He was silent, and I waited for him to beat a retreat, muttering *bitches be crazy* or something.

"It's not a question of enough, pal," he finally said, volleying Gordon Gekko's line right back at me. "It's a zero-sum game. Somebody wins. Somebody loses."

"Touché."

We clinked glasses.

"So what you're getting at is that I look like the evil face of capitalism, is that it?" he asked.

"I think it's the blazer."

"For all you know, I could spend my days building homes for destitute widows in... I don't know, bloody... Kandahar."

"And do you?"

He laughed. "I'm a partner at Mason Mayes & Murray family law firm."

"Ah, so you *are* the evil face of capitalism."

"All right," he said, holding up a hand, "now it's my turn to ask a borderline-offensive question. What are you doing sitting here alone on a Thursday night?"

Fair point. "Looking for my husband," I said, but it came out more self-pityingly than I had intended. "Same as half the women here, probably," I added, thinking that would give me a more *jaded but interesting* air.

"Right," he said. "And what would your husband think if he came in and saw us drinking champagne together?" *We might find out any minute now, Blazer One.*

Although there still was no sign of Richard. Maybe the previous night had been a one-off. Maybe I'd had it all wrong.

But I didn't think so. I was certain he was here. With another woman.

"My husband would probably think the same thing as your wife," I said to my drinking buddy. I gestured toward his ring finger, which was empty but bore a pale indentation against his tanned skin.

His manner changed. "My wife," he said quietly, "would think I was politely making conversation with someone who looked like they needed a bit of company."

Well, that certainly put *me* in my place. "She sounds nice," I said in the end.

"She is," he agreed. "I mean…she's very independent." There was a long pause while he thought about this, then said, "We both work crazy hours. And she travels a lot. A *lot*." Another long pause. "So when she's away, I'm free to enjoy…"

"No-strings champagne?"

"Well, yes."

As bar flies went, he wasn't the worst, but I knew how this would play out. I had met this man before, in every swanky hotel bar I'd ever been in, and I'd been in a lot of swanky hotel bars while touring. By the end of the bottle, he'd start promising he was going to use his connections to get me things he thought I wanted: hook me up with a recording session in his friend's studio or whatever. And then after the second bottle, he'd mention he had taken the penthouse suite for the night, and *would I like to come up for a nightcap?* At least this guy hadn't mentioned a hotel room. Yet.

"Can I ask you something?" I said. "Do you ever feel guilty?"

He looked away and rubbed at the finger where his ring should have been. He shrugged. "Honestly, I don't think about it." He considered what he had said, then gave a nod. He agreed with himself. "I just don't. And I hate to tell you this, but your husband's not thinking about you right now, either." He put his empty glass down. "Anyway," he said, already moving on. He waved his sandy-haired friend over, who downed his whiskey and then stood up. As he walked across the bar toward us, I could see the fold lines of his shirt, fresh out of the packet.

"Let's head on," Sandy said without looking at me. "This place has really gone downhill."

They did indeed head on, but at the last minute, Sandy turned back and leaned in close enough that I could smell his aftershave, which seemed to me to be the lovechild of a musk-rat that had somehow spawned with a Mexican orchid. "That bottle cost one hundred and twenty euros. You could at least put a smile on your face."

Damn my alcohol-befuddled mind. He was gone before I could think of a blistering put-down that would haunt him till the end of his days.

Before long, George arrived back with no sightings of Richard. When the waiter came by to ask if we needed anything, she amused herself by engaging him in borderline flirtatious small talk. "Tell us, Gearóid, how are the tips?"

He shot his name tag a glance, then said, "Pretty good."

Gearóid may have been young, but he had the self-assured air and, indeed, teeth, of someone who was just here to make a bit of pocket change till he took up his Big Four accountancy firm graduate placement. Or got accepted onto *Love Island*. Either one.

"Can you tell when someone comes in?" she asked. "How much they'll tip?"

"You can, yeah."

"What about us? Do we look like good tippers?"

He looked away, seemingly embarrassed, but then he turned his attention back to George with a half smile. He was willing to play the game. Or maybe he really did like her. "Fifteen percent. Maybe twenty, tops. Depending."

"On what?"

"On how many of those you have."

She looked at her cocktail. "You'd better bring me another, so. And one for my friend."

While he went off to do his bidding, I whipped round to George. "What are you doing?" I hissed.

"Eh, prising valuable information out of him?"

"About gratuity rates?"

"It's better than just sitting there mooning, Eliza. You have to do *something*."

"I *am* doing something. I'm brooding. While also numbing my pain with alcohol."

"Oh ye of little faith," she whispered to me as Gearóid approached with two cocktails.

I insisted on paying for the drinks, but then George palmed him an extra twenty.

"I'd say you get a fair few celebrities through here all the same," she said to him, apropos of nothing. "They must be the best tippers."

"You'd be surprised. Sometimes the more famous they are, the tighter they are," he divulged.

"Anyone famous staying here at the moment?"

Oh, God. I saw where this was going. She thought Sasha Jones might be here. In fairness, I had been secretly thinking the same thing myself.

"There's always a few heads around," he said vaguely.

"Go on," she urged, taking a casual sip of her drink. "Impress us."

Either something he had heard on his orientation training clicked in his mind, or it was starting to dawn on him that George wasn't after empty flirtation. He glanced away, trying to find an excuse to get out of this grilling.

"Bloody hell," I found myself suddenly saying, and both George and Gearóid looked at me in alarm. "Bloody good cocktail," I added, sipping on my mojito. But that wasn't it.

I had just spotted Richard.

In plain sight, standing in the lobby, hands jingling coins in

his pockets as he waited for the lift. The lift that one could rea-
sonably assume brought people upstairs to the hotel's bedrooms.

"Excuse me," I said, standing up. But it was too late. Richard was in the lift and the doors had closed. "Back in a sec."

I hurried out to the reception desk.

"Good evening," I said slowly and clearly to the receptionist, to prove I wasn't drunk.

"Good evening," the receptionist replied, slowly and clearly,
to prove she wasn't judgmental.

"I'm staying here tonight but I think my husband used his
name when he made the booking." I lowered my voice. "It's
Sheridan." I lowered my voice even further and leaned in.
"Richard Sheridan."

She began scanning through the bookings on her computer.
"Sheridan, Sheridan. I'm very sorry, madam, but I can't give
out that information. We have some vacancies, though, if you'd
like me to book you a room?"

"I don't want to book a room. We already *have* a room."

"I'm very sorry, madam."

I retreated to the Whiskey Bar and told George the saga.

"We can't just give up, Eliza," she said.

"I'm not saying that, but what am I supposed to do? Wander
round the hotel knocking on every bedroom door? And besides, I can't even do *that*, because you need a key card to get
the lifts to work."

George considered this, then did a little finger waggle at
Gearóid, who dutifully came over. "If a guest orders a bottle
of wine to be delivered to his room," she said to the waiter,
"what happens?"

"Eh…normally, one of the waitstaff collects the bottle and
glasses from the bar here, then brings it up in the service lift?"

"I see," George said. "Because we have a little problem. My
friend Eliza here, her husband is upstairs in their room and
he asked her to get a bottle of house red. But Eliza is such a

featherbrain, she can't remember the room number, and he's not answering the phone. Is there any chance you could check the room number on the system thingummy and bring up the wine to him?"

Then she whispered to me, "Slip him a twenty. *Quick*."

I rummaged around for cash and did as she said. He considered the note. Then he flashed me his Casa Amour smile, pocketed the money and said, "I don't see why that would be a problem." He went over and checked the computer. Then he set a bottle of wine and two glasses on a tray.

So Richard *was* staying here. He had a room booked under his name, after all. Gearóid gave a deliberate nod to us and headed out of the bar.

"Now, Eliza! Go!" George urged me on. "Go now or you'll lose him."

The waiter or my husband?

I could really have done with another cocktail or five, but there was no time. I followed Gearóid to the service lift and when it opened, I stepped in after him. He didn't object. He just seemed to be pretending I wasn't there. The lift went up and up, all the way to the penthouse floor. The doors opened and I followed Gearoid out.

Without a word, he handed me the tray, then disappeared back into the service lift and was gone. I stood alone on the sixth floor.

Shit. Now what? On the tray was a receipt to be signed by Richard. On the top it said Room 651. There was also a key card.

I found the room and stood there listening. Nothing. I put my ear to the door. Murmurs of conversation. A deep man's voice, unintelligible. A woman's voice.

What to do, what to do…

I couldn't just walk in. Or maybe I could? I had the key card, after all.

And some serious liquid courage.

I stepped forward, rapped on the door, opened it and called out loudly, "Room service!"

"Oh! Just a sec!" came a woman's voice full of laughter. The door opened to reveal no other than Sasha Jones, shockingly gorgeous in a hotel toweling robe, which she was now pulling around her. Her hair was adorably tousled, her cheeks flushed, and I was pretty sure she had nothing on underneath.

Maybe it was her beauty, or the sheer horror of what I was doing, but I found myself momentarily unable to speak. What I really wanted to say was, *would you mind awfully if I just lay down on the carpet and quietly died and we said no more about this?*

She tied her robe tighter and called over her shoulder to the man in the depths of the suite. "Honey? Did you order room service?"

In my head, I heard George's voice. *You've got to do something!*

I doubled down. "Could you tell Richard I'd like to speak to him?" I said icily.

She gave me a puzzled look. "Richard?"

This impasse continued until a voice behind me said, "Eliza?" I turned around and lo and behold—*there* was Richard.

Standing in the corridor.

Looking from me to Sasha and back to me again with dismay.

He said my name again, more gently, like the way a hostage negotiator tries to talk down a dangerous criminal—calmly and slowly. Don't startle the lunatic in case they press the detonator. "Eliza, what are you doing here?"

"Oh. My. God!" Sasha said. "I *knew* we'd met somewhere before. It was at the theater that night, wasn't it? I'm so sorry. I couldn't quite place you. You must think me so rude. I thought I heard you say room service when you came in…" Her voice trailed off. I realized she was looking at the key card in my hand and the tray with the wine. Richard followed Sasha's gaze.

"I'm so sorry," I said weakly. "I thought... I thought Richard was here."

Richard took hold of my wrist then, like I was a disobedient child.

"Do you guys want to come in or something?" Sasha asked hesitantly, uncertain of what was going on.

"No!" we both replied at the same time, with equal alarm.

Richard handed an envelope to Sasha. "The rewrites of that scene. If you have thoughts, day or night, drop me a WhatsApp. I'll get straight back to you. You know how much I value your input." He managed to say all this while subtly *shoving* me out into the corridor. Then I heard him say in a low voice to Sasha, "I'm so, so sorry about this. She's been under a lot of stress lately. She's not herself."

"Don't even worry about it. It never happened." I watched as she did a little cutesy my-lips-are-sealed motion.

Richard and I walked in silence down the corridor. We stood side by side waiting for the lift. Again, in silence. I expected him to unleash a torrent of rage, but he seemed too furious to get a word out. I thought I might actually vomit with mortification.

"You said you were going for a walk," I finally said in a small voice.

"I did go for a walk," he snapped. "I walked *here*. To drop off the rewrites to Sasha."

"But you told me you were walking Mr. Pickles every night, and instead you've been dumping him on Mrs. Overend, so I thought..."

He raked a hand through his hair in frustration. "I'm not *pretending* to walk the dog, Eliza. I take him around the block, then sometimes I drop in to Mrs. Overend for a chat because she seems to like the company, and then she offered to do a bit of training with him in the evenings because I mentioned that you're..." He stopped himself.

"What? That I'm what?"

"That the dog seems to stress you out! Like everything else. And that's all there is to it. That's it. No big conspiracy," he said, drawing out the word *big*. "The world is not out to get you, Eliza. You manage that very well all by yourself."

"First, she's not doing an amazing job training him, is she? And second…"

Second, second…

My traitorous brain had deserted me in my hour of need.

"Eliza. When this is all over, when the play is done…"

"I know, I know. Things will be different. It'll be *my* time."

"That's not what I was going to say. After things calm down, I think we should see someone. I can't go on like this."

You can't go on like this? If anyone around here was going to suggest that our relationship was fundamentally and possibly terminally damaged, in a wounding midfight below-the-belt shot, it's supposed to be me.

But I didn't say that. Instead, I said, "Oh. Right."

I quickly texted George to say that I was really sorry, but I had to leave, and that I'd explain everything. Then Richard and I walked out of the hotel together in silence. And walked all the way home in silence. Richard did not suggest we get a taxi, even though I was in heels.

"I'm sorry," I managed to say when we got to our front door.

He breathed in as if to calm himself, then breathed out again, jutting his chin up. "I'm not angry, I'm just—"

"Oh, God, *please* don't say you're just disappointed." He always said that to anyone who worked for him if he wanted them to pull up their socks.

"You really thought I was that guy?" he asked in a hurt voice.

"I got it into my head… I don't know why—"

"Jesus," he said, cutting me off. Richard unlocked the door and let himself into the house.

How had I gotten everything so wrong? How had I ended up here, in this ugly state of suspicion and outrage? Well, I was done. The madness stopped here. From now on, I would stop with all this nonsense.

No more late-night stakeouts with George, no more online snooping, no more truth serum "poitín," no more chasteberry extract.

No more treatments.

And no more Ms. Early.

26

I sat in the Honey Café, hoping to catch George. I hadn't seen her since the disastrous night at the Five Seasons. She spotted me when she came in, hesitated at the entrance as if she was about to leave, but then came and sat down at my table.

I began explaining that I was through with all the scheming and machinations, that from here on in, the only drama would be on the stage in Blind Alley. George held up an index finger to silence me.

"Eliza," she said. "You left me sitting in the hotel like a total pleb the other night. With only Randy Gearóid for company."

"I texted you."

"I know, but what the hell? You just, what, *left*?"

"It turned out it was all a huge mistake. Sasha Jones was in the room, but she was there with someone else, another man. Richard was just dropping rewrites to her. I was mortified."

"So why was the room in his name?"

"I don't know. For privacy? I presume Sasha doesn't like booking rooms in her own name. Celebrities always get their agents to do stuff like that for them."

"He's not her agent, though, is he?"

"George, come on, we got it wrong. And I nearly wrecked everything."

"So you're telling me you genuinely believe he was just there dropping off a script."

"I know he was. I saw him hand it to her."

"He couldn't have done that at work?"

"Maybe she needed to read it overnight."

"He's playing you, Eliza."

Now I was getting annoyed. "You don't know that."

"I know *something's* going on. Why did he pretend he was walking the dog every night if it was all so innocent?"

"Because he knew I'd be on his case about constantly working."

She didn't reply, just raised a skeptical eyebrow.

"George. I know you mean well, but this isn't your fight."

"What's that supposed to mean?"

"It just seems like…it seems like you're taking this very personally and sometimes I wonder if…"

"If what? Go on. Say it."

"If maybe sometimes you're pissed off with your own situation with Mossy, but you don't want to have it out with him, and so you, I don't know, egg me on a bit with Richard."

George raised an eyebrow. "First of all, you don't need *any* egging on when it comes to Richard. You already slag him off all the time."

"But it was your idea to go to the Five Seasons," I said. "I didn't want to do it. You talked me into it."

She went silent, then composed herself and said in an unnervingly calm voice, "What did you mean by my *situation with Mossy*?"

"Well…" Like the time he was off shooting Kalashnikovs in Gdansk while she was giving birth? Like when she found out he actually finished work at five, and not seven o'clock like he had always said, and that he'd been secretly going for a pint every day *for years* to avoid helping give the kids their tea?

But I couldn't say any of that to her.

"Eliza," George said in a warning tone, her eyes narrowed. "Mossy and I are *fine*."

I'd never seen her like this before. She. Was. Fuming.

This was bad. This was very, very bad. In fact, this was nearly worse than Richard being mad at me, because I kind of hated him a good 50 percent of the time anyway, but George? I always liked George.

"Did you even know that I'd just come off a twelve-hour shift that night?" she asked. "All I wanted to do was put on a wash, get the children off to bed, have a bath and a glass of wine and, God forbid, get an early night. But when you rang and said you needed my help, I still made the effort and got dressed up and went out to the hotel with you. Spent money I couldn't afford on cocktails and tips. Because you're my friend and I was worried about you. But now suddenly, what? It's all *grand*? I can't keep up with you, Eliza. You call me when you're all worked up about Richard and I drop everything for you, but then when the drama is over, you…"

"I what?"

"You drop me. And go running back to Mother Hen."

Ah. So that was what this was about. "You know the only reason I'm spending time with Gina is because Richard needs Johnny's help bringing in investors."

"Oh, it's *Gina* now, is it?"

"It just seems a bit disrespectful calling her a nickname behind her back, that's all. Now that I know her."

"You do realize you're just her latest plaything, don't you? It's the same every year. Sooner or later she'll get bored and move on. Especially if Johnny keeps flirting with you."

"He doesn't."

George shrugged. "That's not what I heard."

"What?"

"Are you honestly saying he never flirts with you?"

I thought about this. There had been that moment at Aurora's party. And in the utility room. And leaning on our kitchen island saying maybe he didn't want to stop looking at me. "Possibly," I conceded. "But I'm the flirtee, George. It's not my fault."

"Yeah, well, I hope Mother Hen—sorry, *Gina*—sees it that way."

We lapsed into silence, until I finally said, "I'm sorry I've been spending so much time with Gina lately."

"It's not even about her."

"Then what is it?"

She didn't meet my eye. Whatever she was about to say next was going to hurt, I just knew it. "I'm sorry you're having a hard time with your marriage, Eliza, I really am. And I'm sorry that you feel taken for granted. But if you're not going to do anything about it, then…then I can't listen to it anymore."

There was an awkward silence.

"Has it ever occurred to you that some of us would kill for your situation?" she continued. "That we'd do anything to have the luxury of being home with our kids, to be able to drop them to school and collect them *every day*, to be the ones that bring them swimming and to the park and on playdates? That some of us don't have that choice? Do you really think I *want* to go to work because of my love for dealing with infected stitches and overflowing catheter bags? Sometimes I don't remember driving home because I've been awake for twenty-four hours straight. Sometimes I fall asleep at traffic lights. Do you think I *like* leaving my kids with a childminder who may or may not be using chewing gum to cover the smell of alcohol off her breath? Some of us have no choice, Eliza. Some of us have to work to pay the mortgage. So I'm sorry if I don't have much time for your lack of fulfilment or whatever, but you know, first-world problems and all that."

Her words hit like a slap to the face.

I recalled our very first misfired exchange when I'd expressed gratitude for the school's earlier pickup time and George had taken offense. I thought we'd quashed all that once she got to actually know me.

But apparently, her resentment had been bubbling away this whole time we were friends. And I'd been obliviously heaping fuel on the fire.

George suddenly looked tired, almost pained, as if she was starting to feel bad about coming down heavy on me, but I could tell her stance remained unchanged.

In a quiet voice, she said, "You *chose* this life, Eliza. You *chose* to stay home with Mara. That means Richard has to be the breadwinner. You don't get to complain about it. It was your choice."

27

I had decided to come back after all. There was no one else I could turn to.

Ms. Early listened as I told her everything. About Mrs. Overend and Mr. Pickles, about the hotel stakeout and the blowup with Richard, and the reality check from George. When I was done, she said nothing. Then, she held out her hands toward me, silently commanding me to do the same. I lifted my hands and she took them in hers.

She felt my skin like she was gently testing for something, turning my hands over and examining them. I flinched at the intimacy at first, but then it began to feel relaxing, comforting. "This is good. This is something," she said in the end, as if my hands had surprised her.

"It is?"

Her eyes flicked over me, from the crown of my head down to my runners, taking some mental tally. "You don't wear makeup, it doesn't bother you that your hair is dry and has split ends, you neglect your nails. And you wear all of this almost like a badge of honor."

Um, thanks? "Yeah, I get it. I've let myself go."

"That's not what I mean. Your hands, they're as soft as a child's. You still take care of them."

It was true. I always carried a pot of emollient cream with me. I'd been applying it twice a day since I was a teenager to protect my skin, and I still continued the habit. In the cold weather, when skin tended to dry out and crack from the wind and central heating, I slathered a thick layer of cream onto my hands before bed and slipped mulberry silk gloves on for the night. The warmth of the gloves helped the skin absorb even more of the cream. For some reason I hadn't quite articulated to myself, I did these things furtively now, even hiding the nightly routine from Richard.

"Yes. I still take care of my hands."

She didn't exactly give me a squeeze, but I felt a definite pulse of energy moving from her fingers to mine.

Then she placed my hands back in my lap and stood up. I expected her to take her place behind the desk again and get back to discussing Richard's latest intransigence. But instead, she moved toward the artwork that hung on the wall—the sketch of the woman on the cliff and the seals in the water. It was so detailed, so vivid, you had to double-check that it wasn't a photograph.

"I've seen you noticing this. You like it?" she asked.

"It's beautiful. The most beautiful piece of art I've seen outside of a gallery."

"The artist was a client of mine."

I looked at it again, with more care. I took in the seals gazing with their dark eyes at the woman on the rocks.

"You know the myth of the selkies? Of the selkie bride?" she asked.

"I mean, I might have heard it in school? But it's so long ago…"

She began telling me the myth of the seal who took on the form of a human woman and while on land, was tricked into marrying a handsome young fisherman. He had found her seal-skin, which she needed in order to return to the sea, and re-fused to give it back. But he promised that if, after seven years, she wanted to leave, he would give her back her sealskin and let her go. They had a daughter and, for a time, the selkie bride was happy. But her husband went away more, stayed out drink-ing, didn't come home. Seven years passed, and she asked her husband to give back her sealskin, as he'd promised he would if that was her decision. He refused. Every day after that, the selkie bride went to the cliffs and stared out to sea, where her sisters were, waiting for the bride to come home.

"Gradually, her skin became dull, her hair lost its shine, she was always tired, so tired she must surely have been ill. She grew weaker and weaker. She needed to go back to the sea," Ms. Early reiterated.

I have to admit I was getting the *tiniest* bit impatient. I was sure it was a perfectly good myth but I'd come here to figure out what to do next about my disintegrating marriage, not to dabble in marine mammal–based Celtic parables. "So...the art-ist, your client. Things turned out all right for her? With her marriage?"

Ms. Early's expression changed. "You know, this is our sixth session together now, Eliza."

"Yes..."

"And still you ask the wrong questions."

"Well, what are the right questions?"

"You should know by now."

Should I offer her another squeeze of my pleasingly soft hands to put her back in a good mood? Ask her to continue her les-son on mythology? I didn't understand this swift mood change, this irritation with me.

"You want to ask me now about Richard, don't you?" she continued. "You want me to tell you what to do about Rich-ard, rather."

"But that's what these sessions are for, surely?"

"Oh, I know what you *want* these sessions to be."

Why was she suddenly so frustrated? What did she want from me?

"You're looking at this sketch," she said. "I can see how it affects you, touches you emotionally. In fact, you tell me it's the most beautiful piece of art you've seen outside a gallery. I explain that it's based on the myth of the selkie bride. And yet, the thing you *most* want to know about it is whether I helped the artist fix her marriage."

"But you're my marriage counselor," I reasoned. "And she was your client. Of course I'm going to want to know if you saved her marriage."

She gave a shake of her head to correct me. "I'm your therapist, Eliza. My job is to fix what needs fixing. Not necessarily what you *want* me to fix."

"But I thought we both agreed that it's Richard who needs fixing."

"Eliza," she said, taking a breath. "We have completed the treatment."

Wait, what? "But…that can't be it. I mean, he hasn't changed."

"We've tried adjusting your behavior to elicit a more favorable response. Then we tried an alternative approach, administering a specially formulated tincture designed to reignite the connection between the two of you by reducing inhibitions. And finally, we tried to make it physically impossible for him to be unfaithful. But despite some temporary improvements in his behavior toward you, you must see that the overall trend is not encouraging."

"But, but…you said we'd switch Richard's empathy back on. You said we'd make Richard listen. You said your methods never failed!"

"And they haven't. Eliza, you found out what you needed to know."

"But it didn't bring us closer. It didn't bring him back to me."

"No, it didn't. But that doesn't mean it failed."

"So that's it? You're just going to give up on me?"

"No, Eliza. I'm not giving up on you."

"But we're not going to continue with the treatment."

She didn't say anything. And just like that, it was over.

"I'd better go so."

I had half expected some last rousing words of encouragement, or even a change of heart, but no, she just nodded. "Goodbye, Eliza."

Fine. Abandon me in my hour of need. See if I cared.

I stood and she didn't stop me.

I went down the three flights of stairs, trying not to feel sorry for myself. I had been stupid to think that this woman had more than a professional interest in my situation. Why would she? I was nothing special. Not anymore, anyway.

As I passed the gastropub on the bottom floor of the building, I noticed a piano in the corner. I don't know why, but I slipped inside. There was no one else there but the hipster-chic bartender, wiping the counter. He didn't look up as I walked past and sat down at the old piano. It had surely seen many lock-ins and good times. I supposed I'd just sit there for a while till I'd gathered my thoughts and was ready to get the train home.

I placed my hands on the keys.

My heart was beating fast, my breath wouldn't come, the old familiar nighttime dread rising up my chest like water in a sinking ship.

I began to play. I wasn't happy, but I was playing. I didn't play well, but I was playing. I wasn't able to lose myself in the music like I used to, but I was playing. And I stayed there—playing, playing, *playing*.

When eventually I stopped, I realized the pub had filled up a little, and that several passers-by had paused by the doorway, drawn in by the music. And, to my utter mortification, people were applauding.

Then I saw her. There, sitting at the bar, was Ms. Early.

She stood and walked over to me. Then she reached out and took my hand in hers. This time I felt not just a pulse, but a very definite squeeze.

"You know…" she said in the end. "There *is* something else we could try."

28

I stood at the counter of our kitchen, grinding two tablets into a fine powder using a pestle and mortar. One pill was white, one cerise; as I worked, the colors began to mix into a pastel-pink dust that smelled like strawberry dip dabs. Ms. Early had said that this powder could be stirred into food to hide the bitter taste. She had also suggested taking a look at easypilldog.com for creative ideas, so I had the site open on my phone. There were things called pill pockets, meaty treats with a little cavity in which you could conceal the dose. Maybe I could do something similar with meatballs? There were also pill guns, and I couldn't deny there was an attraction—I mean, it featured a plunger that helped get the pill safely down the throat *without losing fingers in the process*. What's not to love?—but scrolled on.

The site also recommended peanut butter balls as one of the most effective pilling methods. Hmm, that might just about work. Maybe a coffee energy ball: I had never known Richard to turn down (a) caffeine or (b) a snack.

Now, as for what was *in* said pills? That would be estrogen—a *super* high dosage of estrogen, that is. According to Ms. Early, numerous studies have shown that a high concentration of the female hormone in any person's system—but specifically men—

enhanced their emotion-processing abilities through higher level-association neural pathways. In other words: flooding someone's system with estrogen could be expected to turbo-charge their empathy levels. Which Richard desperately needed.

After my impromptu piano performance, Ms. Early had taken me back up to the office and given me the two pill bottles. She said he was to have one of each, every day. Without exception. The pills were fast acting, she'd told me, and would hit his bloodstream quickly, so I should start seeing results almost immediately. On the downside, the drugs would also leave his system rapidly, so it was vital that I kept him on a steady daily dose until the necessary levels of chemicals and neurotransmitters built up.

After ten days of this intensive dosage, the tablets would gradually begin to alter Richard's brain chemistry, making permanent changes we desired.

I will admit that the word *permanent* had given me pause for thought. But did I want to fix this problem or not? I started grinding the pills for the energy balls with renewed vigor. This was my last shot.

What I'd said in Ms. Early's office was true. I wanted the old Richard back, the real Richard. The one who would sit and laugh with me at the end of a hard day, the one who had always had my back, who admired me. I knew he was still there, somewhere. I'd seen glimmers of it these past few weeks. We could still get back to that place. I could fix this, if I just tried hard enough.

I looked down at my work. This powder was as fine as it was going to get. Now all I had to do was finish making the energy balls and wait for Richard to get home.

Then let the dosing begin.

When Richard came home late that night, I didn't hear him immediately go into the study to seclude himself, as he had every night this past week. Instead, right after I heard him lock the front door and kick off his shoes, he walked right into the kitchen and over to *me*. I was shocked, though pleasantly surprised. For one, we could get the treatment started ASAP—I had the energy balls ready to go. Lord knows Richard would be up all night working, anyway, as he had been every night that week.

We'd been avoiding each other like the plague since the hotel incident. For the past couple days, we were reduced to pinging perfunctory emails to each other and sending messages like, "can you pick up chocolate of any kind as we have literally run out" and "sorry, no, have to work late."

And then, even more shockingly, *he* broke the impasse.

But not in a good way.

"Is Mara asleep?" he asked.

"Yes," I said, unsure where he was going with this. It was practically midnight; of course Mara was asleep.

Richard nodded. "Eliza, we need to talk." He then walked toward his beloved study, gesturing for me to follow him. I reluctantly followed suit.

Once we were in the study, he made a point of going over and shutting the door. Then he handed me his iPad, which was open on the *Irish Daily Tattle* site:

Affair Rumors Hit Theater Wunderkind

News has reached our ears that there's quite the drama playing out in the personal life of the theater world's golden boy, Richard Sheridan. While Richard battles to restore the fortunes of one of our national theaters, Blind Alley, he is also battling shocking rumors that he's been playing away from home...with none other than his leading lady, Hollywood A-lister Sasha Jones.

One of the key reasons Richard was hired as Blind Alley's new manager was his wholesome family-man image. The theater's board hoped his appointment would dispel memories of Richard's predecessor, who made Blind Alley a byword for casting-couch misconduct.

However, a source close to the Sheridan family tells us that Richard has grown increasingly close to the Academy Award–winning Ms. Jones, who recently split from her film director husband, and that this closeness has now developed into something considerably more than friendship. If the rumor is true, Richard is jeopardizing more than just his marriage... He is risking his professional reputation—and his job.

Blind Alley's chairman declined to comment when contacted for this article. We were unable to contact Richard Sheridan.

Shit.

I put the iPad down and glanced at Richard. Yep, it was as bad as I'd feared. He was sweating, his face clammy. He was also, it should be noted, livid.

"*You* thought I was having an affair with Sasha," Richard said, pointing a finger at me. "That's why you followed me to the Five Seasons."

"No! I mean, I suppose maybe I *wondered*, but I know now that—"

"Jesus Christ," he said, shaking his head in disbelief. Then he looked up at me. "Was this you, Eliza? Did you leak this?"

"How can you think I would do that to you?" *Especially with my phenomenal track record?*

"Then how do you explain it? Who did you talk to?"

I couldn't explain it. I was as baffled as he was. I racked my brain for who the culprit could have been but came up empty. And then it clicked.

George.

I looked at the floor. "I think I might have mentioned something to George that I...that I thought you and Sasha were possibly... I didn't think..."

He turned away, running a hand through his hair. "Fuck's sake." Then he turned back to me. "What else did you tell her?"

What else did I tell her? Oh, nothing major. Just a detailed blow-by-blow account of pretty much every single problem in our marriage.

"I could get *fired* for this, Eliza," he said, gesturing to the iPad.

"They couldn't fire you. It's not true."

He ignored me, just kept pacing up and down.

"Right," he said finally, in the tone he usually reserved for Mara when she had stolen the laces out of his shoes again. "Here's what's going to happen. We're going to send a lawyer's letter to the paper. And you're going to talk to George and make it crystal clear that if anything else like this appears in the papers, I'll sue her for defamation. Right?"

"Richard. I can't say that to her. She's my friend. I can't threaten her like that. And besides, I really don't think she would do this to us."

"*Somebody* did."

Okay sure, maybe George was pissed off with me, but seriously, who wasn't these days? She wasn't capable of this.

Was she?

I took the Tupperware container of energy balls from the counter and stashed them away on top of the high cabinet. The dosing would have to wait.

29

"Has something happened, Eliza? Between you and George?" Gina asked.

We were on yard duty again. After helping a few children tie their laces, and breaking up a scuffle, Gina steered us to the edge of the yard. I sensed it was because she wanted A Chat. And I was right.

"We just had a bit of a fight, that's all." Not that it was any of her business.

She nodded. "I knew something was off." Then she said, "Can I be honest with you, Eliza?"

Great. More honesty. Just what I needed in my life. "Sure."

"I don't mean this in a bad way, but I never would have put the two of you together. I mean, I get that you both have that sort of… 'sense of humor' thing going on," she said, using air quotes. "But…"

"But what?"

"She basically *hates* us, Eliza."

"What do you mean *us*? You and me?"

"*Us*," she said with an expansive wave of her hand. "Sahms. Stay-at-home moms."

I was about to say I didn't identify as a Sahm, but thought

better of it. "I don't think *hate* is the right word. It's more that she thinks—"

"Eliza, I know you and George call us the Chickadees. And I know you call me Mother Hen."

"What?"

"The Honey Café is pretty small. It's hard not to overhear."

I glanced at her. She was doing a good job of hiding the hurt, but it was there. "God, Gina. I'm sorry. That was before I got to know you."

"It's okay. Really," she said. "I know when people first meet me, I can come across as… I don't know, vain or whatever. I mean, I *am* vain. Johnny goes mad that we're always late for things because it takes me so long to get ready. I like to make an effort. I like a bit of glam, you know? That's just how I am. It makes me feel good. Even if it's a bit shallow."

"I can understand that."

"And I know you hate this whole *Toy Show* situation, and that you're only going along with it for Mara's sake. But that's the thing with you, Eliza. It feels like you're just going along with all of it, just grinning and bearing…*everything.*"

"When? When do I come across like that?"

"Like… Aurora's birthday party? Any playdates we've had. Even in the limo going to the theater that time. It's like you're just forcing yourself to go through the motions and get through it until you can get back to… I don't know, your real life or something? But the thing is, for me, this stuff *is* real life. Whereas for you, it comes off like you think…it's all a bit beneath you?"

"I don't think it's beneath me."

"Eliza," she said. "Remember when I asked if you'd give Aurora piano lessons?"

Okay, so she'd got me there.

"I'm not trying to make you feel bad," she continued. "It just seems like you're forcing yourself to be a hundred percent involved in every part of Mara's life, but it doesn't seem to be making *you* happy."

"But didn't you tell me that you wanted more than anything to be an actress and that you're sorry you never really made that happen?"

She nodded. "Yes. But the difference is that I've made my peace with that. I'm okay that it didn't happen for me. I'm happy with my life now. It's enough for me. But I'm not sure you could honestly say the same. I think...if we're really being honest with each other..."

Oh great, here it comes. Is there anything worse than people being honest? What ever happened to a nice, polite tactful lie?

"I think that's why you're so jealous of Richard's success." *Wait, what?*

"You think I'm *jealous*?"

"Come on, Eliza. You're literally the only person in Ireland who's not proud of Richard. And you're his wife."

"Did he tell you that?"

"You basically roll your eyes whenever someone asks him anything about his play."

Note to self: tone down the eye rolling.

"I'm not trying to be a bitch. What I'm trying to say is, Mara's not a baby anymore. You could let someone else help you. You could get a minder."

"*You* don't have a minder," I said. "If you had a minder you could do more of your influencer work." It was only after I'd said it I remembered what George had told me—that Mother Hen would never allow a minder or an au pair in the house because of Johnny's wandering eye.

She waved this question away. "I get it. I'm annoying you. I should mind my own business. You just seem... I don't know, a bit unfulfilled or something."

"Yeah, well that's a first-world problem and I need to stop complaining about it. According to George anyway."

"Did she say that to you?"

"Well, she *is* working herself into an early grave emptying bedpans just to pay the bills, so I really don't have anything to complain about. I have choices and she doesn't."

Gina shook her head. "She's so full of shit. Eliza, she *chose* to send her three children to one of the most expensive private primary schools in Dublin. Also...when Mossy got drunk at the parents' wine tasting night last year, he told me he wants to move home to Leitrim. They could buy a site and build a big house and their mortgage would still only be half the size it is now. George could give up work. If she *wanted*. Or just do a bit of community nursing. But she doesn't want that. There's no maternity hospital in Leitrim and George has her eye set on becoming director of clinical midwifery when her boss retires. And for the record? George is the hospital's clinical manager—I'm not saying she doesn't work hard, but her days of emptying bedpans are long behind her. So, you know, don't let her get you down."

Later that night, I finally sent the message I'd been sitting on for days: Someone leaked a story about Richard to the Daily Tattle. I want to believe it wasn't you. Please call me.

Weekly Spouse Tracker

Rate the following spousal behaviours from 1 to 5:

1=non-existent,   2=poor/rare,   3=adequate/sometimes,
4=satisfactory/frequent,   5=excellent/always

BEHAVIORS	WEEKLY SCORE
Physical affection	1
Spontaneous acts of kindness	1
Gratitude for Service	1
General attentiveness	1
Reliability	1
Self-Absorption	>5
Helps out around the house	<1
Attentiveness to offspring	1
Answers texts/phone calls	1
Unaccounted-for disappearances	5

*To be completed in between sessions and returned to Ms. Early

30

"Everything's falling apart. My life is falling apart."

"I'm sure it may feel that way," Ms. Early said.

"My husband is giving me the deep freeze and I've lost the one friend I made since moving here, so yes, it does feel that way."

"Have you considered the possibility that things are exactly as they should be at this point?"

At this point of what, exactly? The slow-motion car crash that was my life?

"You know, Eliza," she said, "there is only one way for people to achieve lasting psychological growth."

"LSD?"

This joke irritated her, but she composed herself and continued. "True psychological change only occurs after the self has been broken down."

"But the plan was to make *Richard* change. Not me. And what about reigniting his empathy? What about getting him in touch with his feminine side?"

She waved this aside as if it was ridiculous, as if she hadn't suggested at the last session to artificially flood my husband's system with estrogen. "I've never before encountered a male subject who wasn't broken by my techniques."

"Broken? I want him to stop being an arse, not have a breakdown."

She ignored this. "I see now that he will never change unless he's forced to. The pressure must be such that he has no choice."

"What do you mean?"

"I mean, Eliza, that he must hit rock bottom. He must experience his own *dark night of the soul*. Only then will the ego die."

Tempting though this sounded, I didn't like where Ms. Early was going with this. She appeared to be entirely serious.

"I have to say it sounds a *bit* extreme," I said. "Couldn't he just have, I don't know, a full-moon-but-with-a-bit-of-cloud-cover night of the soul? Like, tough but not utter destruction?"

Ms. Early just shook her head. "If he's not pushed to the point of positive disintegration, we're wasting our time. The darkest nights are followed by the most radiant dawns. This is basic human psychology, Eliza, but do therapists put it into practice? No. And I'll tell you why. Because very few people possess the moral courage to see a process like this through to the end. What do they do instead? They tiptoe around their client's problems and never make any real, lasting progress. And so the clients keep coming back, sometimes even for years— *years!*—thinking their lives are changing for the better because a licensed professional told them so. It's a charming little business model."

Ms. Early stood and walked to the window that looked down over Lincoln Place and across to the National Gallery. She lowered the sash window and I felt a rush of cool air. She stood there, outlined against the hard winter sky. The breeze moved the gray silk of her skirt. Everything about her was so elegant, so poised. Even when she was just standing still, saying nothing, she radiated authority, like an eminent surgeon. Or anyone in a hi-vis jacket. And because of this authority, my treacherous mind automatically believed her, even as another part of me wondered if she might actually be crazy.

She shut the window with a bang. Then she came and sat next to me, a gleam of radicalism in her eye. She gave me an unnerving sort of smile, like we were comrades in some kind of resistance movement. "I believe that you, Eliza, have the moral courage to see this process through. Since our first meeting, you have struck me as exceptional."

"But if things keep going the way they have been, there's a very good chance Richard's going to file for divorce before we reach any radiant dawn."

She considered this. "And you don't think that could be *your* radiant dawn?"

"What? Of course not."

"Tell me about your friend," she said, suddenly bored with this line of conversation. "You said you've fallen out with her. George, is it? What happened?"

From my bag, I took out the newspaper, the one with the article that contained the leaked affair rumors, and handed it to Ms. Early.

"She was the only person who knew about my suspicions," I said.

"Are you sure about that?"

"I've thought about it and thought about it. She's the *only* person who could have leaked it," I said. "I only told you and her."

She said nothing, just sat waiting.

"I only told you and her," I repeated, choosing my words more carefully now.

She remained silent.

"And it couldn't have been you," I said.

There was a slight smile playing on her face now.

"Because that would be a breach of confidentiality."

In the end, she said, "Surely you are aware, Eliza, that there are a number of instances in which a therapist is allowed, in fact is *obliged*, to break confidentiality."

"You never told me that."

"If, for example, the client poses a danger to themselves."

"I'm not a danger to myself."

"In which case, it is my professional duty to take steps to protect you. Even from yourself, if necessary."

"But not by leaking secrets to the paper! That's got to be illegal."

"If you could prove it, perhaps."

"Wait. Is this what you meant about breaking Richard down? By leaking secrets to the press?"

She smiled. I noticed that her pupils had constricted to small dots, giving her an air of focused excitement, like a cat stalking its prey. "What do you think?"

Maybe I stood up too quickly, or maybe I had been hyperventilating, but the room around me began to recede and feel unreal, and I had to sit back down. "You can't do this. You have to stop. You'll ruin Richard."

I realized too late that was the wrong thing to say, because that was probably what she was *trying* to do.

I forced myself to do those breathing exercises that I'd had to do with Mara for her well-being homework, and then I looked her in the eye. "If you leak one single other thing about my life, or Richard's, I'll report you to the authorities. You'll be struck off and you'll never practice again. You are to stay out of my life, and Richard's. This is not to happen ever again. Am I making myself clear?"

She wasn't bothered by this in the slightest. In fact, she seemed delighted. "*Brava!* Finally, we see some chutzpah. The fire is getting stoked. This is very good. You remember what I said? Things are exactly as they should be."

All our sessions together came back to me now, all the intimate details about my life that I had foolishly told her about.

Secrets, memories, my most personal thoughts. I had trusted her. I had been a fool.

"Now do remember, Eliza, what I've told you. The darkest nights are always followed by the most radiant dawns."

I realized in that moment that it wasn't Richard she was trying to drive toward a nervous breakdown or a dark night of the soul or a disintegration of the psyche. It was me.

And she was doing a fucking marvelous job.

I stood up so quickly that my chair toppled backward, but I didn't stop to set it right. I walked straight out of the office and ran down the stairs.

As I dashed out of the building, all I could think was: *What had I done?*

31

As soon as I got home, I flushed the pink and white pills down the toilet, threw the chasteberry powder in the bin and forced myself not to think about Ms. Early and what else she might be capable of. I told myself that once a few days passed and Richard calmed down about the leak, things would blow over and everything would be *fine*.

But things did not blow over. What happened instead was that things got worse. Much, much worse.

That evening, Mara and I came in from the park to hear the sound of a man's voice coming from Richard's study. Johnny.

Something was clearly wrong. He did *not* sound pleased.

Mara ran out to the garden to play with Mr. Pickles, and I moved closer to the door of Richard's office so I could listen unobserved. "Then why the fuck would they put it in the paper, Richard, if it's not true?"

No more Richie. No more backslapping. I remembered what Gina had said about Johnny, that if he was on your side, he was the most generous person in the world, but once he turned against you, forget it. Now I knew what she meant. I hadn't even seen a glimpse of this cold fury before.

Richard began to speak but Johnny cut him off. "I've put

my name on the line here. I've vouched for you to my clients. And we're not talking Peter and Mary wondering where to invest their little nest egg. We're talking big-league guys here. And now they're calling me, f-ing and blinding down the phone at me, asking me what's going on. What am I supposed to tell them?"

"Tell them the truth, Johnny. That it's a complete lie!" Richard said.

"Because if these guys pull out, you realize what it means, right? The whole thing collapses like a fucking Ponzi scheme. Problem is it's not just my *name* on the line here. I plowed half a mill into this shit show so you could afford to hire Sasha. Not so you could have it off with her."

Sorry, half a mill? As in, half a million euro? I had no idea Johnny had already invested in the production, and definitely not at *this* level.

"I've been on the phone for hours trying to convince all the investors that this article is bullshit," Johnny continued. "So please tell me, Richard, that I haven't spent the whole morning lying to my biggest clients. Tell me you're not just some little two-bit hustler who thought he'd ride off into the sunset with my money in his pocket and Sasha Jones on his arm. Tell me we're good to go."

I willed Richard to say what needed to be said, to spin that old patter of his that never failed to charm directors and soothe highly strung actors' nerves, and not to let the *two-bit hustler* get to him.

"We're good to go, Johnny," Richard said in the end. "There's no problem."

"How do you explain the article so?"

"It's like you said. Pack of lies."

"In my experience, there's no smoke without fire."

"You know what the media's like. Trash. They'll print anything."

Johnny considered this, then said, "Why do I get the feeling I'm getting played?"

The door was open a crack so I put my eye to it. Richard was acting cool, but I saw a muscle in his jaw jumping. I knew what this meant—he was struggling to control his temper. He *hated* being given a dressing down. He was only tolerating it with Johnny because there was so much riding on his investment, but I knew Richard. Inside he was fuming. That twitchy jaw was his tell: he was reaching boiling point.

I stepped into the room.

Richard was the first to notice. "We're in the middle of something here, Eliza," he snapped.

I ignored him and turned to Johnny. "Richard's telling the truth. It *is* a pack of lies. I know for sure because...because it was me who leaked the story. I did it." I paused to see how this was landing. Richard looked appalled, but I could explain to him later that I was bluffing. The main thing was that I had Johnny's attention. "I was jealous," I added.

Johnny stared at me, not saying anything, but not dismissing me, either. I had no reason not to keep going. "You see, Richard never told me he'd cast Sasha Jones. He kept it a secret. So you can imagine how I felt when I found out. My imagination ran away with me. I had a few drinks, got myself really worked up and convinced myself there was something going on between them. And then, I mean I hardly remember doing it, I sent a stupid, drunken email to an old friend of mine who works in the *Daily Tattle*. I was so mad with Richard, I just wanted to hurt him. But it was so, so stupid."

I watched Johnny's face. It was impossible to read.

"There's nothing going on between Richard and Sasha. There never was. I've already been on to the *Daily Tattle*. They're taking the story down from their site and there'll be a retraction in tomorrow's print edition," I bluffed. "And as for the investors, why don't we organize a special dress rehearsal night to put their minds at ease? They can come along, see the quality of the production, see where their money is going...maybe even meet Sasha afterward? Full bells and whistles. They'll be blown away. Trust me."

Johnny chewed on this, eyes flicking from me to Richard who, realizing what I was up to, nodded along enthusiastically.

Eventually, Johnny turned to me, a glint in his eye. "You going to be there, Eliza?"

Just like that, the coldness had disappeared from his voice, replaced with innuendo. Like it was the two of us back in the utility room again, him holding on to the bottle of wine, not letting me leave.

"Of course, Johnny," I said. "Wouldn't miss it for the world."

By the time Johnny finally left, it was half past eleven. Richard had holed himself up in his study, presumably still raging with me, but hard at work. He believed me when I told him afterward that I'd obviously been lying about leaking the story. But while I'd bought him a temporary reprieve, I also created another problem: he was now under extreme pressure to figure out the logistics of this whole investor dress rehearsal and how to bring it all together in time. Or else Johnny really would pull the plug. And take his investors with him.

I could hear the clicking and clacking of computer keys from outside the study and knew Richard was *in the zone*, tapping out emails and assigning jobs.

I kept offering to help but this just irritated him, so I stopped. When midnight rolled around, I entered the study and suggested he call it a night, but he dismissed me with a distracted wave of a hand. Before heading to bed, I told him I'd made him a full French press of strong coffee, and this seemed to soften him a bit. I knew he was still furious at me for telling George, but I sensed that the deep freeze was starting to thaw.

I went upstairs to our bedroom and lay in bed, willing myself to sleep, but my racing mind had other plans. I ruminated over the hotel incident, the falling out with George, the suggestive comments from Johnny. But my thought spiral was suddenly interrupted by an incoming text from Gina:

Hey hun can u send Johnny home?

I was going to leave it unanswered. I was most certainly not in the mood to talk to Gina. On the other hand, if I didn't reply, the messages would keep coming.

He left hours ago, I wrote back.

Ok thanx babe. So sorry about the Sasha thing btw. Here for u if u need to talk.

This was followed up by the holding-back-tears emoticon.

The *Sasha thing.* As if it was a commonly accepted truth now that the leak was true. Come to think of it, Johnny was probably already home tucked up in bed, and Gina had just used Johnny as an excuse to text me so she could sprinkle some salt on my wounds. I mean, she could at least *try* to hide her schadenfreude.

But then again, that had never been Gina's style, had it?

32

"Mama, come and look! Daddy's asleep in the kitchen!"

Mara wasn't wrong. It was the next morning and Daddy was indeed asleep in the kitchen, snoring on the old sofa in the corner. The French press was empty; a sandwich crust lay on a plate.

And next to the plate was the container I had used to store the laced energy balls.

The container I had stashed away out of reach in a high cabinet.

Which was now empty.

With the lid off and tucked between Richard and a couch cushion.

"Mara, you didn't eat anything out of this, did you?" I asked nervously, holding up the container.

"Of course not. It smells like feet. But Daddy did. And we had So. Much. Fun!"

I looked at her more closely. She looked simultaneously hyped and exhausted. "What do you mean? *When* did you have all this fun?"

"During the night. I woke up because I heard someone moving around downstairs, so I went down to investigate. It was just Daddy walking around the kitchen. He said he was up late working, but then he *stopped* working! Because he *really* wanted to talk to me. We talked and talked and talked. About the Chickenosaurus. And the Cretaceous Period. And how annoying it is that Mr. Mellon doesn't believe that dinosaurs are still alive today in the form of birds. Daddy says he's going to talk sense into him for me. It was great! We talked for *so* long and he wasn't tired at all but I got so tired that I had to do *this*." Mara showed me how she had held her eyes open with her fingers. "Daddy wanted to keep talking but I had to go back up to bed because I was just *so* tired!"

Oh, Richard. What have you done? I thought.

But the answer was obvious. What he did was this—he had eaten at least nine mocha estrogen balls.

In one sitting.

At first, I wasn't worried. What was the worst Ms. Early had said would happen—enlarged breasts? I snuck a peek at his chest and didn't see any immediate effects. But it *was* continuing to rise up and down as he snored. He was breathing. Everything was fine.

On my way to drop Mara off at school, I was suddenly hit with a very sad thought—this was the first time in as long as I could remember that Richard had shown real, prolonged interest in our daughter.

And it was only because of the energy balls.

I returned home to find Richard awake and still on the couch. He was a bit groggy and definitely grouchy, but I let it slide, since I knew he had a late night. And even if his attentiveness to Mara was inorganic, he still made her feel special and important. That had to count for something.

I discreetly hovered near him, on the lookout for any odd or troubling behavior. It wasn't until later that morning, close to noon, that it became clear that he was not, in point of fact, and by any definition of the word—fine.

There was a slight tremor in his hands, and his eyes were...*off*. Unfocused and spacey. Every so often he did something weird with his face—he ground his teeth, moved his lower jaw from side to side, compulsively licked his lips.

But he didn't seem to notice he was doing anything strange at all. All I knew was that the man in the living room was not Richard. Not even close.

I slipped into our bedroom and called Ms. Early's office.

No one picked up. I rang again and again.

Still no answer.

I couldn't just sit around waiting. I went back downstairs to persuade Richard to go up to bed and rest. For once, he listened.

Then, with my throat growing tight, I drove straight to Ms. Early's office on Lincoln Place. The front door at street level was unlocked. I pushed it open and ran up the stairs.

A cleaner was using one of those rotating waxing machines to polish the floorboards, but there was no sign of the receptionist. The door of Ms. Early's office stood open. I entered.

But the room was empty. The walls were bare, the desk and cabinet gone. I started to question my sense of direction. Then my sanity—could I have gone to the wrong place in my state of distress?

But no. This was her office. I was sure of it. It was the same place I'd gone every week since I first saw that incriminating photo of Richard and Lady Languish. But then why wasn't she here? Why wasn't *anyone* here, and where was all the furniture?

I was just about to leave when I spotted something on one of the shelves—a pale manila folder. On the front was written: *Patient Notes: Eliza Sheridan*.

Ah, so I wasn't completely losing my mind.

I tore through it. Inside was a stack of newspaper clippings, all of them about me. Articles with headlines like, Fourteen-Year-

Old Irish Piano Prodigy Plays the Royal Albert Hall; Seventeen-Year-Old Mullingar Musician Wins International Competition; Local Pianist Signs Contract with Warner Classics; Real-life Romeo Rescues Teenage Musician from Jackson-Five-Style Hell; Award-Winning Pianist Eliza Sheridan Abruptly Cancels European Tour.

There were notes written on some of the clippings in red pen—little comments, things that Ms. Early had asked me about in our sessions.

She clearly did her homework.

I flicked back through the articles once more. And then I noticed it—underneath each of the clippings was the date, alongside her notes. On the very first article in the binder, she'd written: *April twenty-fifth.*

I hadn't started therapy with her until September.

Ms. Early had known about me all along.

I went back out to the corridor and asked the cleaner what had happened, where the therapy practice had relocated and why, but he shook his head. "I don't know about any therapist."

"Ellen Early. The therapist who used to work here."

He shrugged. "I just do the floors."

I ran back down the stairs to the street and noticed the sign for Early Counseling that had been nailed to the wall was gone.

I grabbed my phone and googled "association of therapists Ireland." It brought up the website of the Irish Association of Counseling and Psychotherapy, which had a directory of accredited therapists licensed to practice in Ireland. I searched for Ellen Early in Dublin, then anywhere in the country.

Nothing.

No wonder my threats to report her for professional misconduct hadn't fazed her in the slightest. She was not a licensed therapist.

But then who was she? Who was this woman I shared every

confidential detail of my marriage, my *life*, with? And where did she go?

I needed George.

I tried ringing her again and again on my way home, but she kept shutting the call off before it could even go to voicemail. Once I'd arrived back at the house and she still hadn't called me back, I tapped out a message:

George it's an emergency.

No reply.

Richard is really sick.

When I was halfway through composing my next text, which was going to read, I think he might be dying, she rang.

"Where are you?" George asked.

"At home."

"I'll be there in nine minutes."

33

"All right," George said when she walked through the door. "What's going on?"

I told her about the clammy skin and the drowsiness, and his extreme chattiness with Mara the night before. George took a flashlight from the medicine bag she had with her and shone it in his eyes. He rolled away from her. "Does he have any underlying conditions?"

Apart from possible clinical narcissism? "No."

"Is he on anything? Any medication?"

Funny you should ask. "Well…"

"Eliza, I can't help you if I don't know what's going on."

So I told her about the pink and white tablets, about grinding them down to a fine powder, about lacing the energy balls with them. And about Richard getting the munchies and devouring them—Every. Single. One. In one go.

George looked deeply unimpressed and asked to see the pill bottles. I told her I'd given them back to Ms. Early.

"Can you remember the label?" she asked.

"I think… I think she formulates them herself?"

She let out a long breath. "Eliza."

"I know, I know."

"I thought you were just doing the Stepford Wife thing."

"I was but…he didn't respond well enough to it."

"Did she say anything to you about what was *in* these tablets?"

"She just said something like…it was a blend of naturally occurring compounds?"

George looked exasperated. "*Heroin* is a blend of naturally occurring compounds. So are most medicines on the planet. It means nothing. It's like saying deadly nightshade is grand, as long as it's organic."

"Are you saying I've poisoned him?"

She took a pulse oximeter from her bag, slipped it onto Richard's finger. When the readings flashed up, she inhaled sharply.

"What is it? What's wrong?"

"His oxygen saturation levels are *way* too low. And his heart rate's elevated. He's also developed this rash on his face—" she gestured to his forehead and cheeks "—which is a common side effect of overdose. Known as a drug rash." She turned to me with a grave look on her face. She seemed scared. "Judging by his symptoms… I think it's likely he's overdosed on MDMA."

"*MDMA?* Like, ecstasy?"

"Yes, ecstasy. It's an empathogen. They call it the *love drug*."

I couldn't believe it. Had I really given my husband *ecstasy*? How could I have been so reckless, so trusting of some stranger? I never should have taken Ms. Early's advice so unquestioningly. I never should have gone to her at all.

George reached for her phone.

"What are you doing?"

She ignored me.

"George, please don't. Please don't call an ambulance."

"Eliza, this is serious."

"If we bring him to hospital and the press finds out that Richard Sheridan was rocked up at A&E with a drug overdose, he'll be ruined."

George didn't respond and started tapping in a number.

"And I'll have to tell the doctors everything," I continued. "And then Richard will find out and…and…we'll be finished. Over."

George turned to face me and said in a softer tone, "Would that really be the worst thing?"

The call went through.

"Yes, I need an ambulance," George said, somehow keeping her voice even. "As quickly as possible. It's a drug overdose." Then she gave my home address and hung up.

We locked eyes and it hit me just how serious this was. *What if he didn't make it? What if I'd inadvertently killed my husband? And what would I tell Mara?*

We sat in silence, waiting for the ambulance to arrive. After ten minutes, George called 911 again and was told there were a number of other emergencies in the area. The ambulance would be some time yet, but it was coming.

Fifteen minutes had now passed.

Twenty.

George seemed to sense my panic and took my hand, squeezing it hard. She'd been monitoring Richard constantly while we waited, and taking his readings every five minutes. Her face remained grim, which told me all I needed to know. He wasn't getting better. I paced around the room as she tended to Richard, neither of us speaking.

Thirty minutes. Forty.

I thought I was going to be sick.

But the next time George slipped the pulse oximeter on him, I saw something shift in her face. A relaxing of tension. She turned to me and I saw surprise and relief in her eyes. "His oxygen levels have come back up. They're almost at normal levels now. And his heartbeat is steadying. Still a little faster than I'd like. But…he's stabilizing. He's going to be okay, Eliza."

I covered my face with my hands and allowed myself to breathe. *Thank fuck!*

George rang to cancel the ambulance, and I went to pour us both a drink, even though it was only eight in the morning. We needed it.

"Can you imagine if we *had* gone to the A&E and it got out that the *great Richard Sheridan* had OD'd on ecstasy?" I said, as the full weight of what I'd done began to sink in. "He'd have been ruined."

"And how would it have gotten out, Eliza?"

There was a frosty silence. We both knew what she meant.

"I know it wasn't you who leaked the story about the affair, George. And I never really thought it was you. Honestly."

"Eliza, you literally texted me saying, 'Did you do this?'"

There was nothing I could say to that.

"I would never in a million years," she said in the end.

"I know," I said. "I know."

George sighed, then added, "Well. I shouldn't have said all that stuff to you about your diamond shoes being too tight."

"It's all right. I know I must come across as ungrateful."

"You don't. I said those things in the heat of the moment. I didn't mean it."

"But I do," I said. "Act ungrateful. I know I do. But I want you to understand."

She gave me a curious look.

"You see, I lost a baby," I heard myself say. "I was working too hard and… I lost a baby." I hadn't ever said those words out loud before.

The only sound in the room now was Richard's gentle snoring. I realized my fingers were tingling and my cheeks were going numb.

"He would have been Mara's older brother," I added.

And then I told her everything.

It had happened in Cologne, while I was on my European

tour. The doctors had said flying was all right but had warned that I really needed to avoid stress. But that was like telling a weightlifter not to pick up anything heavy. I needed adrenaline to deliver my best performances.

Richard had suggested I cut the European tour short, maybe just fulfill the Irish and UK dates, but he refused to believe that if I did that, I'd be finished. It would be my first and last tour. My father had drummed it into me from my very first concert. Turn up and deliver. Never disappoint. If you're not reliable, if you make demands, if you cancel dates, you're not asked again. Someone younger and keener will jump straight into your spot. And that's it. You're old news.

And besides, I loved it. I loved the big audiences in the old palaces and beautiful concert halls where I got to play. And I loved it all even more now that my father was no longer in charge, micromanaging every tiny aspect. It was everything I had worked toward.

Afterward, when I finally got back from Germany, Richard was kind. He said not to blame myself. But we both knew the truth—I had caused this. And now I had to live with it.

I never performed again.

Having Mara was the only thing, the *only* thing that made it better. The doctors said I should wait, that it might be dangerous for me to try again, ever. But I knew it was the one thing that would make any of it bearable.

And I was right.

Once I'd finished, George didn't say anything for a very long time. Then she reached out and put her hand on mine.

"God, Eliza," she finally said.

34

Richard's levels continued to stabilize to the point that George felt comfortable enough to leave him with me for the rest of the day. And when she then offered to pick Mara up from school while I kept an eye on him, I gladly accepted. I was in too much of a daze to drive.

When the front door opened, Mara pottered straight into the kitchen and peered at Richard, prone on the battered old sofa. She put her little hand on his forehead. "Hmm…sweaty," she said.

"He just has a tummy bug, my love."

"Then why is there a rash on his face?"

Fair point. It had gone down some as the day went on, but was definitely still there.

"It's the bubonic plague, isn't it?" Mara said, matter-of-factly.

"Of course it's not."

"That man in Mongolia had the bubonic plague last month. Remember I told you?"

Before I could respond, she raced upstairs. When she reappeared a minute later, she was wearing swimming goggles and a snorkel mask—the closest thing she could find to the beak masks that plague doctors wore in medieval times—and holding a container of Mr. Pickles's flea powder. She was all set to start dousing Richard with the powder when I managed to grab it off her.

"But the fleas might still be on him! The infected fleas!"

"Mara, whatever is wrong with Daddy, it's definitely not the bubonic plague. I can promise you that."

Later that night, George swung by the house to do a quick, final assessment of Richard.

"Why am I smelling basil?" she asked when she walked through the front door.

There was, indeed, a very strong smell of basil.

"Because I couldn't find any lavender," Mara said, as if stating the obvious. She had just sprinkled little pieces of crushed basil around Richard and had shoved some into her snorkel mask for good measure, to counter the *miasma* coming off him. She hadn't taken the mask off since she came home from school.

"Mara, it's getting late. Time to get ready for bed," I told her. She hesitated, shooting nervous looks at Richard on the couch.

George read the situation and said, "Your dad's fine, Mara. Trust me—I'm a nurse."

She seemed semipleased with that answer. "Okay, but please make sure you keep checking for fleas. And if you see any, use Mr. Pickles's flea powder," Mara said, pointing to where she'd left it on the kitchen counter. Then she went upstairs.

George raised an eyebrow at me.

"She thinks he's got the bubonic plague," I explained.

"Ah."

George checked Richard's levels one last time and grabbed her bag off the couch. "He's stable. He'll probably need another full night's sleep to get through the comedown phase, but you should stay downstairs with him in case he wakes up in the middle of the night. If he does, he's going to be extremely thirsty but make sure he doesn't drink water. Give him this instead." George reached into her bag for a pack of Dioralyte and handed it to me. "This keeps his electrolytes from getting out of whack and possibly diluting his blood. Otherwise, he's at risk for water intoxication, and if that happened, there'd be no choice but to take him to hospital."

George paused to let this sink in and gave me a long look. "Jesus, Eliza, this has hit you hard, as it would anyone. He's going to be okay, but…are *you* okay? Do you want me to stay?"

I shook my head and persuaded her to go home. I needed to be alone with my thoughts, to try to make sense of what was happening. I was also afraid that if she stayed, I might blurt everything out to her—everything that had transpired since I went to that very first session with Ms. Early. And if I did *that*, I was pretty sure she'd be legally obliged to call the men in white coats.

After George left, I set up shop next to Richard to keep an eye on him, taking his temperature regularly. He did wake up a few times during the night, groggy and confused, and—as George predicted—always asking for water. After several rounds of Dioralyte, he finally fell into a deep slumber around three in the morning.

As I sat there watching over him, my mind began generating an alternative, even more frightening explanation for what the absolute fuck was going on. But not with him—with *me*.

This happens to women around your age, Eliza.

What if Richard had been right? What if I was going through some kind of hormonal breakdown? Was this what female madness looked like? Was I imagining everything?

The cleaner in the Lincoln Street office had known nothing about a therapist when I asked him. No one else had seen this woman apart from me.

Was my melancholy womb, like those Victorian doctors used to say, wandering around my body and messing with my perception of reality? Was it time to start dosing me with uppers and downers like a 1950s starlet so I would behave? *Histrionic. Ungovernable. Hysterical.*

Was it possible…that *I* was the problem?

My thoughts were interrupted by Richard's phone vibrating on the table next to him. He shifted in his sleep but didn't wake. I picked the phone up to see a text notification.

Richard always kept his phone locked and recently he'd switched from using a pattern to unlock it to thumbprint recognition. Which I guess I somewhat understood—after the whole Sasha Jones fiasco at the hotel, it wasn't *unreasonable* for him to assume I'd infringe on his privacy.

Well, if ever there was a time to have a little snoop, then surely it was after you'd accidentally fed your husband a large quantity of disco biscuits?

As gingerly as I could, I lifted Richard's right hand and touched his thumb to the sensor. It rejected the print. I pressed his thumb harder onto the screen. Rejected again. Then I noticed how sweaty his hand was, so I delicately dabbed his thumb with a fresh facecloth and wiped down the screen and gave it one more try. Bingo!

I was in.

I glanced at Richard—still fast asleep—then went straight for the texts. There were a few messages from Majella and other theater staff, but much more interestingly, there were a lot of messages to and from an 083 number that Richard hadn't saved into his contacts.

I scrolled through his exchanges with this number and for the most part, they all seemed to be logistical, coordinating various meeting times.

Then I came across one from the previous night: If u don't pull this off, it's over.

Pull off what? And *what* would be over for him—an affair? I immediately cursed my mind for going there. Again.

I looked at the time stamps and Richard had replied straight away to the texter:

Ok let's talk at investor evening while everyone's watching the first act. I should be able to slip away when the lights go down.

Then he'd texted:

I'll meet u in the old dressing room at the end of green corridor.

My heart sank.

I happened to know from gossipy chats with the girls in the office that the old dressing room at the end of the green corridor was rumored to be a *hookup* spot for actors in need of a little privacy.

Whoever the mystery texter was, they were going to the investor night. My hunch was that it was a woman, which would narrow it down to: Majella, Gina, Sasha Jones—who didn't have any lines until the second act. And basically any of the myriad other actors, stagehands, office and bar staff that would also be there.

I could ring the number and hope that the person on the other end said enough for me to identify their voice. But what if they just said "hi" and then clammed up when they realized it wasn't Richard calling? If I didn't handle this right, I might never find out what was going on. I had to be there to see it for myself.

I scoured the rest of their text exchanges but there was nothing else suspicious—*except* for a strange message from someone called Charles:

I've forwarded on the valuation as requested. Please find attached.

I opened the attachment and saw a document with Precision Pianos at the top. I knew this company; they traded in high-end concert pianos.

In the document, Charles said that following on from his visit to value Richard's Fazioli Brunei concert piano at his Ballsbridge address, they were writing to inform him that although it was difficult to place a precise value on the instrument because it was a one-off, it was still possible to provide a rough valuation of what it would be likely to fetch on the open market. He then gave a range of what he thought it could fetch. He also pointed out that they always had a number of high-end collectors and buyers on their books. He looked forward to hearing from Richard with any further instructions.

My heartbeat quickened and I felt a rush of adrenaline through my body. How fucking *dare* he?

He had absolutely no business going anywhere near my piano, let alone getting it valued. If it was the other way around, if *I* brought an assessor in to value the theater without telling Richard, he'd be livid. Not only was the piano the one thing of value that I owned outright, but it was a one-of-a-kind, made specifically for me.

And fuck it, it was more than just a piano. It was my companion. It was Delphina.

The thought of an assessor's clumsy hands touching my piano without my permission infuriated me. The bloody nerve of Richard!

I was on the brink of ringing George again when I changed my mind and found myself reaching for the business card of Phil, as I liked to call the philandering solicitor I had met in the bar of the Five Seasons Hotel. I had found his card lying on top of the bar's piano after he left. He answered on the second ring and I told him who I was.

I heard a smile come into his voice. "I didn't think you'd call."

"Neither did I. You work in family law, right?"

"You remembered. I'm flattered."

"Can I ask your opinion on something?"

"If I can take you out to dinner."

"Maybe, depending on what your opinion is."

"All right. Shoot."

"So if a client came to you, a somewhat neurotic but ulti-
mately well-meaning woman and she told you that her husband
had been acting suspiciously lately, sneaking out in the evenings,
lying, getting strange text messages, that kind of thing…and
then he got her most cherished possession, in fact, her only possession, which was a concert piano that she won as a prize in a
major international competition, valued. Without telling her.
What would be your reaction to that hypothetical situation?"

He drew his breath and paused for a long time. "Do you really want to know?"

No. "Hit me."

"Okay. On its own, finding out your spouse has had an asset
valued should not necessarily set alarm bells ringing. There
could be any number of explanations. Like getting it valued
for insurance. But put it together with everything else?" He
sighed. "Look, Eliza, from what you told me the other night,
you and your husband seem to be living quite separate lives already. And in my experiences with hundreds of clients, mostly
women, I've seen this pattern over and over again. It's a tactic
used usually by men when they're thinking of leaving. They
get all the marital assets assessed on the quiet and then they
get their tax accountant and a family lawyer to work out how
much they stand to lose if they go ahead and file for divorce.
And they also may start moving assets out of the wife's name
without her realizing it, in order to sell the assets and keep all
the proceeds. And they do this *before* they start divorce proceedings, so that those assets don't go into the pot that's to be
divided between the two spouses."

"He's not taking my piano!"

"No. He couldn't take your piano. But Eliza," he said with
a note of caring that struck me as really very kind, "you need
to start preparing, too, if this is what he's doing. Now, I could
be wrong. There could be an innocent explanation. But the

fact that you rang me, a family law solicitor who hit on you in a bar, rather than going to your husband to talk it through, speaks volumes. Honestly, I'd be happy to meet you for dinner. Not in a date way. Just to advise you. To be frank, you're quite exposed, Eliza. Financially. You need to think of protecting yourself. And your daughter."

35

It was the night of the big investor run-through and, front of house at least, everything was going swimmingly. Fortunately, Richard had not succumbed to his hallucinogenic methamphetamine-induced fug. When he'd woken in the morning, I'd somehow managed to convince him that he'd been so exhausted from overworking that when he lay down to take a brief nap, he ended up sleeping right through till midday. This had actually happened to him before when he'd been really exhausted, which worked in my favor.

And now here he was, drained and washed out, but managing to smile and glad-hand the guests as they arrived.

The bar was buzzing as ancient patrons of the theater mixed with gorgeous young friends of the cast members, alongside plenty of random semiglamorous hangers-on hoping to get snapped by the society magazine photographer circulating through the crowd. The investors were running late but Johnny's crew seemed unbothered, enthusiastically working their way through the free champagne.

With more guests arriving and the drink flowing, it was easy for me to slip away unnoticed. Backstage was a hive of chaotic activity. I could hear actors doing vocal warm-ups and giving each other pep talks. Doors opened and slammed shut. Someone from wardrobe dashed past me, cursing about a missing cummerbund. I glanced into hair and makeup—the girls in there were keeping an eye on Mara for me. She looked content, curled up on a chair, her nose in a book called *Girls Who Slay Monsters*.

No one noticed as I slipped into the unused dressing room, which had become a dumping ground for old furniture and props. I positioned myself behind a rickety dressing screen. My hiding place was not the most pleasant. There was a smell that suggested something had died beneath the floorboards. But this had to be done. I had to know if I was completely losing my mind or not.

I waited and waited and got a cramp in my right calf, then waited some more till I had pins and needles in my legs. Finally, I heard the door open and close again and then I heard footsteps in the room. And now Sasha Jones's voice, followed by her trademark throaty laugh. So I was right yet again—Sasha *was* Lady Languish!

But then I heard a man's low, muffled voice through the door. And it wasn't Richard's.

"Stop, Johnny. I don't have time for that."

Johnny? Seriously?

"Come on, it won't take long."

"God, how romantic. Look, I have to go finish my makeup."

"You don't need to go to makeup just yet. In fact, you look better with no makeup. You look better with nothing at all on."

She gave a little laugh and then there was silence as they, presumably, embraced.

"Don't you have to go schmooze the investors?" she said, after a few moments.

"They're not here yet. Anyway, Majella will look after them. I don't really give a shit right now."

"Do you even realize how arrogant you sound sometimes?"

"That's why you like me."

"No, I like you because you're rich."

A pause. I wondered if he'd get pissed off with this.

"Say that again," Johnny said.

Gross.

"What? I like you because you're rich?"

"That's it. Say it again."

And she did, in that husky voice that made millions for major film studios each and every year.

There was a brief interlude of silence. I peered through the gaps in the screen to see Johnny maneuvering Sasha onto a dusty old chaise longue.

"What if someone walks in?" she said.

"It's fine, it's fine, it's fine," Johnny murmured.

How, *how*, did I get myself into these ludicrous situations?

I began to ease my way out from behind the screen with a view to escaping unnoticed when I saw the door handle begin to turn. Someone was coming in from the corridor. I scuttled back to my hiding place.

Someone whipped open the door and gasped. Shut the front door if it wasn't Gina. The pair on the chaise longue, now *in flagrante*, hadn't noticed her.

"I knew it!" Gina hissed.

There was a flurry of "Oh, shits," from the chaise longue and hasty covering up. But it was too late.

Gina kept repeating, "I knew it, I knew it," over and over, while Johnny told her to stop being hysterical, which obviously just made her more furious.

"You made me think I was crazy!"

"Let's not do this, okay, Geen?" he said.

This enraged her—and me—even further. "I'll do whatever I like."

When Johnny didn't say anything, Gina moved to her next target: Sasha. "How does it feel to be pimped out by your boss?"

Sasha gasped. "Are you going to let her talk to me like this?" she asked Johnny. "She's pretty much calling me a prostitute."

"If the cap fits, babes," Gina said.

Johnny, for his sins, looked genuinely torn. I'd never seen him wrong-footed before. He began to speak but Gina put up a palm to stop him. "You know what? We'll talk about this at home. I'm not doing this here."

"Tell her," Sasha said to Johnny.

Johnny cleared his throat and stared down at his bare feet. There was a long silence. Then he said, "I'm not... I'm not coming home."

Oh no, he did not just say that.

"What, tonight?" Gina said.

They stared at each other. He looked away first.

I saw Gina's chest rising and falling several times. "Well, *you're* going to have to tell Aurora," she shot at him.

"I know," Johnny said evenly. "I'll come round in the morning and explain it to her."

Gina gave a laugh of incredulity. "Oh right. And is there any chance you could explain it to *me*? Your actual wife? Because this *whole* scenario—" she gestured between Johnny and Sasha "—is complete bullshit. For the record."

He turned his face away from her and I caught a glimpse of his side profile. Not surprisingly, he looked like he'd rather be anywhere else in the world than here, with this exact combination of people. And he didn't even know *I* was there.

"I bet *she* knows." Gina nodded toward Sasha. "I bet you tell her all your woes and how you're misunderstood blah blah blah."

"He does, actually," Sasha said. "He says you've turned out just like his first wife. Boring. No ambition."

Gina looked like she'd been slapped across the face.

"Sasha," Johnny warned.

"What?" Sasha said. "You *did* say that."

"You know what?" Gina said. "You're welcome to him. He doesn't care about anyone except for himself. So good luck to you both. You deserve each other."

"Jeez, what a bitch," Sasha said under her breath.

"Don't," Johnny said sharply. "Don't talk about her like that."

"Oh, but it's okay for *you* to call her that?"

And it was at this exact moment I heard Richard say, "What's going on?"

When did *he* get here?

Sasha stared at Richard, as if doing a calculation. Then she whipped round to Gina. "What did you mean, about Richard pimping me out?"

Gina gave a sly smile. "I'll tell you exactly what I meant. Johnny invested half a million in the play. On condition that it would be used to pay your fee. And that Richard would introduce you two, basically do everything he could to set you up with him, whatever it took. Richard knew you were fresh from a breakup, that you never stay single, and that you have a type—men with big egos and even bigger wallets.

"And then when you *did* get together—so predictably, might I add—Richard covered for Johnny. He booked hotel rooms in his name so no one would find out about them. He lied to me, saying Johnny was at his house every evening when actually he was with you."

Sasha was staring down Richard now.

"I bet he sent you presents, right? With little heartfelt notes?" Gina continued. It was all spewing forth in a torrent, like she genuinely could not stop herself. "Richard picked those out. He bought them and he wrote those notes. No point having a writer on the payroll if you're not going to make use of them, right, Johnny?"

"Don't listen to her, Sasha," Johnny said. "She has no idea what she's talking about."

Sasha ignored him, still staring at Richard. "Is it true? What she's saying?"

He hesitated too long before replying. "No. No, of course not. I mean, Johnny's investment meant I could afford to pay your fee, but that's the only part that's true."

"You booked the suite for me at the Five Seasons and you brought him along for dinner every night," Sasha said slowly, as if replaying scenes in her mind and piecing everything together. "And you kept the wine coming and conversation flowing and the good times rolling."

"You were new to Ireland. You didn't know anyone here. I was just trying to make you feel welcome."

"You never brought anyone else along. Only a man who'd paid you half a million."

"Sasha, you were never under any obligation. I never pressured you to do anything you didn't want to."

Sasha went very quiet. She kept staring at Richard, puzzling something over.

And then, I swear to God, my phone, which lay on the floorboards beside me, began to buzz. I had put it on silent but I must have left it on vibrate by accident. A 1-800 number flashed up on the screen. Just my luck. In my haste to grab the phone, my arm jolted the rickety old screen and, as if in slow motion, it came clattering down.

Everyone was staring right at me.

Johnny and Sasha, who now knew I had eavesdropped on their moment of bliss. Gina, who would think I had set up an elaborate sting operation so that she would witness her husband with another woman.

And Richard. I didn't even want to imagine what he was thinking.

I considered trying to explain that although the situation looked bad, *very* bad, I was, in fact, an entirely innocent bystander. But there was no explaining this away.

Sasha looked from me to Richard. Then she gathered herself up, just as I had seen her do onscreen so many times. It was her signature move. I had to admit, even from my not-ideal vantage point, the woman really did have poise. "I'm going home to the States."

Richard and Johnny objected in unison, Richard trying to placate her, Johnny losing the rag.

But it was too late. She was already out the door.

36

"I'm sorry, Richard," I said. "I'm *so* sorry." We were alone now in the old dressing room. Everyone else had stormed out in various stages of outrage. Richard had sat down on the chaise longue and I hadn't the heart to explain that it mightn't be an entirely hygienic move. He had his head in his hands. "You see, I got into your phone. I shouldn't have done it, I know, but anyway this message from an unknown number popped up and, well, curiosity—"

"We're fucked," he said softly to himself, ignoring my rambling. "We. Are. Fucked."

When he didn't say anything else, it all came spilling out. That I'd read the message saying that if Richard didn't pull this off, it was over. And that I'd *also* read Richard's replies arranging a meeting in an out-of-the-way hookup room. And that I'd seen that he'd been secretly meeting up with a woman called Lady Languish for drinks. And that I'd put two and two together and gotten a million.

Without taking his head from his hands, Richard groaned and said, "Lady Languish is *Sasha*, Eliza. I couldn't tell anyone I was meeting her. I told you, I had to sign an NDA. And that message was from Johnny. He meant that if I didn't pull

off the *investor show*, my *career* was over. He wouldn't just with-
draw his own money. He'd ruin my name around town so no
one else would ever consider investing in Blind Alley while I
was in charge."

That actually made sense. A lot of sense. Much more sense
than an affair. *What had I done?* "Johnny can't do that," I tried,
but it sounded weak even to my own ears.

"He can." Richard sounded like he'd already accepted defeat.
"The house, Eliza. The house."

"What do you mean?"

"Our house."

"What about it?" I tried to fight the rising sense of dread.

"We'll lose it now. With Sasha gone, we won't get the investment we need to keep going. The bank won't just take the
theater. They'll take the house."

"They couldn't do that. It's our family home."

"How do you think I raised the capital to fund the production?"

"I've no idea. I don't know how these things work."

"I had to use the house as collateral."

"What? How could you do that without telling me?" Phil
the solicitor's words came back to me: *You're very exposed, Eliza.*

"That's how it works. That's how these things are done."

"I can't believe you've done this to us!"

"Me? *You're* the one who's done this to us, Eliza. If Gina
hadn't discovered Johnny and Sasha here tonight, we would
have been golden."

"If you hadn't been so sleazy setting Johnny up with your
leading lady in the first place, we would have been golden."

"Just one night, that's all I needed to get the investment," he
continued, again ignoring me. "Even if Sasha had quit after tonight, we'd have had the investment locked in. We could have
afforded another big name to replace her. But now the investors are going to run for the hills. Including Johnny." He raised

his head from his hands and looked straight at me. "You're obsessed, Eliza. Obsessed with the idea that I'm cheating on you. You almost ruined everything that night at the Five Seasons, but I managed to salvage the situation. But there's no salvaging this. We're *fucked*. Because of you."

I left the conversation with Richard in a daze. There was only one person I wanted to be with right now: Mara.

I ran all the way to hair and makeup, where the girls had been minding Mara. But she wasn't there. One of the makeup girls smiled and told me everything was fine, Mara had just gone for a *little explore*.

A little explore? In this death trap of a theater?

I rushed down the corridor looking into each dressing room, asking everyone if they'd seen her. No sign. Thinking she might have been drawn back to the thunder run, I ran to the upper level but she wasn't there, either. Maybe she'd gone in search of Richard?

I raced down to his office on the first floor. And there she was. Sitting in Richard's chair, doing her art at his fancy partner's desk, perfectly content.

"I needed paper and I remembered Daddy keeps some in his desk," she said when she saw me. "I wanted to do this drawing for you."

She held out a picture to me.

It was a drawing of a girl standing on a rocky bluff, waves crashing on the cliffs beneath her. The head of a seal was breaking through the surface of the sea below her. The seal had big, dark eyes. The line of its mouth curved upward. The girl's hand was lifted in a wave to the seal.

I stared in disbelief.

"She's a selkie," Mara explained, pointing to the seal. "She got her sealskin back. Her daughter found it for her. The selkie is smiling because she's back in the sea. The sea is her natural habitat. And that's her daughter there on the cliff. She's half-human, half-selkie, so she can choose between land and sea. Do you like it?"

"Mara," I said, trying to keep my voice level. "How do you know about selkies?"

"Do you like my drawing? It's us, Mama."

I let the tears stream down my face. I didn't try to hide them. "Oh, I love it. It's beautiful, Mara." I paused for a moment. "But tell me, Mara, who told you about selkies?"

She shrugged and went back to her art.

As I began to fold the picture up, I noticed that Mara had drawn on the back of a letter that was addressed to Richard. It was from the Honorable Society of the Middle Temple in London, where he had been studying law when I first met him. I checked the date. The letter was fifteen years old.

I read it quickly. And then again, slower this time.

I took a deep breath, then folded it up and put it carefully in my pocket. "Come with me, Mara. There's one last thing we must do tonight."

37

There wasn't much time. I could hear the audience getting restless in the auditorium. There was chaos backstage, but Mara and I pushed out through the maze of corridors until we were standing in the wings. Richard was onstage, and the crowd had fallen silent to hear what he had to say. He began with some made-up excuse, saying that an unavoidable issue had arisen. He seemed to stall there, which was very unlike him. He was usually so confident in high-pressure situations. But for once, he looked uneasy. Anxious, even.

He apologized profusely for the last-minute cancellation of the show, as Sasha Jones was called back to America only moments earlier for a family emergency.

But the crowd was turning against him. Someone shouted something indecipherable, and then someone in another corner of the auditorium began booing. Richard tried to explain himself further, but his attempts were drowned out by the angry audience.

I knelt down to Mara and told her to stay right there where I could see her, and that I loved her. She nodded and looked at me in a way she never had before. Her eyes were alight with glee and…something else.

Awe.

I straightened up, smoothed my dress and walked onto the stage. Richard stared at me in anger first, then utter confusion. I leaned in close to his ear and said I'd take it from here.

Then I turned to the crowd, thanking them for their patience. I could hear my voice tremble. If Mara hadn't been watching, I might have walked right back off the stage.

But I looked to the theater's wing and saw Mara sitting with her legs folded, that same, new expression on her face. Curiosity. Like, who *was* this person who until now has just been my mama?

I would play for her and her alone.

"There's been a change of scheduling tonight," I said. "I hope you enjoy the performance."

An uncertain silence fell on the auditorium as I sat down at the piano. It was a baby grand, meant to be played in the second act by the pianist Richard had hired, had *paid*, when he could've asked his professional pianist wife.

I won't go back to being the pianist's husband.

I played a dramatic opening riff to get everyone's attention, then slid into a comical little piece to lighten the mood. There was a ripple of appreciation from the crowd, and, I noticed, a jump of delight from Mara.

Right so. Let's do this. I took a deep breath, laid my fingers on the keys till I had fully composed myself, and dived straight into Chopin's notoriously difficult *Fantaisie-Impromptu* to show the audience that they were in safe hands.

Now, feeling that I had the crowd with me, I moved into some popular classical pieces and started mixing in some traditional Irish phrasing, snippets of folk songs. Fusing different styles that, on paper, shouldn't go together. Eighteenth century Irish hymn music with a blues rearrangement. Solemn dirges mixed with Gershwin. Then I moved on to some jazz rearrangements of pop music—Britney Spears, Taylor Swift, Lady Gaga. My father would have been apoplectic.

I didn't care. If I was going down, I may as well go down in flames.

I lost track of all time. I might have played for an hour; I might have played for two. There was no way of knowing.

I forgot myself.

I remembered myself.

And finally, it was over, followed by absolute silence. Up until that point, I'd forgotten there was even an audience. But then the crowd erupted in applause. People were on their feet.

It was mortifying.

But really, it wasn't. It was the best I'd felt in eight years. Since that night I had to call myself an ambulance in Cologne.

I stood to take a bow. As I straightened up and took in the audience, I thought I saw a familiar figure in the balcony, right at the top of the theater. There was a flash of gray. Cashmere, no doubt.

But when the house lights went up, there was no one there.

Mara was jumping up and down, clapping her hands in glee. I saw Majella standing next to her, her hands to her cheeks in awe. Several members of the cast were crowded round, clapping furiously. Everyone was there.

Except Richard.

Mara broke free and ran to me, jumping up to give me a bear hug that nearly toppled me over.

Then we stood hand in hand and, together, we took a bow.

As the audience began emptying out of the auditorium, I spotted Gina sitting alone in one of the royal boxes. The box that had been reserved for Johnny and all his hotshot investor pals. She looked quite unlike herself. Pale, uncertain. For once, the mask had slipped. I asked Majella to mind Mara for me and made my way up to Gina.

When Gina heard someone coming into the box, she stood instantly, an expression of hope flitting across her face. Then she saw it was me and slumped back down.

"You've come to gloat, I suppose," she mumbled. "Go ahead. I deserve it."

"You don't deserve it. Johnny's completely in the wrong. It's terrible what he's done to you."

"Karma's a bitch, right? Now I know how Miriam felt."

It took me a moment to remember that Miriam was Johnny's first wife.

"I mean, what did I expect to happen when I married a cheater?" she continued. "I should have known he'd want an upgrade sooner or later. I suppose I thought I was putting in the effort, you know? I kept telling myself that Miriam let herself go. That she didn't... *fulfill* him. I kept myself in shape, made sure I always looked good, kept him satisfied. The house was always perfect, I made a three-course dinner every night. He had *zero* reason to stray. But he lost interest after we had Aurora. I tried everything to get it back, what we'd once had. I even tried to make him jealous. But it was never the same after that. And now I just feel like... I feel like such a fool." There was a catch in her voice as she said this. I could tell she was trying her very best not to fall apart in front of me.

"I'm so sorry, Gina," I said, touching her hand. "I just can't believe Richard also played a part in it."

She gave a humorless laugh. "Can't you?"

If I was honest with myself, I knew he was entirely capable of something like this. Capable of *anything*, really, if it meant saving his precious theater. I now understood that the theater came before everything. Before me, before Mara. Everyone.

"Wait, how did you find out? About the affair? About Richard setting them up?"

Gina sighed and sat back in her seat. "You remember Aurora's birthday party?" I nodded. "Well, after Johnny did the whole tennis court palaver and everyone else headed back to the house, I overheard Richard and Johnny talking about it. They didn't know I was listening."

Classic. When I'd seen Richard hanging back at the tennis court and asked him about it, he'd snapped at me for being nosy. Another lie.

"At the time, I thought it was a joke," Gina said, shaking her head.

"Why? What did they say?"

"Richard was talking about the next funding round he was going to run to raise more money for the theater. It was very obvious he was trying to get Johnny on board, but Johnny wasn't biting. That's when Richard dropped Sasha Jones's name. He told Johnny to keep it to himself because the contracts weren't signed yet, but he'd managed to land her for the lead role. Now *that* got Johnny's attention, I can tell you."

"So…what, then? He said he'd invest?"

"He joked that he'd put half a million in if Richard could hook him up with Sasha." Gina laughed despite herself. "Or at least, I had thought it was a joke." She took a deep breath. "But then a couple weeks passed and I started wondering if maybe it wasn't a joke at all. Johnny was becoming increasingly slippery and hard to pin down about things. Whenever he was late home in the evenings, he always claimed to be at 'Richie and Eliza's house—'" she paused for us to roll our eyes in unison "—and going over details of the investment with Richard. Doing his due diligence, that kind of thing. For a while, I let myself believe this. After all, what did *I* know about business transactions?

"But then that evening when I'd texted you to send Johnny home, and you'd replied saying he'd left hours earlier, that's when I knew. He had been lying to me. And there were other little things, too. He's begun working out, started wearing aftershave again, jumped in the shower as soon as he came in the door in the evenings… I knew what signs to look out for because I remembered how he acted when he was cheating with me. It's just I was used to being *the other woman*, not the wife." She paused to look up at me and I squeezed her hand. "Anyway," she continued, "I began to connect the dots. I went through Johnny's home office and found the paperwork for his investment. He put in *500,000 euros*, the exact amount he'd 'joked' he'd invest if Richard would set him up with Sasha. I wanted so badly to be wrong. But you saw for yourself this evening." Gina gestured in the direction of backstage. "I just can't believe how long he's been lying to me," she said, her voice cracking. "I think it started up soon after Richard and Johnny talked at Aurora's birthday party. That's three months ago. Three months he's been sneaking behind my back, making a fool of me. And now he's leaving me. When he should be the one begging for *me* to take *him* back!"

"Do you want me to get Richard to talk sense into him?" I offered.

"No," she said firmly, regaining some of her usual composure. "You shouldn't be trying to help me, Eliza. Not after what I did to you."

"What are you talking about?"

She hesitated. "You remember the story that was leaked to the *Daily Tattle*? About Richard and Sasha?"

"How could I forget?"

"That was me. I… I leaked it."

Wait, what? "But why? Why would you do that? You knew it wasn't true."

"It was a shit thing to do. I know that. But you have to understand, Eliza, I was desperate. I had to protect my marriage, and it seemed like the only way to do that was to get Sasha off the scene. And, well…it seemed like things were already pretty rocky between you and Richard. I honestly thought you wouldn't really care that much if he was having an affair."

I laughed in disbelief. "You didn't think I would *care* if my husband was having an affair?"

She plowed on. "I thought the story in the *Daily Tattle* would cause such a scandal that Sasha would have to step down and that she'd hightail it back to the States. But that didn't happen. Instead, it just made Johnny more possessive. It made him want her *more*."

I remembered the uproar when Johnny had come storming into our house on the day of the leak, furious with Richard. I'd assumed it was purely because he had a lot of money riding on the play, and that this scandal could derail it. But no, no, no. He'd also been burning with jealousy. Because he—like me—thought Richard had stolen Sasha for himself. She paused and checked the time. "I better go home," Gina said, almost to herself. She abruptly got to her feet. "Johnny might change his mind. He might come back to me. I better be there."

I wanted to object, to tell her not to give him another chance, that she was better off without him. But who was *I* to be giving marital advice? So instead, I just nodded.

Gina was halfway out the theater when a thought came to me. "Gina, wait!" I called out. She turned around in surprise, and I jogged over to her. "Did you leave this for me?" I paused to catch my breath. "That day in the Honey Café?" I reached into my bag and pulled out Ms. Early's business card.

She assessed the card, her eyebrows scrunched in confusion. "No, that wasn't me," Gina said, handing it back to me. "I don't know an Ellen Early."

38

Everyone was finally gone. The cast, all the invited guests, Majella. Just a few bar staff moving about quietly, clearing up glasses, setting things to rights. Mara was asleep on a banquette, covered with my jacket. Richard had gone behind the bar and found a bottle of wine. We sat side by side, drinking. He ran the palms of his hands down his cheeks.

"Quite the night," he said, staring down into his drink. Then he started laughing so hard I thought that he might cry.

"So you really weren't having an affair," I said.

"You could have just asked me."

"What would be the fun in that?"

He nodded, a wry smile on his face. "You always did like to do things your own way."

"What did the investors say?" I asked, nervous for his response.

"They're going ahead. With the investment."

I looked at him in shock. "*Really?* That's great!" I waited for him to share in my excitement, but he didn't look up from his drink. Didn't say anything. "Right?" I prompted.

He shrugged. "They'll put in the money, but not for my play."

"Um, okay... For what, so?"

He turned back to his drink. "For you."

"*Me?*"

"They want you to do a run of solo performances."

"But I couldn't fill a theater."

"You're already doing the rounds on the socials. People in the audience were videoing you. Posting clips. Creating a 'buzz,'" he said, using finger quotes. "These guys eat all that stuff up."

"But if they're willing to put the money in, that means we'd save the house?"

"Yes. We'd save the house."

"Well, then."

He said nothing. His play was to be his crowning achievement. He was to be feted in his hometown. He would finally win the admiration of his father. And I had stolen all that away from him.

"With the investments and the profit from the concerts, you could stage your play, even cast a big name to replace Sasha."

"Maybe."

We sat without speaking for a long time until I broke the silence. "There's one thing I have to ask…" He gave me a look that said, *what is it now?* "My piano. You got it valued."

"Yes. I got it valued."

"Did you use it as collateral, too? To help you buy the theater?"

He stayed silent and my heart plummeted.

"Why would you do that without telling me?"

"Because it had to be done."

Months ago, maybe I would have just let this go. But not anymore. "How would *you* like if I used your share in the theater as collateral for a loan? Without telling you?"

"Jesus, are we back to the piano again? The difference, Eliza, is that the theater is my livelihood."

"And that piano is *my* livelihood."

"If Blind Alley fails, I'm finished in theater. And I have nothing else to fall back on." He gave me a very pointed look and I knew exactly what he was thinking: *Because I flunked out of law school for you.* Somehow, we always ended up back here. And though he'd never actually articulated this, he'd implied that I was to blame countless times.

But this time was different. Because *this* time, I had read the letter—the one on the back of Mara's selkie drawing:

Dear Mr. Sheridan,

It is with regret that we must write to inform you that you have not passed the Bar Professional Training Course, having failed three modules. Therefore you will not be Called to the Bar this term.

Sincerely,
The Honorable Society of the Middle Temple

The letter was dated August 2004.

Which was before Richard persuaded me to run away with him to France.

Which meant that he had *not* sacrificed his career in law to save me. He had already flunked the Bar. But he had made me think it was my fault. And then he'd played on my guilt the whole way through our marriage so that every time he put himself first—again and again and again—I couldn't say anything. After all, he *had* given everything up for me. What right did I have to complain?

Every right, it turned out.

"I think we've talked enough, Richard," I said to him now.

I placed the Middle Temple letter on the bar beside him. He scanned it, then glanced at me. We looked at each other, finally, probably for the first time ever, with understanding.

George had kindly offered up her spare room to Mara and me for the night. Though it was cozy and peaceful with Mara sleeping next to me, my thoughts were racing. Every time I was about to drift off, yet another flashback from the evening's dramatics popped into my mind, setting off a flare of adrenaline. How Richard had misled me for all these years. How much I had put up with out of guilt. Guilt that was never mine to hold.

But of everything that had happened, it was the conversation with Gina that kept nagging at me. Something didn't add up. She'd said that the affair between Johnny and Sasha started shortly after Aurora's birthday party at the end of September. Sasha had been in Ireland for about two weeks at that point.

Richard had said that Lady Languish was Sasha. That he'd been meeting her to persuade her to take the role. But now that I thought about it, the diary dates had shown that Richard had been meeting up with Lady Languish all through June and July. Sasha wasn't even in the *country* then.

And another thing—who was the 083 mystery texter? Richard had claimed it was Johnny. That he'd been threatening to ruin him if Richard didn't pull off the investor rehearsal. But if Johnny had arranged to meet Richard in the old green dressing room, why on earth would he bring Sasha there for a spot of extramarital fun at the same time? And why wouldn't Richard have Johnny's contact saved on his phone, especially since they'd been all buddy-buddy after Aurora's birthday party? It made zero sense.

I pulled my phone out and scrolled back through texts till I found the original message that had kicked off this whole saga. Underneath the photo of Richard and the mystery woman, the sender had typed July 25, confirming my suspicions.

Sasha couldn't have been Lady Languish. But then who *was*?

I continued to pore over the photograph for what felt like the millionth time, willing myself to find an answer. *Think, Eliza, think.* But I'd spent months ruminating over the picture, assessing every specific detail to try to identify this mystery woman by the small of her back. And it had gotten me nowhere. My heart sank as I realized I may never know who "Lady Languish" was. And I had to come to peace with that.

But right as I went to turn off my phone, I noticed something on the screen that looked familiar. Very familiar.

And it had nothing to do with the picture.

39

I sat in Richard's study, waiting for him to come home. It was the evening after the disastrous investor rehearsal. Mara was still at George's house. I needed to do this alone.

I sat down in his fancy adjustable chair, just as I had done months earlier, the night I'd tried, and failed, to make myself confront him over the photo. If I'd just had the nerve to have it out with him back then, maybe things would have been different. But here we were, and no champagne this time. I would do this sober.

Eventually, the front door opened and shut. I heard Richard drop his keys on the hall sideboard and walk toward the study. He rounded the door deep in thought and was startled to see me.

"Oh," was all he said.

We hadn't spoken since the blowup in the theater bar. Mara and I were still staying with George.

"Can you sit down for a minute?" I said. "I need to talk to you about something."

He sighed.

I let the silence build between us. He caved first and said, "I already apologized for not telling you about failing out of law school. Are we going to keep doing this? Because if you can't move on, then…then we might not make it, Eliza."

"You didn't, actually."

He looked confused. "Didn't what?"

"You didn't apologize. But that doesn't matter now."

"You're right. It doesn't. Because my career has just imploded, in case you hadn't noticed."

"No, it doesn't matter because of this." I handed him my phone. The photo of him and the woman in the backless dress was open on the screen.

Richard frowned, then took a closer look. I saw the recognition all over his face, but then also saw his expression transform into disapproval. *Let's see you try to bluff your way through this.* He gave a dismissive shake of his head, and I saw him start to puff himself up into a state of anger.

Before he could say anything, I held up a hand. "Save your energy, Richard. I know about the affair." I looked at him, my partner of so many years. My husband. The father of my daughter. He had made me think I was bat-shit crazy. And he had done so *knowingly.* Deliberately. He had gotten angry with me, had belittled and humiliated me, had figured out my weak spots, had played me. Whatever it took to make me be a good, quiet, docile wife. The look in his eye told me he still thought he could win this, could somehow turn it all back on me.

"This again? Eliza, how many times do I have to tell you, Sasha and I were just—"

"Not Sasha, Richard. Gina."

His expression shifted and he was silent. *Check. Fucking. Mate.*

That night at George's, right when I'd begun to accept defeat on the mystery of Lady Languish, my eyes floated up to the sender's phone number.

An 083 phone number, to be exact.

Fortunately, I'd taken a picture of Richard's text messages on my own phone while he was still unconscious, so I wouldn't forget the time and place of the meetup during the investor show. Sure enough, the sender's number in those text messages matched the one that had first sent me the photograph.

Once I'd identified that Richard and I had the *same* mystery texter, a score of details began to rearrange themselves in my mind. How Gina came up to me at the Honey Café only *minutes* after I'd received the incriminating photo to ask if everything was okay. How she'd never wanted Aurora and Mara to hang out but had no issue fawning over Richard at Aurora's birthday party. How she'd latched on to us as a couple, how she'd accused me of not being proud of Richard. How she and Richard had been so touchy-feely at our house the night we'd had that impromptu party. How she'd leaked the news of Richard's alleged affair with Sasha.

She didn't only want to end things between Johnny and Sasha. She *also* wanted to end things between me and Richard.

But one detail in particular was the final nail in the coffin— Gina had turned up at the dressing room at the *exact same time* the mystery texter had told Richard to meet them there. Gina was Lady Languish.

"Aren't you going to say anything?" I said now.

I could see his mind working, flicking through his options. "Well, what did you expect, Eliza?" he burst out. "We hardly sleep together anymore. You don't even seem to like me. Affairs don't happen in a vacuum, you know."

Unbelievable. Even when he was so clearly in the wrong, he still thought he could foist the blame elsewhere. The old me would have taken the bait. But instead, I took a deep breath and didn't say a word, instead letting the silence build and build and build between us, letting him know that his tactics weren't going to work on me.

Not anymore.

"I'm sorry," he said finally, breaking down, putting his head in his hands. "I fucked up, all right? I'm sorry."

He *seemed* to be sobbing into his hands now, but were his tears genuine? Was he truly sorry? Sorry he'd been caught, for sure. Sorry he now had to face the consequences of his actions, definitely. But sorry he'd hurt me? I doubted it.

"It's over anyway. With Gina," he eventually said, his voice *actually* full of self-pity.

Translation: Gina dumped his broke ass. Sure, maybe part of her had had genuine feelings for the man sitting across from me, but that would never be enough for her. It was also his showbiz connections, the glitz of the theater. But no glitz, no Gina. That was how it worked.

I was never in it for the glitz. I was in it for love. But there was no love left here. I remembered what my father had said to me years ago, when I'd phoned him up to tell him I was marrying Richard—the first time I'd spoken to him since running away.

He's a pup, Eliza. A pup.

My father, flawed as he was, had seen through Richard's act right away. But not me.

Instead, I'd gone ahead and married him.

Richard dropped his head in his hands, anxiously rubbing his temples.

Poor, poor Richard. I took a nice, long look at him. This man—this stranger—I had once so deeply loved. My husband, the father of my child. This man who didn't do anything but *take, take, take,* but no matter how much I gave him, it was never enough. And it would never be enough.

Finally, I spoke. "You want my advice?"

He looked up at me in surprise but meekly nodded.

"I think you should go fuck yourself."

40

In the end, it was Majella who delivered the final blow to Richard.

Once she'd found out about his role in coercing Sasha into an intimate relationship with Johnny—in return for funding—Majella went straight to the board. That *was* her job, after all. The board deemed that Richard had placed his lead actor in a compromised position. The chairman informed Richard that he couldn't keep his job, even if the board wanted to save him. He was too great a risk.

I, however, accepted their offer for my concert run.

Richard moved out. Permanently.

As for George? She had handed in her notice and withdrew the boys from Alexis. She, Mossy and the kids were relocating to Leitrim, where they would live with his mother on the family dairy farm while their house was being built. Mossy was going to take over running the dairy and George had been hired by a team of local doctors to set up a new community medical practice. "We're getting out of Dublin just in time," she'd told me, then lowered her voice. "The kids won't be stuck with the accents."

I withdrew Mara from Alexis, too, and enrolled her in a

regular down-the-road non-fee-paying school. It suited Mara better. Her new teacher noticed and encouraged Mara's growing interest in art and allowed her to draw in class if she seemed anxious or withdrawn. She even gave Mara a sketchbook to bring out to yard so she had something to occupy herself with if she didn't feel confident enough to join in with the other kids.

News quickly spread about *child prodigy Eliza Sheridan's* concert revival. Orchestras in cities all around the world began reaching out to me, inviting me to perform.

And then I got the email in my inbox—it was Decca Records, inviting me to record at their studio in New York City.

This time, I said yes.

As I drove to the airport, I thought about the adventure that awaited us. Our suitcases were packed, the online check-in done. Mara and I had every little step planned. We had jellies to stop our ears from popping, and Maltesers to crunch while we watched a movie; then I was going to read an Agatha Christie, and Mara was planning on catching up on *Dilbert*.

It would be her first time flying over an ocean, my first time since she was born. And when the plane touched down in JFK, someone from Decca would meet us and bring us to our hotel in downtown Manhattan. We were allotted substantial free time to acclimatize to the city, so I had promised Mara we'd spend the entire first day in the Hall of Saurischian Dinosaurs near Central Park. And then she would come with me to the recording studio for each of the ten days that it was booked, where I was to record my album of Celtic-classical fusion piano music.

I looked in the rearview mirror and smiled. Mara was asleep, her hands still clutching her precious cargo—an encyclopedia on dinosaurs. She had recently made a new friend at school, a boy her age, after he'd noticed her sketching a dinosaur in yard. He'd lent her his encyclopedia so she could brush up on her facts before our big trip to the museum.

Finally, Mara had said when she got home from school that day. *Someone who knew their pteranodons from their pterodactyls.*

Epilogue

For months and months, I'd put Ms. Early out of my mind and focused entirely on Mara and my concerts and building our new life. I tried my best not to look back. But every so often, I would catch sight of a woman with a sleek, short hairstyle, or a particularly elegant bearing, and the memories would flood my mind in a rush. Those almond-shaped nails tapping on her desk while she considered what to do with me; that low, persuasive voice; her stillness; the hint of radicalism in her eye. Sometimes, she even appeared in my dreams.

I needed to know who this woman was who had swept into my life, shaken it asunder and then passed on just as swiftly. Who'd known about me for months before I'd even set foot in her office. Richard made me question my reality through the entirety of our relationship. I needed proof that she existed. That she was real.

So I got to work. I spent hours online, running Google searches that confirmed she wasn't a registered therapist, but barely gave me any additional information. In my research, I stumbled upon a link to an obscure Irish history blog. I clicked through and saw the phrase "the *bean feasa* Early." I looked up the meaning of *bean feasa*—it was the Celtic name for a woman of knowledge; a wise woman, descended from the ever-living ones; a walker between worlds.

Intrigued, I did *more* research, reading books on Celtic mythology and the *bean feasa* phenomenon. I trawled through online archives, searching for information, trying to piece together a picture of who she really was. And then I found what I was looking for: a specific reference to one Bridget Ellen Early. It was an article about a nineteenth century traditional healer who had defied priests and police officers to continue treating locals in County Clare. She had lived till she was eighty and had three husbands. It was said that all three husbands had died from the drink.

Some people said she was Ireland's last witch.

One night, on a Celtic history archive site, way down in the comments section of a post on Irish witchcraft, I came across a woman who said she'd grown up in Clare near where Bridget "Biddy" Early was rumored to have lived. This commenter went on to say that Biddy lived on in her own family folklore, as she'd allegedly cured her great-grandmother of a terrible fever. The woman said her family had even once made a vigil to Biddy Early's old cottage, which, legend had it, still existed to this day.

Several other women had responded to this comment and shared their own stories about this Irish witch and how she had helped their own female forebears. How they, too, had made vigils to keep Biddy's memory alive.

Just when I was about to shut down the laptop and go to bed, I saw that the original commenter said she would like to pay a vigil to the cottage herself, out of respect for what Biddy Early did for her great-grandmother, and *did anyone know how to find it?*

Underneath the query—posted only a day prior from an anonymous account—were exact directions and GPS coordinates to Biddy Early's cottage.

★ ★ ★

One spring day, I set off, driving west for Clare. Mrs. Overend was minding Mara for the day. Our house had been sold to free up money so that Richard and I could buy two smaller places as part of the separation, and our neighbor had gently insisted that Mara and I move in with her. At least until we found something more permanent. And it turned out she wasn't all that bad-tempered.

She'd just been lonely. Same as me.

I drove for hours, growing more and more aware of how far I was from Mara. We'd never been farther than a couple of miles apart before. The tug was strong to get back to her, to be there in case of an emergency, a worst-case scenario. But I forced myself to keep driving, on past Feakle and then finally just before the village of Faha, I took the tiny lane that Google maps insisted was the right way, unlikely though it seemed. Brambles scratched against the paintwork of my car as I nudged it through the undergrowth that had taken over the lane. Eventually, the terrain became so unforgiving that I had to abandon the car and continue on foot. The phone told me to take a right, onto a boreen that I never would have noticed otherwise. I pushed on. I worried I shouldn't have been there on my own, but I'd come too far to give up now.

The GPS was insisting that I had reached my destination, but I could see nothing but a wilderness of brambles and bushes. The cottage was, apparently, just to my left.

The springtime birdsong was loud. There were bursts of yellow and purple primroses as I pushed through the trees. A gentle drizzle started up, pattering on leaves and there was a faint scent of wood smoke in the air.

And there, at the end of the trail, was a completely derelict cottage.

It was a simple stone-built laborer's house, centuries old, and it was on the verge of being subsumed back into the earth.

The roof had long since caved in and saplings were now growing out through the open space. The walls were choked with dead ivy vines as thick as my wrist. I put my hand on one of the stones of the front wall. Cool, soft with moss. Through one of the windows, I could see that one of the inside sills was crowded with objects.

I entered.

There were lots of little colorful stones that I knew Mara would have loved, but there were also coins, one small, rusted pot and a shard of blue glass. I could see lots of other trinkets and offerings, not just on the sill, but wedged between the stones of the cottage. A rotting St. Bridget's cross, burnt-out tea lights, shells, a white quartz pebble.

It was then that I saw the blue bottles—hundreds of them—of all different shapes and sizes, thick with decades of dust and dirt. I picked up one bottle after another and found that several of them were marked with a name and a date.

My mind strained to make sense of the situation, but I needed more information. In a corner of the windowsill, I discovered business cards identical to the one I'd received in the Honey Café. They each had a short note written on the back. Many of the cards had started to soften and decay, the written words unintelligible. But some were more legible:

Ellen, you changed my life—Sarah S
I finally have peace—Anna May
I was lost until I met you. Thank you.—Saoirse M

I stood there for quite a while, waiting. For what, I don't know. It was silent except for the birdsong.

From my bag, I took out the blue poitín bottle and wrote Eliza Linley on it—I had since gone back to my maiden name—with today's date. I placed it on the windowsill next to the others. But I kept my business card. I would save it just in case I came across a woman in need of help, a way out. And I would pass it on to her, just as someone, whoever it was, had passed it on to me. I said a silent goodbye to Ms. Early, to the cottage, to all the women who had visited before me, and slowly walked back to the car.

A twig snapped somewhere. A bird fought its way up toward the sky.

As I started to walk away, I glanced back. The sun's rays cast a warm, iridescent glow on the cottage.

And it was radiant.

★ ★ ★ ★ ★

Author's Note

I first came upon the story of the real-life Eliza Sheridan many years ago when I was going through a big historical fiction–writing phase. Born Elizabeth Linley in 1754 into a family of extraordinary musical talent in Bath, she went on to become one of the most celebrated singers of her time. Eliza's life was remarkable in many ways, but one aspect of it stuck with me and inspired me to start writing about her: her husband, the famous Irish playwright and politician Richard Brinsley Sheridan, forbade her from performing in public after their marriage. Why? Because he felt that having a wife on the stage would make it impossible for him to be considered a gentleman. In other words, they could not both fulfill their potential.

I tried to bring Eliza's story to life through a historical novel, but no matter what way I came at it (and I came at it *many, many* ways with the help of two different literary agents), the problem remained the same: the ending was just too sad. Eliza and Richard's relationship may have started in a "romantic" way, with an escape to France, but it was not a happy marriage. Because of the social constraints on women at that time, there was no possibility of Eliza transcending her situation. As their marriage deteriorated, the Sheridans began to live pretty much separate lives, and Eliza, who had never been physically strong, died at the age of thirty-seven from tuberculosis.

Despite all my failed attempts to bring Eliza's story to life, I couldn't get her out of my mind. I decided to look at it differently: Would Eliza be able to find fulfillment in a modern setting, or would she still find herself as the supporting act to her husband's all-consuming ambition? Some might argue that there's nothing stopping women from reaching their potential now, but if you've read books like *MILF* by Paloma Faith, it's clear that the truth is complex, particularly for mothers.

So I transported Eliza and Richard to contemporary Dublin (and, for various reasons, made Eliza a pianist rather than a soprano) and set them in motion. To my delight, fictional modern Eliza rejected the traditional version of a happy ending for something much braver and more fulfilling. She found, or created, peace for herself and her daughter in an ending that I hope would have made the real Eliza Linley happy.

Acknowledgments

I'd like to thank the two funniest and most fascinating people I've ever met (who just happen to be my children), R and J, and our very own little Mr. Pickles, Benji Madden (our dog, not Cameron Diaz's husband).

Thanks to my parents, Pat and Fionnuala Madden, for filling my childhood with books, laughter, love and pet ducks; and to my childhood companion and brother, D, particularly for your support in recent years; to Claire Flynn, thank you for making me laugh pretty much constantly since we met at the age of twelve. You haven't just been a friend, you've been like a sister to me.

Kesia Lupo, how can I thank you enough? You've been the literary agent every writer hopes to find, and for a moment there we had the dream team going. Your integrity and kindness are so rare and I hope that we can work together again some day.

And a huge thanks to Trinity McFadden of the Bindery Agency for all your support and help.

They say that when the student is ready, the mentor will appear, and that's what happened when I saw a tweet years ago about a writing course being run by John Givens: thank you,

John, for keeping the faith despite all my unpublished manuscripts and fondness for exclamation points! Your writing group has been one of the best things to happen to me. A huge thanks to all of its members over the years, in particular Serena Molloy, who has the biggest heart—thank you for always being there, through all the ups and downs—and Andrew Hughes: your endless kindness and friendship have meant so much to me. And thanks also to Mary Barnecutt, Maura O'Brien, the Flitcrofts, Oliver Murphy and Antain MacLochlainn.

Thanks to Laura Slattery for all those companionable writing sessions in coffee shops and our lovely writing weekends away with Fiona Reddan. Fiona, I had decided against writing this book but you encouraged me to go for it. I'm hugely indebted to you for that and for all the wonderful *Irish Times* work you passed my way when I needed it most—you'll never know how much that meant to me.

There are no words to express my gratitude to Nicole Luongo, my stellar Park Row editor, but I'll give it a try: Nicole, your knowledge, intelligence and vision blew my mind from that very first Zoom meeting. You then worked some kind of editorial magic, transforming this book into something so much better than I could ever have imagined. I still can't believe my luck that we got to work together on this book. In fact, *work* is the wrong word—it has been a complete joy!

Thanks also to the rest of the team at HarperCollins, especially to the eagle-eyed copy editors Kathleen Mancini and Stephanie Van de Vooren for taking such care with the manuscript, to Yordanka Poleganova for the stunning cover illustration and to Tara Scarcello for the beautiful cover design.

Huge thanks also to my wonderful Eriu editor, Deirdre Nolan: I had been watching with admiration the beautiful new Irish imprint you've been building, so to become part of that imprint has been a dream come true. Your belief in this book has meant the world to me, and thanks, too, for your whip-smart insights into improving the manuscript. Thanks also to Lisa Gilmour and to the brilliant Eriu authors I've gotten to know, particularly Miriam Mulcahy.

Thanks also to Berni Vann and Will Watkins at CAA for their belief in this book and for their encouragement.

It took a lot of experts to wrestle my manuscript into shape before it was ready to send out into the world. Catherine Gough helped me enormously, not only by advising me on how to improve the opening section, but also because she told me that I wasn't barking up the wrong tree with this book, which gave me a confidence boost when I most needed it. When I got stuck at thirty thousand words, a brainstorming session with Vanessa Fox O'Loughlin got me unstuck—thank you, Vanessa! And thanks to Katherine Mezzacappa for her encouraging feedback after doing a manuscript assessment. Anna Barrett's experience as a former agent was incredibly helpful when it came to refining my agent submission package. And I am massively indebted to Lisa Cron, whose book *Story Genius* made all the difference.

I'm still blown away by the kindness and generosity of the early readers of this book, in particular: William Wall, Alan Glynn, Joseph Murray, Colin Walsh, Emma Murray, Disha Bose, Lauren Mackenzie, Michelle McDonagh, Joseph O'Connor and Sinead Crowley.

Thank you to all the writers (including those just listed) I was lucky enough to interview for *The Irish Times* and my blog, *www.myfirstbookdeal.com*—each of you inspired me, in different ways, to keep writing. None has been more inspiring than the young neurodiverse writer Roisín Coyne—it has been an honor to get to know you, Roisín, and your wonderful mother, Anne. Thanks also to the journalists Yvonne Reddin and Sarah Harte—I have nothing but admiration for you both.

To the oldest friendships that have kept me going all through the years: Siobhain McGuinness, Jean Seagrave, Michelle Fitzpatrick, Noelle Harvey, Nuala and Vinnie Crimmins, and Claire Malone.

And to my children's extended family: your continuing kindness means so much to us.